DEATH SHALL REIGN

Gemma Ashborne

PLAYLIST

"Do I Wanna Know?" by Arctic Monkeys
"Somewhere I Belong" by Linkin Park
"Wasted Love" by City and Colour
"Alkaline" by Sleep Token
"Lose Control" by Teddy Swims
"Number 13" by Nothing But Thieves
"Addicted" by One True God
"Arsonist's Lullaby" by Hozier
"Passion's Killing Floor" by HIM
"Seven Nation Army – The Glitch Mob Remix" by The White Stripes
"Landing in the Dark" by Aaron Martin
"Iris" by The Goo Goo Dolls
"Jaws" by Sleep Token
"Natural Born Killer" by Highly Suspect
"Use Somebody" by Kings of Leon
"Mine" by Sleep Token

WARNING

Death Shall Reign contains content that may be triggering or disturbing to some. This book is a work of fiction, and I in no way condone or encourage such behaviors in real life. If you wish to go in blind, know you have been warned.

Your mental health matters.

Trigger warnings include, but are not limited to:

Strong language, sexually explicit content, attempted rape (not between FMC/MMC), sexual assault, references to childhood SA (not depicted on page & ends in revenge), cannibalism, sex trafficking (again, ends in revenge), parental loss, parental neglect (not depicted on page), substance use, brief suicidal ideation, self-harm (blood pacts), and copious amounts of murder.

If you have any questions regarding the content of this book, please feel free to reach out: Gemma_Ashborne@att.net

Enter at your own risk.

And welcome BACK to Anathema, dear one.

To anyone who has ever felt like they don't belong:
I see you, dear one. I hope you find a home between these pages.

PROLOGUE

The night I realized I was in love with my best friend, I came face to face with Death for the first time.

At eighteen and twenty, we were still trying to find our way in a world that didn't understand us. We'd always been a little...other. While most feared the dark, we thrived in the shadows—chased them—consumed by questions regarding the universe and how we fit in it. The night's reverence held such promise for us. There, we could be our true selves, away from prying eyes that deemed us unfit. *Broken.*

The moon radiated a strange glow that night, haloed by golden light which seemed to whisper that Fate's eyes rested on us. Destiny carried on the wind, tangled in a perfume of fresh pine and moist soil. The woods called to me as they often did in my early years after my powers had manifested, but I knew better than to sneak out without Kim. She would've had my head if I did; she was vicious in her desires, even back then.

I'd recently had my heart eviscerated by a tall, charming—albeit a bit pretentious—guy three-quarters of the town population either lusted after or championed as some great overachiever on the rise. What started as a daring touch at a house party had turned into late-night meetups laced with whiskey and wandering hands. I'd known I wasn't in love with him, but being his secret felt good for a while; it had given me a reason to live, however small. He'd offered me something I craved, body and soul, though I denied it: a chance to be wanted. *Me.* The parentless, vacant shadow who habitually distanced himself from any connection that might leave him open and vulnerable. I wasn't oblivious to that side of myself—don't get me wrong—but I didn't care to change it. When your past was as packed full of death as mine was, well...getting lost inside yourself comes easy. It keeps you safe. But I'd believed he'd seen me. *Really* seen me.

Turned out the dude was a filthy fucking liar.

Looking back years later, I realized envy had driven our first interactions. Wanting to be *with* him was never as strong as wanting to *be* him. He had everything I'd always wanted: a gentle father who taught him everything he knew and a mother who doted on him, promising he could be anything his heart desired. He had a family, a home, and a future. He belonged.

We'd met up in the old cemetery like we often did, my heart clapping in anticipation. With a blanket laid out under the stars and snacks packed in my backpack, I'd waited. When he finally showed, I'd assumed we'd spend time together. Talk maybe. I know, a ridiculous thing to want from a sneaky hookup. Especially one hiding malevolent desires. By the rough end, my hands shook as I buttoned my shirt back up while he'd carried on about how he wasn't queer and how disgusted he felt in having let me "convince" him to do such a thing. To think I'd given him a chance—torn my walls down to let him in—only to be reminded why I'd built them in the first place. I'd been such an idiot. I'd allowed him to get close, to see into the real me. Guess he hadn't liked what he found. He'd left me there in a confused fog, drowning in the overwhelming realization that I was unwanted. *Again.*

I would have paid a pretty penny for a shot at breaking the dude's jaw, but his parents shipped him away to a conservative college in the south to "get his head straight" before I'd had the chance. For someone hellbent on not being into dudes, rumor had it he'd been caught mid-act with the star running back of Cottage Grove Community Collage on his parent's bed just days after our last hookup. Apparently his picturesque family wasn't so shiny and perfect when it came to their son being queer. They'd pried, and he'd lied. I heard he'd gone as far as to say he'd been with Kimber on the nights he'd met up with me, attempting to pin his sneaking around on being into plus-sized chicks. My jealousy had reared its ugly head after hearing that bit. It's true we all have to find our way—sometimes breaking a heart or two along the journey to self-discovery—but he'd been a merciless dick in his attempts to hide his true self. At least he'd given me a gift intermixed in the lies. A revelation. It wasn't *him* I'd yearned for. No, my jealousy had never been on his account.

It had been *her*. Kim.

Though I had no family to call my own—a guardian who popped by on occasion to put food on the table and make sure I still had a pulse was better than nothing, I guess—there was one person I knew I could always count on no matter what. For weeks, I'd denied my feelings surrounding his betrayal until I couldn't any longer. Slinking up the vines to Kimber's bedroom like some grim twist on Romeo and Juliet, I had knocked on her window until the light flickered on. With concern in her eyes, she'd parted the curtains and didn't hesitate to follow me into the night. I'd like to say I regretted stealing the truck from her mom—the lady was incredibly kind—but with whiskey on my tongue and the wind nipping in through the windows? Nah, I'd needed it. And so, Kim and I did what we always did when life landed a sucker punch.

We threw rocks down in the quarry to blow off steam.

After a mile walk in, we found our usual lookout spot. The treetops danced against the midnight sky as we sat wrapped in the silence for some time, entirely comfortable in the shared quiet. No pressure or need to speak until we were ready. I dug my fingers into the gravel—the bits of rough stone against my palms calming me with each throw. Finally, Kim leaned her head against my shoulder, and my rapid thoughts slowed. Stilled.

"It's his loss, you know," she said, bumping my shoulder. "You're a catch."

I chucked another rock into the abyss below, counting the seconds before it clattered at the bottom. "Of course you'd say that. You're my best friend. You have to."

She slapped my arm. "I do not!"

"Right, 'cause 'moody' and 'emotionally unavailable' are such turn-ons. Who wouldn't want me?"

"I think you meant to say 'mysterious' and 'alluring.'"

I laughed, her head bobbing against me. "Sure."

"Are you calling me a liar, Cooper Rollins?"

She stood, placed one hand on her hip, and pulled me to my feet with the other. Even in her hole-ridden sweatpants and faded band t-shirt, she commanded attention. Demanded it. The moonlight kissed her ashen hair, and I couldn't help but step closer, drawn to her like a moth to a flame. My steps faltered. How had I not noticed the dusting of freckles on her nose before? Like a sea of stars on her skin as if the night had claimed her for its own. I drank her in anew. Her gaze pinned me in place, and I dreamed of what it might be like to— I shook my head. What the hell was wrong with me? *Friends. We are friends.*

"A liar?" I scoffed. "No. I've never met anyone as honest as you. Less brutal in the approach maybe, but never more honest."

She pursed her lips—their plumpness drawing my focus—and searched my face. An infectious smile overcame her as she spun me about, her laughter hitting home in my gut. We danced to the music in her mind, and I found myself curious as to what tune drove her. I fought the urge to ask, in fear she'd stop and I'd have to remove my hold on her hips.

"I purpose a toast to us," she declared.

"To us?" I asked, dipping her back. "What for?"

"To us being mysterious, and desirable, and honest, and all the things."

"All the things. Pretty vague there, don't you think?"

"Fine then." She raised the whiskey bottle high. "Then to you. To the guy who never gives up, despite his haunting past. To the person I can always count on, no matter what time it is or how ridiculous my current meltdown might be."

I stole the bottle, raising it out of her reach in jest. "And to you. To your brilliant mind and twisted dark humor. To the way you would die, maybe even *kill,* to protect the people you love."

"You're damn right, I would!" She hopped up to steal the bottle back again and downed a sip, wincing at the liquor's harsh bite. "To the way you make me laugh until my stomach hurts."

"To the way your nose wrinkles when you smell a person's bullshit."

A challenge rose in her stare. "To the way you pretend you're heartless, even though you care more than you let on."

"Wrong, I couldn't give two shits about most things, but—" I grabbed the bottle, taking a swig. "To the way *you* see me."

Her brow tensed. "I'm not the only one who sees how awesome you are. You know that, right?"

"Nobody sees me the way you do, Kim. All they see are my sharp edges and messy past. They judge me before they even get a chance to know me. Which, honestly? Fine by me. Screw 'em. But you..."

Her hand cemented around my cheek, forcing my chin up to look me straight in the eyes.

"Other people are idiots," she bit out. "Anyone who doesn't see you for the strong, capable, kind person you are is blind. And you're right: screw them, because they don't deserve you."

Her words started a fever in me, heating my core more than whiskey ever could. "To the way you speak your mind."

"To the way you encourage me to," she said, "and to the way you listen."

Head full of liquor, I drew closer, a feral desire building in me. Suddenly I knew: I didn't want to be friends anymore. I wanted to be much, much more. I wanted to touch her, hold her, breathe her in, and do anything in my power to make her smile at me again and again. My mouth went dry. Holy shit...I—I was *in love with her.*

My pulse pounded as I reached out, but the twist in my chest made me stop shy. What if she didn't feel the same? Rejection was one thing, but if it came from her, I might never recover. Despite my fears, the need in me grew too charged to ignore. I leaned in—my fingers playing with the fabric hugging her curves—and my gaze fell to her lips. "To the way you feel like home."

"I'll always be your home." Her breath hitched. "And you will always be mine."

My nose brushed against hers, the ache in me doubling. More so, I realized I believed her. Heart and soul, I believed her. Tomorrow wasn't promised, but to know I wouldn't be alone in this hellscape of a fucked-up world meant everything. Just like that, she became the driving hope for my future.

"I might kiss you," I muttered.

"Coop, we can't." She stiffened but didn't pull away. "You mean way too much to me to risk—"

"I'm not asking you to commit or promise me anything, but if I don't kiss you right-fucking-now, I might lose my mind."

Our lips crashed into one another, desperate. Her kiss was electric, her mouth soft and laced in the sharp tang of alcohol. A taste I committed to memory. She began to mirror my hungry touch, her need pushing me a step back on the rocky ledge. I dug my heels in as her body pressed against mine and our hands wandered. I knew then that I'd been forever changed. Remade and claimed. I feared for a moment that I'd fallen asleep—my stomach dropping at the thought of waking from such a dream—but her teeth nipped my bottom lip, and the gentle ache of her bite sent a shock wave through me. This was real. Carefully, I guided her to the ground, propping her up. Her chest heaved, and her eyes grew wild.

I traced a hand along the sliver of skin peeking below her shirt. "Do you want this?"

Her head fell back, breath heavy. "Yes."

"Are you sure?" I traced a hand lower. "Because if not—"

She fisted a hand around my shirt collar. "Shut up and kiss me."

Her tongue swirled around mine, and I slipped her bottoms down, tossing them to the ground in reckless abandon. With a pointed finger, I guided one knee to the side, then the next—her moan of approval making me throb. Chills rose up my arms as I beheld her, devastatingly beautiful in her vulnerability. I'd never been so hard in my *life*. The urge to please her rose to near catastrophic levels, and I brushed my touch along her inner thigh, grabbing her hand to wrap it around mine. "Show me how you like it?"

She smirked and took my fingers between hers. With gentle strokes, she guided my fingers in circles about her swollen clit, slow and steady at first. I watched in amazement, rubbing my cock through my pants in tandem with her. So hot: the way her knees shook the closer she got, her dominance moving me to her pleasure. The speed increased, her hips grinding against my fingertips.

"Don't stop," she whimpered.

But I did. I wanted to try something. I wanted...no, *needed*, to taste her.

"No," she whined. "I was so close. Why'd you stop?"

"Because your pussy looks like a goddamn snack, and I want a taste."

My lips devoured her—her hips bucking—and I drove my tongue in and out to swirl around her center. Her back arched beneath me as her hands knotted in my hair.

"Shit," she moaned.

I nipped her clit with my teeth, and her sweetness spilled across my tongue as she crashed over the edge. Pure heaven. But I was nowhere near satiated, tipping from hungry to ravenous.

Without warning, she snatched me by the throat and forced me underneath her, removing my pants frantically. Wasting no time, she straddled me and settled her warmth over my length. She began to glide back and forth while her thumb teased the tip of my cock.

"You want this?" she asked, positioning me at her entrance.

My entire body ignited beneath her. "Gods, yes. Put it in."

"Then beg for it."

"Please," I whimpered.

Her mouth gaped, and she pushed me inside. Just the tip. Absolute torture...and I loved every second of it. The sheer *power* she held over me was intoxicating as she leaned down to bite my neck, her tongue tickling my ear.

"Mmm, beg harder," she ordered.

"Please, I need to be inside you."

She slid down my length a little more, and I buckled under the sensation. Her softness tightened around me.

"Better, but I don't quite feel your desperation." She pinned my hands over my head. "I said, 'Beg.'"

"Please, Kim, fuck me."

"There it is."

She drove me in all at once, stealing the air from my lungs. Her gasp at my entrance fueled me, and I slammed her back down on my cock. A second time. And a third. Each blow brought me closer to the edge, had me throbbing inside her. Her brows pinched as she neared her second climax, her hand cementing around my throat. Pure, addictive lust radiated in her eyes, and I wrapped my hand around hers, encouraging her tight grip. She rode me harder and harder until we were a mess of moans and sighs and breaths and—

"Oh gods, I'm coming," I growled, pounding into her.

My sights locked onto her pretty, pink mouth as she cried out in pleasure. I knew then what my purpose was: to serve her; to protect her; to treasure her. She owned me.

And I was damn proud to let her.

She collapsed, her breathing labored. "I can't believe we just did that..."

"Me either."

But to say I was glad it happened would have been the understatement of the century. We laid there in a heap beneath the stars for some time. Content in the silence—neither of us eager to tackle the loaded question drifting between us—we sipped what remained of the whiskey.

A scuffle in the tree line sent me reeling. My lungs tightened, and the hair on the back of my neck bristled at the sudden thickness in the air. The scent of decay permeated. But animals died in the forest every day, right? It was probably a half-eaten kill left to rot, and I chalked it up to a nearby squirrel or rabbit. But I couldn't shake the undeniable feeling that we were being watched, and not by a harmless woodland creature. A predator. I brushed if off as nothing more than drunken paranoia.

Still, if some crazy drunk stumbled up in the middle of the night, I wasn't about to be caught with my balls out, seeing as Kim owned them now. I snatched my pants and shimmied them on alongside Kim when my zipper snagged, the bent metal slicing my thumb.

"Ah," I hissed, and sucked the cut clean. "I know you think I'm sexy, and you just *had* to get in my pants, but damn lady. Do you have to dominate *and* destroy? These are my favorite jeans."

"Eh, it's more fun with a little destruction," she teased back. "And for the record, it was *you* who begged *me*. So really, you're the thirsty one here."

I chuckled. "Oh, is that so? Because from my view, it looked like you couldn't get enough, *Miss Beg-for-it.*"

"Don't move."

"What, knees still quivering? I have to admit, the way you take control is hot as—"

I looked up to find her frozen in fear.

"Kim, what's wrong?"

"Look," she whispered. "There's someone in the woods. They're...watching us."

I turned to catch a glimpse, and my stomach dropped. The silhouette of a rather large man lingered with his sights on us, apparently not the least bit concerned that we saw him. Like deer caught in the headlights, we sat frozen in place until I couldn't take it anymore. I jumped to my feet. "Hey asshole, take a picture. It'll last longer!"

Kim shot to her feet and snagged my wrist. "Cooper, don't—"

The world stilled. In time with the man's disappearance into the trees, Kim's foot slipped against the gravel, and her body arched towards the abyss below. I reacted on impulse and swept her back on solid ground, but my own feet betrayed me.

One, two, three, four, five seconds to the bottom.

I hit the ground with a loud thud, my bones breaking in tandem against the rocky ground. Unbeknownst to me, a severe fall does strange things to the body. All I could think as I stared up at the cliff's edge was, *"What just happened?"*

Vision blurry, I laid there in shock. I waited for the pain—Kim's panicked screams reverberating downward—and slid a hand into my hair, prodding a jagged gash along my skull. Warmth ran down my fingertips. Fresh blood, but still no pain. I was dead. I had to be. I mean, what other explanation could there be?

"You saved her," a layered voice called from somewhere in the dark.

Yup, definitely dead. "God?"

The man snickered. "Not even close, boy. I am more akin to a nightmare than a deity."

"I—I need help." I pushed to sit, but my body defied me. My head spun as I attempted to make out where the voice hailed from. "I think I'm dying."

"You are. Rapidly, in fact."

"Please...help me?"

"I can do that. It is well within my power. But tell me, are you willing to pay the cost?"

As mental haziness closed in, I struggled to find my answer. Cost? Who was this person who'd found me in such perfect timing? And why? How?

"Time is ticking," he *tsked*. "I've not long before I must leave this plane behind. Make your choice. Death or a debt owed."

"I—" Light began to fade. Sound and color disappeared. "I—I don't want to die."

An aura of destruction and judgment carried on the man's coattail as he emerged on the edge of my vision. The feeling of being completely at his mercy stripped me down to nothing; my soul laid bare at his feet. I shivered. How could he bring me the salvation he promised? Mortality was inescapable, no matter who you were.

"Finding you was nothing short of divine intervention. An act of Fate, some might say. And so I shall grant you life. But know this, boy: your destiny is forever entwined with hers now."

In my peripheral, I watched the man slice his palm open, find the crevice in my skull, and place his wound on mine. A buzz settled in my ears, heat spreading out across my limbs on contact. "Entwined with who?"

Kim's cries ricocheted from the canyon floor, her footsteps pounding closer. My strength returned, and my vision settled. I stood—a million new questions rattling through my mind—as the sight of my savior took morbid shape. A crown of bone sat atop his head, and his eyes burned like hellfire. Evil incarnate.

I recoiled. "Who are you?"

The wicked grin on his face widened as he replied, "I am Death. And you, dear boy, are indebted to me."

Chapter One

OUR SHARED DARKNESS

Two Years Later

I owed Death my life.

That sentiment haunted me for years, lingering over my shoulder like a hooded figure determined to swallow me whole. Each step, each move from that moment on had been shaped by the fact. Questions surrounding my fate plagued me, awake and asleep. When would he return? What would he demand of me? What was a soul *truly* worth to Death himself? And would that cost be worth it? The only answer I'd found in my relentless studies surrounding the realm of eternal night and its inner workings was simple: he would return. And I would pay.

Yet, I wouldn't change a thing. The night I'd bartered my life held more than dark fears. It had allotted me my most treasured memories too. Kim's soft skin against mine. Her laughter. The way she leaned her head on my chest as she promised I'd never be alone again, because *she* would be my home. And the way our bodies fit together like perfect puzzle pieces. I'd bound myself to her then. Sworn to protect her happiness, no matter how I fit into the picture. In the end, Death's mention of our entwined fates had been meaningless, because the second those big, round eyes rimmed in starry light met mine, I'd made my choice.

I'd serve her until my last breath.

With the blood moon looming above and the perfume of the departed afternoon rain lingering in the breeze, I reminded myself of that commitment as Kim and I set out to summon the very being I'd fought so hard to evade. Her father. I jutted my hand out the truck window—the cool night air kissing my skin—and steadied my breath. Kim lay unconscious beside me, spirited away to the astral. Her whimpers tickled my ear. She'd needed to tell Juniper about our plan and communicate the risk involved, which I supported entirely. While I envied her lover, I'd never wish her distress. From all I'd heard, the woman was walking perfection. I mean, Kimber practically *glowed* when she told me about their first meeting. Love at first sight. They made each other happy; I knew it beyond a shadow of a doubt. But still my blood boiled, because the pleasured moan that slipped past her lips as I veered onto the highway wasn't for me. And damn, how I wanted it to be. My body responded despite my objection: throbbing, all-consuming need to bury myself inside her—*no. Fuck, no.*

I rerouted my focus and let my sights slip to the trees, righting myself just in time for Kimber to return to our plane of existence. My white-knuckle hold on the steering wheel threatened to undo me, rat me out.

"What?" she asked, honing in on my tight grip.

"Sounds like *somebody* was having a good time."

She slapped my arm. "Oh, whatever. You're just jealous."

"And if I was?"

Before I could convince myself what a monumental mistake it would be, my hand ran up her inner thigh. Soft as velvet. She shuddered under my touch; and shit, if everything in me didn't beg to pull that truck off the road and slide her onto my lap. To press against her most sensitive space. To claim her.

Mine.

But she wasn't and might never be. If there's one thing to be said about my best friend: the woman doesn't do a damn thing she doesn't want to do. And though it broke me, it seemed I was one of those things. She removed my hand from her thigh, lacing her fingers through mine.

"Have I told you lately how much I fucking love you?" She smiled up at me.

"Not nearly enough, tease," I joked, despite the ache in my chest.

In her renewed silence, her true feelings rang through at deafening volume: she didn't want me the way I wanted her, and the rejection stabbed me the same way it had years before.

After the night we'd shared, I'd waited for her to bring up what had bloomed between us so we could sort through it; but as time dwindled away, so did my courage. The call for a new start hung heavy that next morning—Kim's sleeping frame an inch from mine, so close and yet so far away. I'd stared up at her bedroom ceiling, envisioning what it might be like to leave it all behind and find solace in a simple, mundane existence: to become a faceless stranger in a random town where nobody knew or cared to know me. A do-over to give my shattered heart a chance to heal. In time, maybe I'd even meet someone to live out that new life with; and though I might not burn for their touch the way I did for Kim's, I might be able to forge a future I enjoyed well enough. Nothing shiny or grand, but a means of escape nonetheless.

Then the early morning light seeped in through the window to kiss Kim's eyelids. Her lashes fluttered—immersed in a seemingly perfect dream. With one hand on the door, I'd paused, unable to tear my gaze away from the rise and fall of her steady breath. The way the sheets draped over her hip, revealing the gentle slope of her curves. How could I leave her behind? And would I be able to live with myself if I did?

In that moment, I'd visualized such a future and the things I'd miss most. Her sarcastic wit and the way she made me feel irreplaceable, or how she refused to shy away from the darkness I'd always had lurking beneath the surface. Hell, how she *encouraged* such darkness. Found it beautiful. In truth, the mortal world's cruelty hadn't vexed me alone. It'd broken her too, leaving her stranded on the sidelines of society. How could I abandon her? I'd stood in that doorway, teetering on redefining my fate, only to end up in the exact place I'd started.

Lost in her.

I'd been an idiot for even considering it. A life without Kim would be no life at all. And so, I'd signed on to help her reclaim what was rightfully hers. To lead her back to the place I'd ran from long ago: Anathema, the realm of eternal night. The place where my people were slaughtered and chased from their homes. Because in truth, she was the realm's only hope for change. I knew it in every fiber of my being. I'd die to see a crown upon her head: regal and respected by all. She deserved nothing less.

I snapped back to reality as her hand squeezed mine.

"So," I said, shuffling in my seat, "think this will work?"

"It has to. I'm ending that piece of shit, no matter what it takes," she ground out.

"That's my girl. Give 'em hell."

After pulling the truck into a shadowed alcove at the forest's edge, we hopped out—backpack full of monstrous goodies in tow. Trapping a demon was sure to be one hell of a good time, but as always, I'd have to play it down. She couldn't know what I truly was. *Who* I was. To Kim, I had to be nothing more than a human; because if she found out I was the last remaining pureblood shapeshifter when someone had fought so hard to wipe us all off the map, well...that's the sort of thing that gets you tortured. Killed. I couldn't risk it.

I cracked my knuckles in the moon's dense red glow as my nerves knotted up tight.

"Care for some liquid courage?" she asked, a wicked smile on her face.

Damn right, I did. But it wasn't the fear of the impending fight that had me on edge; it was the simple fact that everything we'd worked towards could very well mean I'd never see her again. After all, Death held the power to seal me out and lock my best friend away for all time. Not to mention the payment due for our little bargain. I took a swig from the bottle, and fiery, warm liquor ignited my taste buds. Let him come. I'd slit his throat before I let him tear us apart.

Time ticked by without any signs that a demon lay hiding in the darkened woods. We listened intently for the usual signs: sporadic footsteps from behind—always behind, no matter how many times you turned around—or a lingering silhouette in our peripheral. Demons got off on that shit: terrifying their target before a kill. Power-hungry assholes. I rubbed my eyes impatiently. We had one chance to nail this sucker. If he didn't show, years of meticulous research and planning went right down the drain, just like that.

Kim's knee bobbed as she scanned the scene. A minute later, I broke the silence.

"This isn't working," I said, resting a hand on her shoulder. "If he doesn't know we're here, he won't reveal himself. He's probably waiting for some lonely hiker to wander past. It's about the thrill of the hunt for monsters like this."

She tapped her chin. "Yeah...maybe you're right."

"Aren't I always?"

"Well, I certainly wouldn't call you humble, that's for sure," she teased.

I gasped, placing a hand over my heart. "You wound me so."

"Something tells me you'll survive."

We chuckled and slipped farther into the night, slow and steady, careful to keep our conversations to a minimum. A nearby owl screeched, followed by a potential mate's call in the distance, but no signs of demonic activity. Farther in it was. Winding through the trees, we came to a ravine, and I internally cursed. Months of dried leaves had accumulated alongside its entrance, making the incline slippery after the recent rainfall. I positioned myself in front of Kim and motioned for her to steady herself against the large oak's coarse bark in passing. Of course she mouthed for me to "fuck off" because the woman could handle herself, but I digress. Finally, we approached an outcropping of rocks and set up shop. But still, nothing. We couldn't afford to wait any longer or leave it up to chance as the morning loomed closer. If the blood moon passed, Kim would lose her opportunity to summon Death, which simply wasn't an option.

I sat up straight and turned to find her picking at a plant in the rock face. "I have an idea. I'll bait him."

"Hell no!" she burst, scrunching her nose. "Way too risky!"

"If we don't nail this guy, you'll never get your chance, Kim. Please let me do this." But I wasn't asking, not really. I would do this for her whether she liked it or not.

"Fine," she sighed. "But the second that asshole comes into view, you run, you hear me?"

"You'll need me to hold him down."

"You forget, he isn't the only one more powerful on a blood moon."

Her shadows writhed, making my stomach jump. After a few more swigs of liquid courage, I headed into the open field and clasped my hands around my mouth. Time to put this feral bastard down.

"Help!" I screamed. "Anybody out there? I lost the path."

To the target hunting me, I needed to embody the frightened, weak, perfect victim. Which couldn't have been further from the truth, because in reality, I was bloodthirsty and raring to go. How many innocent mortal lives had been forfeited strictly for this prick's sick enjoyment? We'd confirmed at least a handful marked by his calling card: a coin; but there had been more. There always were when it came to those who had acquired a taste for human flesh. It drove them mad; and while most demons no longer ate liver, it seemed this specific one had an insatiable lust for it.

Chills crawled up my neck, but it wasn't from the wind. I felt him. There, just outside my line of vision, ready and waiting. I fought a grin, trading it instead for the show I knew the monster craved. *Come and get me, asshole.*

"Help, please!" I yelled.

A screech, shrill and scratchy, tore through the open field. *Got him.* The demon emerged, his face concealed by an ornate mask.

"Lost, are we?" he taunted.

"I...yes," I lied, feigning fear. "Please, can you help me find my way back?"

"I'm afraid you've come to the wrong person if you wish for help. You see, I'm not here to decide if you should live or die, let alone be worthy of my help. No. That I'll leave up to Fate."

He began to circle me: predator and prey...or so he thought. Fool. All the while Kim hunted him from the shadows, and I fought to keep his attention on me. He really believed he was in control. Joke was on him, because I'd taken far crueler beasts down before, laying them at my feet as they pleaded for the same mercy they'd callously denied their own victims.

The demon flipped a coin, catching it between his palms. "Call it."

"Call what?" I asked.

"Call it: heads or tails. Heads, you live, and I'll decide if that includes my help. Tails, well…"

He sauntered close, calm and confident, and the urge to break him made my pulse pound. My bones shifted, my instincts threatening to take over. He stepped within arm's reach, close enough that I could easily lock my fingers around his neck, squeeze until the light drained from his eyes and—

Kim's blade gleamed in the moonlight as she lowered herself into position, and my breath hitched. Gods, how was it possible for murderous rage to look so damn sexy? Such a vicious thing. This fight belonged to her; all I had to do was lure him into position.

I slipped off to the left, drawing his gaze. "Tails, and you kill me, right?"

"Oh, no, no." He chuckled. "Tails, and I hunt you. I know, I'm far too gracious, giving you two chances at potential salvation. So, mortal. Call it. Heads or—"

In the blink of an eye, she was there—blade thirsty—but quick as she was, the demon was faster. Older. *No…* I watched his foot movement, noting the regality in his posture. He dodged with minimal effort, even feigning a yawn as if Kim's ruthless strikes were mere child's play. Who *was* this guy? Stepping to the sidelines, I studied the hilt of his dagger and found a ruby-encrusted moon inlay. I swallowed hard. Only the elite carried weapons engraved with Anathema's sigil. This was no rogue demon; he was royalty, and well-trained royalty at that.

I started towards him, ready to step into my power and blow my most closely held secret if it meant protecting Kimber. She wouldn't fight this battle alone; I would be her blade. Her weapon to wield. Her shield. A low growl rattled the earth beneath my feet and stopped me in my tracks. *What the hell?* Following the guttural sound, I locked onto a set of golden eyes in the tree line, and my heart sank. No. *Oh, no, no, no.* Not good! As if we weren't screwed enough already, a brutish nightmare emerged. A hellhound: huge and hungry and one thousand percent set on eating me alive. Awesome.

"Kim!" I called, holding my hand out to her.

"You were supposed to run! Why are you still here—"

The beast bared its fangs, stalking towards us.

I fought to stay by her side. "I can't leave you."

"You can, and you will." She stepped in front of me. "I'm not asking."

Spoken like a true queen. On her command, I took off like a shot, but not for my own safety: for hers. Predators enjoyed the thrill of the hunt, and I was ready to give it to him. I caught a glimpse of Kimber's brutality—the wind twisting tendrils of ashen hair about her—and couldn't help but grin. Here I thought she needed me. Ridiculous. The woman was born to be Death. Though I'd always watch for her enemies, hell if I'd steal her thunder. She lived for this: the kill.

Cutting through the trees, I thrashed through the leaves with intention, making my moves trackable. Each footfall echoed, and my heavy breaths carried. I needed the hound to give chase to ensure Kim had the chance to circle back and take it down. Her sudden scream made my blood run cold, and I skidded to a stop. I looped straight back the way I'd come, screaming and waving. "Over here, you mangy shit!"

Now *that* got its attention. I ignored Kim's curse—something about me being a dumbass for coming back—and waited a second longer than was comfortable to make sure the hound was, in fact, following me this time. *Good puppy.* I narrowly avoided its jaws as it took a bite at me. Like a wraith in the night, Kimber slid between us, determination radiating from her. But me? Unabashed fear crashed over me as the hound took her to the ground. "No!"

This was not her time. Fate could take me instead, the selfish bitch. In one swift move, I rolled Kim to the side away from the beast's reach, but I knew I wasn't fast enough to save us both. The hound had already locked onto me, ready to fill its unholy belly with my still warm flesh. Its teeth pierced my shoulder. Muscle tore and bone cracked, the heinous sound rattling through me as cold penetrated my soul and spread out across my chest. The hound readjusted its bite, sinking its fangs deeper, and I couldn't hold back my scream.

Venom seeped into my veins—the un-fucking-believable sear ripping through me like acid—and I knew. I knew my fate right then and there, because nobody—supernatural or otherwise—could survive hellhound toxins once in the bloodstream. The shit was more lethal than cyanide.

I'm a dead man.

My heartbeat boomed in my skull so loud that I feared my eardrums might burst. A pleasured snarl slipped past the monster's lips, and the world began to spin as warmth rolled down my arm. Blood...an ungodly amount of it. My time was running out. Quickly.

But I couldn't go yet. Not without knowing she was safe. Letting adrenaline take over, I fixed my stance, summoned every last bit of strength I had left, and cocked my fist back, landing a hard blow to the beast's snout. With a whimper, it released me. I pivoted, placing myself between Kimber's seemingly unconscious body and the hound.

"You can pick my bones clean," I growled, "but if you touch her, I'll crawl out of my damn grave to filet you alive."

The look reflected in the creature's stare confirmed my suspicions: this was no feral animal. Consciousness and calculation danced behind those eyes. This was the hound of legend: bound to one demon and ready to defend to the death; but so too was I bound. Claimed by one I would kill for. Or die trying. My inevitable end called to me as I looked down at Kim's still motionless body and noticed her chest rise and fall steadily. Relief rushed over me. She was alive, but I needed to buy her time to wake up. To fight. To run.

Ready to strangle the hound with my bare hands if necessary, I started back towards it; and my knees buckled, taking me to the ground. My vision grew hazy. Fuck. Not yet.

"Take me." I dragged myself through the dirt. "Let my bones serve as penance, but...spare her, *please.*"

The beast cocked its head, and in a breathy whisper I swear I heard it say, "No."

My stomach dropped as I frantically searched the woods for something, *anything* that might beat the beast back a step. Buy a little more time for Kim to stir. I snatched a thick branch off the ground and jabbed it towards the hound, but it bit the brittle wood in two with a snarl as if it were a mere twig. *Think, Coop. Think!*

In an unexpected burst of fury, Kim hopped to her feet and buried her blade to the hilt between the monster's shoulders, its cry of agony reverberating through the trees. A death blow. *That's my girl.* My laughter rose as darkness crept in, though I fought it. My back against the hard earth, I cast my sights to the stars, pleading with the heavens for just a little longer. I hadn't fulfilled my duty yet. Hadn't protected her as I'd sworn to; and while I still had breath, it belonged to her.

The demon was still out there, hunting her, and yet my cursed body wouldn't move. *Get up, get up, get up!* Harsh reality crashed over me like an avalanche ready to bury me alive, my spirit leaching from its mortal coil with every passing second. Despite my desires, my promises, my hopes...Death was coming.

For me.

CHAPTER TWO

A DEAL WITH DEATH

Dying is frigid. It's the sort of chill that touches parts buried so deep inside, you didn't even know they existed. A permeating cold sinking into every nook and cranny. There's no escaping it: the loneliness between life and death. Not quite in your body, not quite separated from it. But worst of all...I could still hear her. My best friend's cries and screams as she performed the summoning spell she never should have attempted alone. I tried to call out to her, to slip back into my body, but I couldn't. Fuck, I was supposed to be there! By her side, backing her up if Death decided he had no intention of sharing his throne with his heir. From what I'd researched, Cadagon was a less-than-gracious ruler who cared little for what anyone else thought, let alone what they desired. And Kim was alone in the forest, accompanied by a demon and—based on the sizzle of flame tickling my barely conscious ears—Death himself.

I'd failed her.

Red light danced behind my eyelids as complex galaxies began to spin about, giving way to supernovas that stretched out farther than the human eye should be able to perceive. My soul began to writhe—the sensation of being swept away by a waning wave overcoming me with a rush to the head. What was happening? Panic gripped me. I didn't fear death, not really. But any sort of consciousness which didn't include Kim? The notion had me clawing back into my bones. To be truly alone...there was no worse fate or torment. I *needed* her. We needed each other. I screamed into the unfurling void and begged for it to release me, but it held sharp and firm, ready to drag me into oblivion. I thrashed, though my body remained fixed and motionless. Why couldn't I *move*? All sound evaporated, the silence deafening.

No. No!

A voice called to me then, the darkness skittering away in its wake to create a path in my mind's eye. On one end: a hooded figure stood at the bow of a boat rocking on a crimson sea. On the other: an ornate door encased in bright yellow light. I turned back to the silhouetted man. His presence needed no formal introduction. Only one being could overshadow the dread presented at the afterlife crossroads.

Death: returned to claim my payment.

"You're here," I said, despite my lips never moving somehow.

He nodded and pointed to my hands. *Choose.*

I followed his gaze and watched in stunned horror as my fingertips dissolved into cosmic stardust. The remnants flitted away on an invisible wind. Each passing second whittled me away further, but the heavens stirred with promise, galaxies shifting overhead. Beautiful. A strange peace settled around me like a blanket, blocking out the chill. Maybe...maybe I could stay. Here in this warmth and comfort. I met Death's sights again. A knot formed in my throat as my feet turned towards the light at the opposite end of the path.

Choose wisely! He barked into my head.

My stomach jumped. Wait, no. I needed to get back. To something...but...to what again? The door began to sing a familiar melody, summoning me nearer. My soul knew it well: the harmony of the universe. Synchronicity of all things. I'd forgotten it after binding myself to this mortal coil; but now, here, I remembered it clear as day. The answers to life's great mysteries resided beyond that door. Every question could be answered. All I had to do was choose it. There would be no loneliness there, no pain. There, I'd be whole again, connected to the source. An internal magnet called me nearer, murmuring how I could leave everything behind: my pain, my grief, my—

She needs you, Cooper.

She...wait...Kim! The door's melody rose as if it knew I wavered. I stared at the golden door handle and considered taking hold, but fought the temptation as an ache settled in my chest. While peace surely resided within, true rest wasn't attainable without her. I'd be leaving half my heart behind, constantly wondering if my leaving had doomed her. I took a step back. The closer I got to Death, the more the light dimmed. The door cracked open wider with each step, attempting to call me back towards it, but I'd made my decision. Waves lapped at my feet as I settled at Death's side.

Meeting his flame-filled eyes, I whispered, "I choose life."

The path beneath me crumbled, dropping me into a violent sea. I thrashed to the surface time and again fighting for air, but the bloody waters filled my lungs, burning deep. As I sank to the murky depths devoid of warmth, I wondered. Had I been fooled? Was the abyss my punishment for walking away from the light? My toes skimmed the ocean bottom, knocking a rotten bone loose from a corpse's chest cavity. I'd chosen life, and yet here I was: dying. Again. Dread threatened to consume me. The door to peace had closed, and I was lost. Forever.

"Awaken," Death said, his voice drifting about like vapor.

The waters hurled me back through time and space towards a light, but not an ethereal one. It was softer somehow. Moonlight? No, torchlight—a mere sliver. Only...why couldn't I move? If I didn't know any better, I'd have confused the blood in my veins for concrete. Something wasn't right. I was stuck, trapped. Not breathing. Why wasn't I *breathing*? And then, life came—a thousand needles stabbing through my chest. My eyes flew open, and my lungs labored as I took in the blurry scene. Darkness, but...

"I—I'm alive?"

"Indeed," Death responded from somewhere in the shadows. "Though you cut it far too close for comfort with your insufferable uncertainty. The Sea of

Lost Souls nearly devoured you. And what's worse, my most treasured cloak is now ruined. Centuries old. Congealed blood is impossible to remove."

A swish of wet fabric tickled my ears, and my body shot up; but a hard crack to the head knocked me back down in an instant. *The hell?* I poked a fresh cut above my eye; my vision stained red. The world sharpened and came into focus. Glass. Wood. Nails. A coffin.

I was trapped in a fucking coffin!

Despite the fact that every bone in my body, every muscle and organ, seized with the pains of having stopped working for however long I'd lain dead in the dirt, I couldn't stay still. Small spaces, especially those lacking air, were among the few things that could seriously freak me out. To be confined in that way: stuck with nowhere to go while hyperventilation threatened to soak up your very last breath before you even had time to consider how you might escape...yeah, the stuff of nightmares right there. But I couldn't regain control. What was the point in bringing me back only to let me die another slow death? Cadagon was a serious piece of—

The coffin lid snapped open, and I thrust up, heaving in big lungfuls of moist, night air. When my head finally stopped spinning, I surveyed the room. A crypt. Based on the gold and intricate carvings surrounding the winding hallways to my left, I'd bet serious money that this was a resting place for royalty. A crescent moon carved into the granite ceiling snagged my attention: the symbol for Anathema. Yeah, this wasn't just any royal crypt. Death's family line was laid to rest here. A chill ran up my spine.

"How do you feel?" Death asked, concealed in shadow.

My head turned to find the corner now empty. "Cadagon..."

"That's 'Death' to you, boy," he called out, again from behind. "But I see someone has done their research. Good, I do dread wasting time on frivolous details."

"Guess that means you don't want to hear my life story then, huh?" I hopped out of the coffin—my jellylike legs nearly taking me to the ground—and righted myself against the coarse stone wall. Shit, I must have been dead long enough for rigor mortis to set in, because *damn,* my muscles were useless.

"On the contrary. I already know precisely who you are, Copernicus Talonborn. Or has the debt you owe me been forgotten so easily?"

As if my body wasn't already stiff as a board, his words turned my bones to ice. That name...I hadn't heard it uttered since I was a child. "Of course I remember my debt, but how do you know *that* name?"

Death emerged; the hood of his dripping robe hung down over his face. He began to circle me—watching—and pressed his black-stained fingertips together the same way he had upon our first meeting. "Naturally, I grew curious after striking our bargain as to whom I had bound my blood. It did not take long to realize who, or rather *what*, you are."

I squared my shoulders. "Huh. Here I thought you'd remember me based on having slaughtered and chased my people from their homes. Or are you really stupid enough to believe you killed the last of the Talonborns?"

"Lies and slander," Cadagon snarled. "Seems you've learned well from the mortals. Good. Kimberly will need you to utilize such lying abilities moving forward. That is, if you wish to repay her for the steep bargain she struck to save your life."

Bargain? But what— Reality sucker-punched me in the face: she'd struck a blood pact to save me. Shit! What a reckless little thing she was. I told her to always save herself, to not worry about me. But then again, if she'd listened then she wouldn't be the woman I fell in love with. Figures she'd sacrifice on my account. Brat.

"What did she offer you?" I asked.

Death tilted his head up just enough to flash a wicked grin my way. "I'm not at liberty to discuss such details. Even if she is the object of your unrequited love."

His words hit hard, and my sights slipped to the floor. He wasn't wrong, but I hated to admit part of me still hoped that one day Kim would learn to love me. That she'd find her home in my arms. A ridiculous wish. But her affections or lack thereof wouldn't sway my mission. I'd protect her down to my last breath, even if it meant she would find happiness in another's arms. In Juniper's arms. I swallowed hard, lifting my gaze. Based on Cadagon's prideful stare, he knew he'd hit a nerve, and I'd be damned if I let him have the satisfaction. I righted my face, donning an even expression.

"Fuck you." I stepped closer. "You don't know a thing about us or how we feel for each other."

"Oh, but I most certainly do. You see, I have eyes everywhere." He motioned about the room. "Even in the mortal world. How do you think Kimberly has gone this long without being attacked? Lived unharmed and peacefully among the rogue creatures of the night who have hunted her these years past?"

Memories—dark and twisted—traced their claws across my brain. The first time I'd killed in Kim's name, I'd been fourteen. We'd snuck out that night, trailing about the woods in search of a distraction from our monotonous lives, when the hair on the back of my neck stood up. I'd searched the area and found nothing, yet I'd known someone was watching us. Watching *her*. Based on the pull in my gut, the lurker had malicious intent. Careful not to alert Kimber—she'd have thrown hands despite her gifts lying dormant still—I'd taken her home. Made sure she was tucked into bed safe and sound before sneaking back out the window and heading straight to the garden shed.

Looking back on it, I felt bad for him: my inner child. The way his hands shook around the shovel handle as he'd waltzed into the tree line, entirely unprepared for what he'd find or the sudden awakening of his magic thereafter. Turned out someone in Anathema knew Kimber hadn't died in the massacre, knew she'd escaped. My guess at the time was someone had put a bounty on her head, considering the failed attacks that ramped up soon after. I'd found the stalking reaper—demented and torn from his purpose to bring balance based on the crazed look in his eye—hunched over, rocking back and forth as he glared up at her bedroom window. Circling back, I'd whispered from behind, "Hey, pervert. You make it a habit of watching underage girls sleep?"

He'd spun on me and buried a blade in my thigh before I could blink. That was the first time I'd known real pain. To my surprise—and future list of kinks—I'd discovered pain fueled me. With time, I'd learned to love it. Crave it: the submission pain demands. Asshole had only managed to get one cut in before my shovel cracked against his skull, knocking him out. Shock froze me in place until he'd started to stir again, writhing in the dirt, and it'd became clear what I had to do. Cocking the shovel back over my shoulder, I'd made his death quick and clean, but for my own sanity, not his. I hadn't had the stomach for murder yet. That would come later. After throwing up violently for gods knows how long, I'd buried him in the family pet cemetery and never looked back.

I fixed my eyes on Death. "She survived because I protected her."

The room darkened as he threw his hood off, his irises burning with living flame. "She survived because *I* allowed you to live!"

A laugh slipped past my lips. "So you admit it. *I* was the one who stayed and watched out for her, unlike her useless father who tossed her to the wolves—"

"Silence! I have done everything in my power to keep her safe!"

My jaw locked; words stuck in my throat despite my attempts to free them. Black smoke crept from Cadagon's fingertips, spilling across the floor to circle my ankles and hold me in place.

"Listen closely, *boy,*" he said pointedly. "What happened in the past will come to light in due time, but I have one clear, concise mission for you. One you will neither deviate from nor alter. If you do as you are told, I will consider both Kimberly's and your debts paid, but I expect your full cooperation. Do you understand me?"

With a snap, my lips were free.

I rubbed my sore cheeks. "Both our debts?"

"Both. But do not test me, or I may be inclined to retract my kind offer and deliver you to the Shroud instead."

"Is that supposed to scare me?"

"It should, if you have any sense whatsoever." He circled me again, stopping to run his finger through a candle flame. "I am certain you have heard the tales, have you not?"

Kim had mentioned the Shroud on more than one occasion. It's where she and June met, somewhere within the astral plane. Never once had she said anything to make me concerned for her safety there, but given the conviction in Death's eyes, it grew painfully obvious that I'd been naive in this. "I can tell you're dying to fill me in on what I missed, Death. Go on then, tell me."

With a nod, he drifted to sit on a carved stone bench in the corner. Gold and alabaster inlays along the bench's arms shone in the blinking candlelight. "The Shroud is an odious place. Those of us with any true sense residing in the adjacent realms remain vigilant in avoiding it as it harbors great destruction and chaos. You see, at the beginning of time, the Old Gods—the original Fate and Death—fell in love. A burning, all-consuming connection. With time, they hoped to create what most do: a family." Cadagon's face grew still, and a sliver of horror slipped through his calm demeanor. "These 'children,' as the delusional Gods called them, were simple beings at the start. But then humanity was born, and Fate and Death grew curious about those strange, fleeting beings."

The hair on my neck stood up.

"With Fate and Death's attention stolen," he continued, ambling towards me, "their creations grew jealous. That jealously gave way to murderous and ravenous tendencies. Only when the Old Gods' children had pushed humanity to near extinction did Fate and Death lock them away in the Shroud."

Disturbing, sure, but I hadn't a clue why Cadagon felt the need to share this little fairy tale. "What are you getting at?"

"Our gifts, Cooper. Kim's and mine. Where do you think such abilities came from?"

"They descended from the Old Gods. It's in your blood."

Cadagon laughed. "Hardly. It was a gift. A weapon. Fate bestowed part of her light to Elysium, and Death reluctantly presented part of his darkness to Anathema. They cut out threads of their inherent powers and wove them into chosen, mortal bloodlines to ensure humanity would never be pushed to the verge again. But such power comes with a cost."

My eyes narrowed on him. "Why are you telling me all this?"

"It is important for you to know. Should those sinister beings confined in the Shroud find release from their prison, leaders of the adjacent planes would be called to fight. With imbalance brewing in the realms as we see here in Anathema, humanity is already at risk. Kimberly *must* restore balance before it taints the other planes bordering the Shroud. If not, we risk history repeating itself, and innocent people will die. Kimberly very well could be one of them."

"I won't let that happen," I bit out, grabbing Cadagon's cloak sleeve.

He brushed my hand away but met my gaze with conviction. "Are you willing to bet your life on that?"

"I would do anything for her."

"For the sake of all things we hold dear, I hope that is true, because what I am about to ask of you should not be considered lightly." Death reached into his cloak, returning with a gem-encrusted scythe. His stare burned hotter than before as he slid the blade across his palm and extended it to me. "Do you promise to weed out Kimberly's enemies? To uphold her honor at all costs and see to her survival, even if it should cost you your life?"

The steady drip of blood echoed about the room, and I weighed his words. Cadagon was not known for being forthcoming, let alone truthful. He could very well be hiding something. Playing me. "And if I deny the terms of your deal?"

"Then I will return you to the Sea of Lost Souls or better yet, the Shroud. I will even allow you to choose your fate. But you will not deny me, because you care too greatly for her. It is what brought you back from the brink, what brought you here to Anathema."

He was right. I would strike the deal regardless of the fine print, but knowing I had no choice—that I served another's will for my own life—made it difficult to simply grab his hand and agree. In the end though, it was easy: make the deal or die. Not to mention, I'd be damned before Kim succumbed to another realm's corruption when enough surely awaited in her own. I met Death's stare, and it struck me: the reason he'd saved my life two years ago was because he'd *had* to.

"You can't protect your own daughter...why? I thought you were the big, bad Death himself. Why drag a shifter into the mix?"

"I will say this only once, so listen closely." Something akin to regret reflected in his expression as he huffed out a breath. "I have made mistakes. Done things I am not proud of. But always in the name of my family. While they will never understand or truly know me, that is not my concern. I am bound, Cooper, but I can offer you a chance at the happiness I never got. At love."

"I—I don't understand."

Blood ran down his wrist as he pinched the bridge of his nose. "I've made deals to ensure Kimberly and her mother remained safe until my daughter could return and claim her rightful place. The time has come to pay the price for those deals. I won't be around to protect her, and she will be forced into situations I've no power to revoke or change."

"What kind of situations we talkin' here?"

"For one..." He hesitated, his lips forming a tight line. "She has been promised."

The ground shook beneath me. No, that—that couldn't be. Losing her to another because she chose them was one thing. But for her to be forced into a loveless marriage? Like hell I'd let that happen.

I paced the room, my hands fisted at my sides. "Promised? This isn't gods-damned Elizabethan England! Nobody has a right to a woman's body or heart unless *she* chooses it. I'll fucking kill him!"

Death's smile grew wild. "How I hoped you'd say that. Now, do we have a deal?"

We stood there; our eyes locked. Trusting someone like him came at a cost, but if he was telling the truth—if he really had boxed himself into blood pacts to ensure her safety—then I might be the only one looking out for her. A vision of Kim facing this brutal kingdom alone swept in, scaring the shit out of me. I lifted my chin. I knew what had to be done. My best friend's safety far outweighed the risks. From here on out, I would be her shadow. Her blade.

I offered my hand to Death. "Yes. We have a deal."

In a heartbeat, he snatched my wrist, dragged his dagger down my palm, and clapped our hands together. A blood pact. Unbreakable. Binding.

"Let it be known," he said with a laugh that boomed through the stone enclosure, "the deal with Death has been struck. You have your mission, Copernicus. You will kill the vampire Lord. You will kill Lyvias Kraven."

Chapter Three

THIS FUCKING GUY

Slinking through the castle halls, I found my way to the servant's quarters. First order of business: find a way to blend in unnoticed. Shifting was always an option, but I wasn't entirely sure what forms were considered normal in this realm yet. Based on what little information I'd come across in my research on Anathema, few mortal creatures still resided within its borders—most having died off from lack of sunlight—and if caught in a form which wasn't organic, I risked getting caught before I even set eyes on my target. Better to play it safe.

Careful to avoid detection, I stuck to the shadowed corners, but the splendor of the castle was not lost on me. Carved stone pillars, towering ceilings, crimson stair runners, and half-melted candles dripping from their ornate candelabras drew my eye. Stunning, to say the very least. I knew if I gave myself time, I could wander these halls for hours marveling at the art, not to mention the literature packed in the study bookshelves. It struck me: the history of my people was within reach. Accessible for the first time. Questions I'd battled my entire life could be laid to rest with some dedication and time. What really happened to the shapeshifters and why? But my own desires would have to wait.

Servants ran about the halls, each in a rush to their required locations. Dawn—while you wouldn't know it given the crescent moon hanging high in the night sky—was upon us. Royalty was waking, and based on the palpable tension in the air, nobody intended to keep their charges waiting. My gaze slid down my frame: acid-washed jeans, band t-shirt, leather jacket. Gods, could I look any more like a human? I needed a wardrobe change. ASAP. I took a step forward, but paused as someone approached. The woman's bright fuchsia eyes radiated in the low light. A demon.

"Go," she said in a kind tone and guided a timid, young demon down the hall. "I'll find them, I promise. But for now, you must attend to the advisor. Keep up the façade. Keep him happy."

The girl—who upon closer inspection couldn't be more than fifteen years old—shook her head fiercely. "I—I can't. I don't know how to do this. Suri, I'm scared."

"Fear is normal," Suri responded, taking the girl's hand in hers. "But you cannot let fear win. You cannot let *him* win. Play the role; be his right hand until we can find a way to get you home. Fake it like your life depends on it. Can you do that for me?"

The young girl nodded—her chin trembling—and Suri ushered her towards the far end of the hall.

"Good. Now go before you're late. And Lana..."

Lana turned, wiping the remaining tears from her cheeks. "Yes?"

"You are far stronger than anything he throws at you. Do you hear me?"

With a strained smile, Lana disappeared into the shadows, and Suri turned...heading straight towards me. *Fuck.* Before I could curve around the next corner out of sight, she was there. Her eyes drilled into me. She knew I didn't belong—that I was an invader in this kingdom—given my appearance alone. Her hands tightened at her sides as she turned to run, a scream clawing up her throat.

"Guards! Intruder—"

I clamped a hand over her mouth and dragged her dainty frame into the nearest room off the main hall. Pressing her to the wall, I lowered myself into her sight line.

"I am not your enemy. You're safe."

She looked me over frantically, panic evident in her stare.

I raised my free hand in submission, showing her I bore no weapons. "I promise, I'm no threat to you."

Her expression relaxed slightly.

"Good," I said. "Now, if you swear not to yell, I'll—"

Her teeth sank into my palm, drawing blood, and I instinctively released my hold. With speed I'd not anticipated, she was nearly out the door before I brought her to the ground and placed one knee on each side of her, pinning her in place. I clapped my hand back over her mouth.

"That wasn't very nice, was it?" I whispered. "Here I thought we were becoming friends."

She thrashed beneath my hold, determined for freedom at any cost. I couldn't help but marvel at her for a moment. That rage, the wrath...it was all too familiar. A flicker of Kim's conviction in my current rival reminded me of my mission. I heaved a deep breath.

"Look, I saw what you did for that girl back there. Lana, was it?"

Upon hearing the young demon's name, Suri stilled beneath me.

"I am no stranger to the malicious intents of royalty," I continued, "which is precisely why I'm here. I have someone I need to protect as well. I don't want to hurt you, Suri."

Her flailing settled, and I gave her a moment to find her center.

"Okay, I'm going to remove my hand now. Please don't scream." Slow and steady, I did as I said I would.

When her breath evened out, she asked, "Who are you?"

"Who I am doesn't matter. I am no one to concern yourself with."

A deep voice cut through the quiet, reverberating down the halls. "Suri! Death has summoned you! You must hurry!"

Fear flickered across her face, and I stood, pulling her to her feet. "You're Death's right hand?"

"No." She shook her head. "I am to be the new queen's royal dresser."

The admission hit me square in the chest. "Kimberly?"

She nodded. Another voice echoed down the hall. Followed by another and another.

"I must go," she said, and headed for the door.

I caught her arm gently, turning her towards me. "What happened to Lana? I'm assuming she didn't have a say?"

Suri's face fell, and she shook her head again. That poor girl played no part in her own future, the same way Kimber had no say in her betrothal. The notion burned me up inside. To force such a fate on anyone, to take away their autonomy, their choice...it was beyond cruel. Dehumanizing. Evil men thrived best in darkness where their sins were easily concealed, and Anathema provided them a hunting ground enveloped in eternal night.

"Your future queen would never allow such a thing. She seeks to right the wrongs brewing here in Anathema." I stepped closer to Suri. "You don't owe me anything, I know, but if you give me the chance, I will dedicate myself to helping Kim do just that."

Another gruff call from a castle guard ricocheted down the hall. Death was losing his patience.

"Really, I must go," she said, ripping her arm free.

"Please, no one can know I'm here. Not if I have any hope of ensuring your future queen has the chance to fix the imbalance in this kingdom. For you. For Lana."

"The future queen, she is your charge?"

"Yes, I serve her will."

"I see." She looked me up and down. Her nose wrinkled when she came to my ripped jeans. "Three doors down to the left, you'll find a small room. We keep extra servant uniforms there." She turned to leave but stopped to peer back over her shoulder. "Do not make me regret this. Mistaking my kindness for weakness has led men to an early grave on more than one occasion."

With that, she was gone.

After donning my new attire—a scratchy-as-hell black ensemble—I began my search of the castle. Knowing where things were located, especially good hiding places, was a must if I hoped to take out a gods-knows-how-old vampire Lord. Sure, I had my strengths, but something told me he wouldn't be my easiest kill to date. Good thing I loved a challenge. I familiarized myself with the main wings: washrooms, studies, ballrooms, the usual. Upon my turn towards the south tower, a soft voice stopped me in my tracks. The girl from before: Lana. I ducked into the nearest study and pressed my ear to the door frame.

"Please," she begged. "I can't do that. I just...can't."

A man—his tone full of venom—responded, "You will do as your royal advisor commands, or you'll secure a new permanent residence where you'll be...put to better use, shall we say."

"A new place doesn't sound so bad—"

"You foolish girl," he seethed. "You will find no kindness there. No joy. You would be nothing more than a fresh slab of meat outside these walls. Prey. Have you forgotten the mercy I bestowed upon you? How I plucked you from your miserable life and allowed you to serve me here in these grand halls?"

I snuck a glance to find Lana's hands knotted in her skirt. I convinced myself to stay put despite everything in me yearning to rip this asshole a new one. Who talks to a *kid* that way? The dude deserved to have his tongue cut out.

She cowered under his stare. "No sir, I—I haven't forgotten. I just, I've never offered my blood to anyone before. I'm scared."

"It is an honor to appease the future king's needs. We can't very well have him focused on his thirst while he aims to charm the future queen in battle, can we?" The demon advisor jerked Lana's chin up. "A thing like that could easily be defined as treason: refusal to attend to your royal duties."

Tears slid down her cheeks. "Will it hurt?"

"Oh, very much so." A wicked grin spread across his face as he slid a single finger down her cheek, wiping her tears. He stepped closer to Lana. "But to lend your virgin blood to the next king of Anathema is a pain worth enduring. Would you not agree?"

My hands shook, and my teeth gnashed together. Sick bastard! The look in his eyes told me that given the chance and privacy, he'd be willing to go a lot further than what I'd just witnessed. Probably had. Something told me Kim might already have dibs on this guy—my girl had fantastic intuition when it came to identifying monsters—but if she didn't, he would die by my hand. Oh, how I'd make it slow, draw it out.

His hand tightened around Lana's arm, and she recoiled with a sharp breath. That was it. Screw him! I turned the corner with clenched fists, ready to beat the prick black and blue, when a shadow eclipsed the hall. I flattened myself against the wall, motionless. Based on his garb, the deep crimson of his eyes, and the fang-filled smirk, it didn't take long to realize who I'd happened to bump into. A murderous urge pumped through me.

"Lord Lyvias," the advisor greeted. "We were just coming to find you, Highness."

"Could have fooled me, Nasheesh," Lyvias responded, the vein beneath his neck tattoo bulging. "Looks to me as if you were playing with my meal. And I don't take kindly to seconds."

"My apologies. I only wished to make sure she was prepared to serve you adequately."

"Not necessary. Going in blind causes panic, increases fear. Terror makes the blood all the sweeter." The vampire Lord let out a dark chuckle and honed in on Lana. "Come, child."

With a quickness I hadn't anticipated, Lyvias and his prey were gone, leaving Nasheesh grimacing in the hall. My heart sank into my gut. Shit. I should have saved her. Should have stepped out and beat them both senseless. But if something like this was going on within the castle walls in plain view, I'd bet it'd trickled in from the outside. There could be more like her. On my mother's grave, I swore then and there that I'd not only save Lana, return her to her family, and murder the men who'd caused her pain; but I would also do everything in my power to prevent such tragedies from befalling another woman or child in Anathema. So I'd bide my time to save as many as I could. And while I waited,

I'd relish the thought of Nasheesh's and Lyvias's blood on my hands, the life seeping out of them.

You don't fuck with kids. *Period.*

Nasheesh smoothed his robes before snapping at a passing guard. "You. Escort me to the training grounds. I wish to be present when the future queen arrives."

"Yes, sir," the guard responded.

I followed close, but not too close, attempting to blend in. When onlookers passed, I stopped to polish a nearby statue with my sleeve or straighten a picture like a good servant would. Nobody appeared to notice me, let alone question whether I belonged, and the realization saddened me. How many of the castle staff had been forced into a life like this as Lana had? Been bent to another's whims above their own desires? It sickened me. Why did Death allow it? No doubt he'd have countless people willing to serve him by choice. It was a prestigious position to most: serving the king. Why steal a child from her home? He had some serious explaining to do upon our next meeting, but I logged the thought away and turned my focus to the present. *Stay sharp.*

I made it through the gardens and into the training grounds, scouring the scene before finding the servant's tent tucked away from the group of well-dressed aristocrats. Death mingled among the crowd, and I scooped up a rogue serving platter packed with a variety of drinks. Blood sloshed in a golden goblet. For Lyvias, surely. Wading into the crowd, I kept my head down until I brushed elbows with Cadagon.

His sights honed in on me as he lifted a glass of red wine from my tray. "You may go now."

"Your Highness, might I have a word—"

"I said, 'Go.' Servants are to be mere shadows." Cadagon shooed me away.

A hint. *Don't let anyone of importance see you.* If Kim found out I was here, or Lyvias caught onto Death's and my deal, everything would be ruined.

"Yes, Your Highness. I'll be just around that corner should you need me."

His eyes narrowed. "I won't."

I resigned myself to a nearby outcropping in the tree line where I could easily disappear if need be. Though at the crowd's synchronized head turn in anticipation of Lyvias's appearance, I knew it'd be impossible for me to look away. He began his sparring match with a thick-muscled reaper. The vampire Lord swung his axe around as if it weighed little more than a feather, nearly decapitating his opponent in the first minute. I studied his foot placements, his grip on his weapon, committing it all to memory. While I hated to admit it, the asshole was good at what he did. He'd be a challenge to defeat even on my best day.

Every head but his turned towards the grounds' entrance, and my heart skipped a beat, reminding me exactly why I had come in the first place.

Kim walked in with her head held high like the queen she was. Her gown's plunging neckline drew the eye to her perfect breasts. My gaze slid about her, down to where the pleated fabric hugged her curves. I imagined my hands laced around those hips, digging my fingertips into her soft flesh, while my lips pushed hard against hers to absorb her pleading moan. Ruby clips dotted the gentle waves of her hair, glittering in the moonlight's glow, and I forgot how to breathe. I lost myself in her. Stunning. Absolutely stunning in every way. My body reacted the same way it always did in her presence, and I carefully adjusted my arousal, tucking the evidence into my waistband. That's all I needed was to have a noticeable boner over the future queen. I'm sure that'd win me an overnight stay in the dungeon at the very least.

I never took my eyes off her as she conversed with Death and Nasheesh; never looked away when she feigned interest in her new betrothed. For a moment, I feared she might actually be entertaining the idea. Lyvias and her. Sure, he was easy on the eyes, not going to lie. If I hadn't seen what I had with Lana, and say, stumbled across him in a club instead, he would have caught my eye. But I knew better. The deadliest predators usually came wrapped in beautiful packages. And after seeing Kim that close to him—a smug, disinterested grimace on his face as she appeared to be pleading with him about something—I had to remind myself that this was a marathon, not a sprint. Slitting his throat in front of so many important assets to the throne that Kim would certainly need to remain in good standing with...well, that wouldn't do.

As I stepped out of my secluded watching area, the crowd gasped in tandem, their feet shuffling together and blocking my view. Their panicked tones gave me pause; talk of death and murder and ill intentions rolled through the mass.

"What is he doing?" muttered someone.

With a scoff, another responded, "Lyvias won't let her go so easily."

My blood ran cold. What the hell was going on? Had he hurt her? With hurried steps, I rounded the guests, attempting to catch a glimpse through the hysteria. I swore if he'd laid a fucking hand on her, I'd kill him right then and there.

When I finally saw what they'd been murmuring about, the only thing I could do was laugh. There, splayed out below his own weapon, laid the big, bad vampire Lord. Kim pressed the edge of the axe down harder, spilling fresh blood on Lyvias's throat—the sharpness of the blade dull in comparison to the wrath in her stare. I bit my lip.

"That's my girl," I whispered.

"What did you say?" a cerulean-eyed demon asked, his sudden proximity making me jump.

"Shit—uhh. I mean, my apologies. I said, 'Would you like more wine, sir?'"

He raised a brow, his sights drifting about as if he could see right through me. "Right. I will pretend you didn't just lie to me then."

"I promise you, I—"

"Ah, ah." He raised a hand, the gold bangles around his wrist jingling. "Lie to me once, and I am prone to forgiveness. But nobody lies to Adari Melontin-Wentworth twice."

His attention lingered between me and some unforeseen image above my head before he ambled into the crowd. What *was* he staring at? *Old kook.* No wonder he hadn't wanted any more wine; the dude was already having drunken hallucinations. He slid his hand into a man's wearing a dapper, tailored suit and stole one final glance towards me before pressing a kiss to his partner's cheek. Odd. I never took the elite to be ones to let things go. Especially when my dumbass let something so personal slip. The crowd parted—Adari disappearing in the mix—and I dismissed the curious interaction.

Instead I set my sights on Lyvias as he pouted his way off the training grounds in a dramatic display of poor sportsmanship. With little consideration, he began removing his battle gear and tossed it aside in his walk of shame back towards the castle. A young man in servant attire much more worn than my own trailed after him, leaning down to pick up each individual piece in time with the Lord's tantrum. I followed suit, helping collect the abandoned armor.

"Thank you," the man said quietly. "He's fast and impatient."

"Who, Lyvias?"

The man's face went white. "*Lord* Lyvias, you mean."

"Lord, yes. My apologies."

"Silence your incessant yapping, would you?" Lyvias barked. He spun on us—his attention landing on me—and a flicker of something dark and familiar flashed in his crimson eyes. "And who might you be?"

I swallowed hard. I hadn't considered a name; what a rookie move. *Umm...*

"This," Death's voice interrupted as he pushed me forward, "is your new servant. He's quite keen on stress relief, and I thought you might be in need of a good massage after such an intense battle."

"He is mine to command?" Lyvias asked, raising a brow.

"Indeed, he is. Consider him a gift. He will do whatever you require of him."

Lyvias looked me over, hungry. "Anything?"

My hands began to shake. "What is that supposed to—"

"Yes," Cadagon cut in, stepping between us to glare down at me. "*Addison* will do whatever it is you ask of him. Correct, boy?"

Death's burning eyes reflected a murderous spark back at me, but not my own. He'd provided me an opening alongside a warning: bide my time, study my target. The hunt had begun, and *damn* was I excited to learn this asshole's weaknesses. I licked my lips, my heartbeat amping up. "Yes, Lord Lyvias. I am at your service."

With that, Death snapped for the other servant to follow and went on his way, leaving me and my prey alone.

So very, very alone.

CHAPTER FOUR

A VIOLENT HEART

I followed the vampire Lord closely through the winding hallways back into the castle's recesses. All the while, my blood boiled. How would I do it? Take the fucker out. Countless scenarios swam in my mind. Decapitation? No, too messy. Fire? Nah, I'd never get the smell of burnt hair out of my nose. Despite mortal belief, a stake to the heart wasn't necessary unless the vampire came from old lineages: pureblood. And based on the slightly dulled ends I'd seen on Lyvias's fangs, he was nothing of the sort.

"Sit," Lyvias demanded upon entry to his lavish suite overlooking the courtyard.

He pointed to the leather chair nearest the window. I bit my tongue and obeyed. I'd play along, if only to learn him better. His eyes never left me as he began to unbutton his shirt, pulling it away to reveal a plethora of vine tattoos winding up his neck and slithering back down his chest. They held an eerie resemblance to the poison ivy inked on my own arms. I studied the scars marring his rib cage, his shoulder, his forearm. Clearly he was no stranger to battle, and I wondered how many of those marks had ended in death for his opponents.

My chest tightened. Would I become one of them? A fallen, forgotten memory at the hands of this monster? Vampires were worthy adversaries, especially when trained in battle as he was, which made him a bit of a wild card. At least he didn't come equipped with rapid-moving venom like my last target; and without the need for a stake through the heart, I might stand a chance. His speed and strength would be a bit of a challenge, sure. But what he didn't know? Pureblood shifters were used to broken bones. My rubber ligaments were practically *made* to take a beating.

You can do this. Don't let him get in your head; just stay focused.

"What?" he asked, pulling me back to reality. "Do you like what you see?"

I dropped my gaze, my muscles tensing. "My apologies, sir."

He sauntered over—his dick perfectly aligned at my eye level—with an expectant smirk on his face. The arrogance.

"No need to apologize." He lifted my chin. "You wish to serve your future king, do you not?"

Shit. I swallowed hard. Death had offered me up as a personal masseuse, but he hadn't mentioned anything about a happy ending. My hands clenched at the memory of Lyvias looming over Lana's trembling frame. The only way I would *ever* touch him would be to wrap my hands around his throat and squeeze until bone snapped. Oh, *there* was a thought. Strangulation. I'd hold onto that one for later. Because if I allowed my mind to wander? Allowed my imagination to fill in the blanks on what may have occurred in private after he'd taken the girl away...my rage would win out. A rash choice could land me in the dungeon or worse, six feet under. I heaved a breath. I needed to remain focused, no matter how much I wanted to bury my fist in his face.

"Soothe me," Lyvias demanded, lying face down on the bed. "Show me what those hands can do."

The filth looming in his stare told me that with time, he'd demand much more of me than a simple rubdown. After all, a vampire's appetite was ravenous, and blood wasn't their sole means of sustenance. Some—not all—savored the emotional drain of breaking a person down to little more than a vessel on which to feast. Stealing a person's dignity first fed their predatory instinct. Their ego. It made them feel powerful and superior. I fought the bile rising up. An emotional vampire was just as dangerous as a starved one. Maybe more so.

"Come now," he cooed. "I don't bite...much."

A war raged within me. Serving him went against everything I believed in, but if I didn't play along, I risked blowing my cover. *Kim,* I reminded myself. This was all for her. And for *her,* I'd do anything.

"Yes, sir," I said, reluctantly making my way over to the bed.

I would be patient, for now. I placed my hands on his bare shoulders, and he flinched against my cold fingertips. Nausea swept over me on contact. Dark energy leached off him like thick tar set to consume. Devour. Intuition—a skill I'd worked hard to hone since discovering my lineage—told me this man was hiding much more than a simple sinister desire or kink. Whatever he was mixed up with had tainted his soul so deeply, it radiated against my fingertips. A sick, twisted evil controlled him. He bred anguish, spread it like a plague. I shoved hard against his shoulders, envisioning the ways I'd love to repay the pain he'd dispensed.

He moaned into the pillow. "Strong grip. I like that."

"I aim to serve," I lied through my teeth.

With a laugh, his hand snaked up my leg. "As you should. Tell me, how far would you go to earn my favor?"

His hand came to rest on my inner thigh, and I froze.

"I don't know what you mean, sir."

"Oh, don't play coy now." He pursed his lips, pushing to sit. "A man with such skillful hands has clearly pleasured another in his lifetime."

"I don't offer such services, I'm afraid."

I stepped back, his hold on me dropping. With a quickness imperceptible to the naked eye, he stood to glare down at me, snatching my jaw in a firm grip. I fought his touch, but his fingertips only buried themselves deeper in my skin the more I struggled.

"If you won't offer me pleasure freely, I could simply force your hand. Is that what you want? To be taken by force?" He grew eerily still, a grin splaying across his cheeks. "I do enjoy breaking a man, Addison."

I dared another step back, and his shoulders squared. *Oh fuck.* His sights locked onto me like a lion ready to attack. Not good. Not. Good! I hadn't planned to kill him so soon, but if this asshole was prepared to do what I thought he was, I'd have no choice but to fight. I planted my feet, narrowing my stare.

"I don't break."

In a flash, he pinned me against the wall, trailing his tongue up my throat, and I thrashed in his hold. His lips came to rest against my ear.

"You will bend to my will. No one says 'no' to Lyvias Kraven."

His fangs punctured my neck, sending an unwelcome rush through me. A vampire's bite was known to cause euphoria, but like this...against my will? How could my own body betray me? Warmth washed down my shoulder, a throb emanating where his fangs tore through my flesh. I snatched his wrists, burying my nails in his skin.

He groaned and licked my blood off his lips. "I like them with a little fight. It makes my triumph far more satisfying."

"Get off me," I snarled.

Violent urges reared up in me. Murderous, demanding urges that warred with the mounting heat in my cheeks. *Holy hell, his strength...* I'd thought him pompous and narcissistic, certainly, maybe even a bit tougher than others in his league, but the lavish lifestyle of a royal oftentimes made one soft. Yet the sheer force in his grip had me reeling.

Don't be a pussy! Show him who he's messing with!

My confidence returned, and I shoved him hard, creating space between us. One foot over the other, we mirrored each other's steps. "Your move, *sir*."

"I'm done with your games." He closed in. "Submit or—"

Three hard knocks silenced his demands. His eyes shot towards the door.

"Lord Lyvias." Lana's familiar voice rang through. "I've come to attend to you before your meeting with the advisor."

Lyvias's attention fell back on me, and he dismissed me with a wave. "Go. We will finish our dance tonight."

Head spinning, I took my chance and started for the door. Like hell we would finish later, psycho!

He caught my wrist and stopped me in my tracks. "And do not even think about leaving me waiting. Your life is of no consequence to me aside from pleasure. If that pleasure was to end? Well, I simply would have no use for you anymore, now, would I?"

He threw me against the door, my hand catching on the doorknob to break my fall. Oh, yeah, this fucker would *pay*. As I passed Lana—Suri waiting outside in the shadows—it took everything in me not to beat the son-of-a-bitch to death right then and there, even if it meant my own demise. Which it very well could. I pinched my brow, trying to silence the stupid voice in the back of my mind telling me that I was in over my head. That I was no match for Lyvias. Sure, he had me in the strength department, but I'd find a way, damn it.

"I know that look," Suri said, her expression even.

"I want his head on a fucking platter!"

She yanked my sleeve, ushering us around the nearest corner. "You'd be wise to keep your voice down. There are eyes and ears all over this place."

"I don't give a shit what anyone hears. He's a predator! How are you okay letting Lana attend to him?"

"Okay with it?" A cynical laugh slipped through her. "I am anything but okay with what happens behind those closed doors! But I'm not a fool. I know how little sway people like you and I have. We have to be sharper, smarter. We can't allow a momentary lapse in judgment ruin her chances at true freedom."

"She's at his mercy! What if he—"

"Breathe," Suri demanded. "I've taken great care in preparing Lana for this moment. She is a master of diversion and evasion. Do not underestimate her."

"But she's just a child!"

"She is no mere child, I assure you. That girl is a sharpened blade. We all become a weapon at one point or another in our service to the crown of Death. She knows how to protect herself, Addison."

I ground my teeth. "She shouldn't have to."

Suri rested a hand on my arm—a plea to calm down—and in that small touch, her energy coursed through me. She...she was letting me in. Letting me feel her true power. My skin pebbled; my heartbeat slowed. Profound pain—the kind that mars the soul and demands retribution—flowed in her veins. Whatever she'd seen and the things she'd been *forced* to partake in during her years in the castle had led her here to this moment, attending to Lana. Protecting her the best way Suri could at every turn. This woman...she'd seen some shit; and while her rage rivaled mine, an eerie peace encased her heart. I looked her over. Beneath the ache in her fuchsia stare lay a blatant truth: she wasn't about to let the sins of Anathema's elite go without a fight. She would have her revenge. And as I rested a hand over hers, I decided I was going to help her get it.

"Cooper," I finally corrected, running a hand through my hair.

She raised a brow.

"My name is Cooper."

"Ah, I see," she said with a nod. "And you're a shapeshifter."

I faltered. *How the...* "No, I'm—"

"Oh, hush. You can trust me. Your energy reading proved that much, did it not?"

She'd felt that? But that would mean... "You're a pureblood?"

"No, witch. Half, on my mother's side." She smiled, pride in her stance. "A tinctured witch to be exact, gifted in clairvoyance. I knew someone was coming who would help me, though I must say I didn't expect you this soon. Why do you think I let you go upon our first meeting?"

Her words settled around me. Tinctured magic. So she dabbled in the spiritual realm, unlike an elemental witch with an affinity for the physical. My mind recalled when I'd pinned her to the floor, how her eyes had drilled into me. She'd been reading me then too. Only this time, she had dropped her internal barriers so I could read her back in an exchange of fragile trust. Clever woman.

"Besides," Suri continued, "those sharp cheekbones give you away. Typical shifter trait. Others might have forgotten your people, your court, but not me. The corruption didn't end after the massacre; that was only the beginning. Nevertheless, we have to suss out our enemies before we can strike."

I turned to Suri, pointing towards Lyvias's door. "This bastard—"

"Will get what's coming to him," she finished.

"But Lana...we can't just leave her there."

"She's strong. Has to be, given her role."

"Role?"

"Spy. What, you think I'd allow her to attend to Lyvias without her consent? While the elite give no such option, those serving royalty are under *my* supervision." Her jaw flexed. "*My* protection. Lana serves the vampire Lord to unearth his weaknesses. She knows doing so will bring freedom to many, including her, and help end this blight of darkness once and for all. And now look, the Goddess brought us together. You and me: we can end him."

A child. A damn *child* had to make the choice to sacrifice a part of her young heart to set others free. Had to choose to leave behind her childish wonder before her time in order to strike down a "blight of darkness." I paced about the narrow hall, hands balled into fists at my sides. It wasn't fucking fair. I landed a harsh blow to the nearest granite stone; then another and another until my knuckles split and I could regain my breath.

Suri lifted an eyebrow with a quirk of her lips. "Are you finished with your tantrum, then?"

"Yes." I crossed my arms. "I'm done."

"Good. Now go. Find your leverage, *Addison*. I will alert you when the time is right, after I attend to the future queen."

A semblance of peace washed over me. Having Suri by Kim's side—watching out for her with a trained eye that was no stranger to the corruption lingering in Anathema—dulled the fear of Kim alone with Lyvias. At his mercy. With a nod, I took my leave. My attention would be better served in laying my trap than stewing in my anger. Though picturing Lyvias bleeding out at my feet did bring a smile to my face.

Shifting—while I'd done it more times than I could count—never got easier. The breaking and reforming of bone, the throb in my skull, the urge to throw up my guts: a torment.

But upon finding Suri and Kim in the castle courtyard prepared to embark on a tour about the courts, I had no choice but to take my alternate form: a raven. *Poe*, as Kimber had so deemed me. Transitioning back into my human form was bearable, mostly. But phasing *into* another form? That shit was *rough*. You know, considering the human body has two hundred six bones that have to fuse and condense into the mere twenty-six bones of a bird. That, and the size variation I suppose; but once the anguish subsided, I enjoyed my winged form. Flying was freedom.

I kept close watch, surveying the kingdom I'd been forced to flee far too young. Riding the wind, I soared over the towering buildings in the demon court, swept through the moonbeams in the vampire court, and savored a wild raspberry in the reaper court. To my surprise, things almost seemed safe, balanced. *Almost.*

But my girl didn't play it safe.

Barging her way into the shifter realm—well, I guess I should have expected it. Kim would never be satisfied with secondhand accounts of the events there. She had to see it for herself. But me? I was wildly unprepared for the devastation.

Flames. Screams. Death.

My people. I'd known about the desolation my court faced under Cadagon's rule, but reliving it in real time proved far worse than any portrayals I'd read. And Kim's anguish—the way her heart shattered in front of me—killed me inside. Death had handed her a broken kingdom. He had let her enemies infiltrate his ranks, setting her up for failure. I watched from a nearby tree as the two argued over the event leading to the brutal energetic imprint surrounding us.

"You expect me to turn a blind eye to all of this and join you for some damn dinner party?" Kim said with a cynical laugh.

"Please, Kimberly," Death sighed, "do not make me get harsh with you."

"Harsh? Is that what you call it to make yourself feel better in that shithead brain of yours?"

She rattled on, her sharp tongue jabbing at his failures and twisting the metaphorical knife until he'd had enough. Being on the receiving end of Kim's anger was not a place anyone wanted to be. The woman knew how to break you down, that's for damn sure.

"Watch yourself," he warned.

"You can't do anything to me." Her jaw tensed. "You need me. Tell me what the hell happened."

"Or what?" Death's shadows billowed around him. I am in control here, not you. Now accept your fate and join your guests for dinner."

Cadagon snapped once, and Kim's feet betrayed her, marching her back towards the courtyard. As I trailed them back to the castle—Kim's mouth sealed by Cadagon's unholy powers—the reality of my own uselessness ate at me. I was no match for Death himself. Regardless of how much I wanted to step in, to push back against the king's control, I couldn't. But wrapped in the silhouette of the castle towers, I realized I had a say in what happened next. I could watch for her enemies, strike them down in the shadows.

For example: the pompous vampire Lord awaiting her on the front steps.

As if I weren't already set on ending Lyvias's life, hearing the vulgar lies he spewed upon Kim's return set my resolve in stone. *A disease,* he'd called her. Screw finding answers. If I had to, I'd stab until the dude had no more blood to spill. Maybe I'd start with severing his fingers, then his toes, then his tongue. But as I watched Kimber crumble—tears trailing down her cheeks—I knew my revenge would have to wait a little longer. She needed me.

Catching a gust of wind, I found my place at her side. If I'd had arms, they would have sheltered her. Comforted her. My lips would have sung her praises to soothe every harsh lie spilled between the vampire Lord's fangs in an attempt to break her. It was a cruel joke. Because Kim? She didn't break. When presented with cruelty, she always took it in, letting it fester and strengthen her. Death's daughter was forged in fire. Alone, she let the tears fall and allowed herself to feel. I'd always envied her for that. At least it seemed—as small a gesture as it was—Poe's familiar presence brought her a modicum of solace, and her eyes widened at my approach.

"What are you doing here?" she chastised, shoving me under her skirt.

While getting in her pants consumed my thoughts a solid eighty percent of the time, I can't say I'd imagined it'd happen in such a way. A chuckle rattled through my mind, escaping as a croaky caw. After Kim saw to my safe travel to her suite and put me under the protection of Suri—who seemed to be in the right place at the right time more often than not—I heaved a breath and returned to my natural form. It was an easier transition considering my body was used to taking on my inherent shape, but not entirely painless. A dull ache. Nothing a long night's rest couldn't fix, whenever the hell I'd be able to do *that*.

"Holy—" Suri heaved, grasping her chest. "What in the damned did I just witness?"

"What, never seen a shifter in action?"

I cracked my neck and arms, turning to find a blush on her cheeks. I followed her sight line...straight to my naked frame. Clapping a hand over my junk, I snagged the throw from Kim's bed and tied it around my waist.

"Sorry about that." I laughed, tucking my hair into a knot atop my head.

Her smirk widened. "Don't be."

This little vixen. *Of course* Kim and Suri would form a friendship. She was totally Kim's type, which both turned me on and made me unnecessarily jealous all at once. "Hey now, don't go giving me those googly eyes. My heart is already spoken for."

"Who said the heart only has the capacity to feel for one person?" She winked. "But really, what *was* that?"

"Poe is my alternate form. I do it to keep an eye on Kim."

"You were with us during the tour?"

"Every step of the way. Or...wing flap, I guess?" I dropped my sore bones into the leather chair nearest me, cracked the window, and allowed the cool night air to sweep about my achy muscles. The scent of fresh rain tangled in my senses. Heavenly. Raindrops pelted the stained glass, almost lulling me to sleep. "After seeing what Lyvias was capable of? There's no way I was about to let you two wander the realm without protection."

"Mmm, a protector. Sexy."

"Sex appeal: it's a heavy cross to bear, but someone has to do it." I stretched, tucking my arms behind my head.

Suri snickered. "You poor thing. Well, sorry to inform you, but you must get off that tight ass of yours and get going. *Now*. Lyvias will be expecting Addison's presence before the ball tonight."

Of course. Royalty: ever obsessed with their social engagements.

She shuffled me to my feet, ushering me towards the door. Oh, I couldn't *wait* to teach him a lesson in respect, but I'd make him my bitch soon enough. Powerful vampire Lord my ass. I cracked my knuckles and reached for the door handle.

Suri cleared her throat. "Ahem. Forgetting something, are we?"

Clothes. Right. We wound down one level into what appeared to be her room, and she immediately starting digging through a clothes pile in the corner.

"Wait, you live in the princess's tower?" I asked.

"Yes. Kimber demanded it."

"Sounds like her." My fierce queen.

Suri froze for a second. "I've never had anyone care for me like she does. Is she always like that?"

"Always."

With a muffled "hmm," she tossed a towel at me and snatched a half-drank water glass from her side table. She motioned for me to turn around and guided my head back.

"What are you doing?" I asked.

"Addison had to bathe before being in the presence of his Lord. Uncleanliness would simply be unacceptable in the future king's presence. Hence why he showed up late, right?"

Ah, smart. I chuckled as I tied the towel around my hips and set out into the hall, hair dripping wet.

Suri stepped out behind me. "Listen, Lana confirmed Lyvias has no pureblood relation. How she found that out, I'm not entirely sure, but I trust her."

"So no stake necessary then?"

"Correct. You can take him out however that violent heart of yours deems fit. Play the helpless, fearful servant. Sell it. And then, when he lets his guard down, make that asshole pay for what he's done."

"With pleasure."

Murderous energy pounded through me with each step. Guards chastised as I passed, belittling me for my late arrival and lack of clothing. When that heavy mahogany door came into view, the world around me stilled. All noise fell away. My target lay just beyond, unaware I held his life in my hands; and while I hadn't planned on killing him yet, some opportunities were just too juicy to pass up. Time to end this prick. I knocked twice.

"Come in," Lyvias barked.

A crooked grin cinched across my face. Game on.

Chapter Five

Cannibalism?

I entered to find Lyvias perched at his vanity, prodding and primping his cheeks as if he were the most devastatingly beautiful thing in the world. Entranced by his own reflection, he gave no notice of my arrival. I lingered in the doorway, my stomach in knots. To think this man had the world at his feet—surrounded by riches and adoration—while he concealed sinister desires behind closed doors. His birthright had ensured he reaped reward after reward without consequences. And for what? Being born royal and handsome? I guess it's true what they say: beauty is power. My body jittered in anticipation at the thought of marring that beautiful face and reminding him that nobody was untouchable. I shuffled a step forward, and his eyes crashed into mine through the mirror, a scowl plastered on his face.

"You're late," he snarled. His sights carried down my body, transfixed on the towel hung around my hips. "And why in hell's name are you not clothed?"

"My apologies, sir. I wanted to make sure I was presentable for you and lost track of time in the washrooms. I felt it...inappropriate to be unclean in your presence."

Take the bait, asshole.

"Mmm, I see. I did warn you not to keep me waiting, did I not?"

"Yes, sir. I am truly sorry for my tardiness."

"Enough." He sauntered over, conceited energy leaching off him like a plague. Pushing me to sit on the bed, he started undoing his belt. "You will attend to my needs before tonight's events. Immediately."

"What are you—"

"Stop talking. It turns me off."

"I already told you I don't offer such services."

"Playing hard to get then, are we?" He pushed in closer, his hardened dick nearly touching my face.

I averted my eyes, heartbeat pounding in my ears. I forgot how to speak, how to breathe. How many others had he taken without consent? My chest tightened. The way he forced himself on a man of equal stature mixed with his lustful grin told me it had been too many. Sick fuck.

He pinched my jaw between his forefinger and thumb. "Cat got your tongue?"

I tore his hand away but remained silent. The way he held himself—his shoulders back, staring down his nose at me—burrowed under my skin like a parasite. A slinky, slimy thing.

"You truly think you can deny your future king what is rightfully his?" He knotted his fingers in my hair, jerking my head back. "Answer me!"

"Rightfully yours?" I snapped. "I hate to knock you off your high horse, *Lord Lyvias*, but simply because you want something does not mean it is yours to take."

"You would defy a direct order?"

"If it means sucking your dick? Then yes, I will defy your order." I stood, stepping into his space, our sight lines even with one another. "You see, I don't bottom. At least not for men."

A hard slap landed against my cheek, my skin burning in its wake.

"You will do as you are ordered, peasant!"

Wind rushed past my ears as Lyvias pinned me to the wall and ripped my towel free in two seconds flat. A murderous chuckle slipped up my throat. Well, I didn't have *Killing a Vampire Lord Butt-Ass-Naked* on my bingo card; but hey, here we were. Fine by me, really. Naked or clothed, I'd deliver on my promise to put this rabid dog down for every innocent who'd been forced to submit to his prickish whims.

I fought against his hold, but he managed to snake a hand down my stomach. My limp cock in his hand, he began to pump. Despite the insatiable desire to rip his throat out, my body reacted to his touch.

"Is this what you want?" he whispered into my ear, sending goosebumps across my skin. "To be broken before your king?"

I gripped his shoulders, shoving him backwards. "Fuck off!"

Shock wrinkled his brow, replaced in a split second by unabashed anger. He descended upon me: a wall of muscle and brutality. To my unfortunate surprise, he took me to the ground with ease and pinned my hands above my head, pressing my face to the floor.

"You will take it," he growled, "and you will like it!"

I bucked, and my skull cracked against his chin, inducing a snarl from his lips. I hopped to my feet to find him wiping away a trickle of blood from his split lip. He started back towards me, something adjacent to pure evil surging in his crimson stare.

"As I said, I like a challenge. I. Will. Break. You!"

I raised my fists, landing a solid blow to his jaw on approach, followed by another. He spit the blood now pouring from his mouth, and I stole a glance about the room. There, as if Fate had placed it just for me, a blade shone in the moonlight. This was it: my chance. I began to circle, Lyvias mirroring my steps. His eyes darkened to near-black depths, and I knew one of us wasn't leaving this room alive. It was me or him. I positioned myself in front of the side table, the blade nipping my finger as I slid it into my palm.

"You forget, Lyvias," I said, "I am not your usual target. Or have you gotten so used to preying on children you don't know how to handle your own in a fight?"

"Why you little—"

Before he could reconsider his charge, I whipped the dagger out, sinking its tip into his gut. The Lord's shocked breath swept across my cheek, and his eyes widened at the fresh wound. *That's right, asshole. You lose.* A shudder ran up my spine at the tear of muscle and gush of blood. Making wicked men pay for their atrocities never got old: a hobby Kim and I shared.

A laugh built in Lyvias's chest until it rose to maniacal levels.

"You fool! You think *this* will kill me?" He grasped the hilt, ripped the blade out without so much as a grimace, and tossed it aside. "I am a gods-damned warrior! I have fought men twice your size and bent them to my will! And to think, I was prepared to go easy on you."

Oh, shit. Again he charged, this time nailing me to the bedpost. The wood splintered on impact, a shard burying itself in my spine and sending shock waves down my limbs. Yeah, that definitely cracked a rib. His fangs sank deep into my throat. I pushed and shoved as he began draining me faster than I could fight him off, but to no avail. My head spun; hands shook. At the rate of his frantic mouthfuls, I'd be unconscious before I could land another blow. But to my benefit, his thirst was his undoing. He reared back with a satisfied grin to behold his prey, blood dripping from the corners of his mouth.

"You taste divine," he panted.

His lips crashed into mine, his tongue sliding into my mouth frantically. Dumb fucking move. I bit down hard, nearly severing his tongue, and iron danced on my taste buds. This, it seemed, was enough to throw him off kilter, and I took him to the floor, burying my knee in his chest. Hands secured around his throat, I squeezed. And squeezed. His face flushed a most intoxicating shade of purple, and red flooded my vision as my bloodlust took root. My body tingled at the blatant fear refracted in his stare. *Finally.* He flailed under me—the hairs on the back of my neck standing on end—but I allowed him no leniency.

There it was: the life fade I'd been so hungry for. Almost done. One hand still cemented on his throat, I reached for the blade. My fingertips brushed the smooth hilt. Just a little farther. With another shift, I snatched the dagger, pressing it to his throat. A stab to the gut wasn't enough to take him out, but no being—supernatural or otherwise—could survive without blood. I'd drain him the same way he'd drained his helpless victims.

"This is for Lana," I snarled through clenched teeth. "For every person whose innocence you have stolen, you *disease!*"

Spit foamed on the sides of his lips, and he shoved at my throat. The pressure in my skull built as he pushed my head back farther—the tear of muscle echoing in my ears—but I'd be damned if I let him win. I slashed his wrist, severing tendons. His hand hung limp, and his arms recoiled, leaving him wide open. So like the gentleman I am, I offered him a final smile to carry with him to the afterlife.

And with a firm slash, I slit his throat wide open.

Blood gushed, pooling around us as he choked and pawed at his throat with the hand I'd so graciously allowed him to keep. Such a delicious sight. I pinned him harder to the floor and savored every second. He'd lost. He knew it. I knew it. *That's right. Die, fucker.*

He went motionless under me.

My lungs heaved. I'd done it: fulfilled my promise to Death and cut down the threat Kim faced. No longer would his shadow haunt hers or any other's doorstep. I cracked my sore neck and scrambled off Lyvias's dead frame, making my way to the nearest window to spit until the remnants of his blood no longer haunted my senses. Then reality set in.

How the hell was I going to hide a six-foot-something vampire warrior without attracting attention? Anyone awaiting his arrival for the night's event would assume him fashionably late. At least I hoped, anyway. Sure, he'd never show up in the end, but one step at a time.

The door crashed open a second later. Great. Caught red-handed. I snatched a blanket from the bed to cover myself and backed into the corner. Suri strolled in, her expression tense as she surveyed the scene. Her sights carried from the dead Lord to me, and back again. How long we stood there in thick silence, I'm not sure. But finally, Suri's laughter broke through. It started slow, transforming into a raspy giggle.

"You actually pulled it off!" She wiped away a tear.

"Yeah, but the douche put up a good fight."

I rubbed my back, attempting to catch an edge and free the splinter buried in my rib cage. No luck. Suri pursed her lips, sidestepped the crimson pool at our feet, and motioned for me to spin about.

"Oof, that's deep."

I winced at her touch. "Eh, I've had worse."

"Take a deep breath."

Despite my best attempts, a guttural moan escaped me as the shard broke free, heat radiating through my legs.

"That's going to need stitches." Suri dug in her pockets and removed a small box with needles and suture thread.

"What, you just walk around ready to sew up anyone who needs it?" I asked.

"Never know when you'll need them. Better safe than sorry, right?"

After sterilizing the needle in candle flame, she went to work. In and out. The sensation of thread slithering through fatty tissue made my skin crawl, and I gritted my teeth through sharp bite after bite. A necessary discomfort, but one I'd rather avoid in the future.

"There, all done," Suri said.

"Thank you." I rolled my shoulders. "How did you know?"

"Know what?"

"Know when to show up—" I paused. "Clairvoyant, right."

"Figured you'd need help disposing of the prick." She stood over the Lord's body, kicked his lifeless thigh, and tapped her chin. "Well, we can't very well bring him out the front doors."

"We could chuck him out the window? Make it look like an accident?"

She shook her head. "Too risky. Plenty of people saw you heading here to attend to him. You'd be in shackles before we could blink. Not to mention the gaping hole where his throat used to be."

Right. And being locked in the dungeon didn't fare well for my plans to look out for Kim. "We could sneak him out through the servant's quarters?"

"With all the elites attending tonight's ball? I think not. We deal with him later, when the majority of the attendees are tucked away in their rooms. For now, we have to figure out how not to arouse suspicion." She turned to me, placing her hands on her hips. "Lyvias is expected in the ballroom in an hour. Did you have a plan on how to explain his absence? Or did that detail simply slip your mind when you decided to kill him *tonight* of all nights?"

"Yeah…I hadn't really gotten that far."

"Of course not. Cooper, if he doesn't show, the guards will come snooping. You do know that, right?" Her breaths grew ragged. "I swear, if this gets out, and it lands me in the dungeon for the rest of my life, I'll have your head! I've worked too damn hard flying under the radar in order to free these girls."

I grasped her shoulders. "That's not going to happen."

There was one way to make this all disappear: the body, the murder, the missing vampire Lord. I'd considered it, though I wasn't sure I had the strength to pull it off. While an ugly, unsettling option, I had to try. I bit the meat of my cheek. "I have an idea, but I can't guarantee it'll work."

Suri crossed her arms over her chest. "What are you talking about?"

"I'm a shapeshifter."

"Right…and?"

"And a pureblood," Death's voice boomed, making us both jump. He loomed in the shadowed corner, flames swaying in his irises.

Suri's body went ridged as her gaze fell to Lyvias. "Your Highness. I—I can explain. We didn't mean—"

"Silence," Cadagon interjected, raising a dismissive hand. "I could care less what or who caused the Lord's death. He was a plague upon this kingdom. What I *do* care about is making sure Lyvias is dressed to perfection for tonight's event. I ensured a tailored suit be delivered earlier today; it's hanging there in the closet."

She cleared her throat. "With all due respect, Highness, he's kind of…"

"Dead?" Cadagon finished. "Precisely. But that doesn't mean he will not be in attendance tonight. Correct, Cooper?"

So I truly didn't have an option. Perfect. "Right, *if* I can pull it off."

"I don't understand," Suri said.

"A pureblood has the ability to wear another's face," Cadagon explained. "It's a particularly ruthless ritual, but if performed correctly—"

"Cooper will be Lyvias."

"For all intents and purposes, yes," Death responded.

"What kind of ritual?"

"I have to eat his heart," I whispered, snatching the dagger off the floor.

Suri clapped a hand over her mouth. "You *what*?"

"It's the only way," Death confirmed, and looked to me. "And you know the consequences, boy?"

I nodded. Taking another's identity meant I would always carry a part of them with me. *What* piece exactly was a roll of the dice, but I'd cross that bridge when I came to it. Before I lost my nerve, I heaved a breath and raised the dagger above my head, bringing it down hard. The blade cracked through ribs, bouncing back against the muscles below. I shoved in farther, all the while my heart thundered. Here I thought committing a murder in the buff hadn't been on the agenda for the day. But cannibalism? That for *sure* hadn't been part of the plan. My hands soaked in cooling blood, I pried the blade upward, breaking bone free. Time passed slowly; every second a lifetime as I severed arteries and veins until, finally, I could pull the heart free. The mass rested heavy like a stone in my clutch, and I swallowed hard.

"Good thing I had a light lunch, huh?" I forced a laugh.

Suri gagged and averted her eyes. But Death? He didn't blink as his sights burned into me.

The first bite into the firm, stringy organ was the worst, like my body knew. This? This was *not* for consumption. I closed my eyes and cleared my mind. A steak. It was just a bloody, raw steak. From there, I let my instincts take over. I forced my teeth through, tearing a meaty chunk free.

"Oh, I'm going to be sick." Suri ran to the window to spew her guts.

Which didn't exactly help my gag reflex. Then Kimber's sweet face tickled my mind. If I assumed Lyvias's identity, I'd be able to be by her side in the open. Watch out for her in ways I hadn't been able to so far. That was all the motivation I needed to finish the last course, rubbery bite.

"There," I forced out. "That wasn't so bad—"

My body seized all at once. Acid burned in my veins. I lifted my hand to behold skin rippling over breaking finger bones, and I collapsed, my head cracking hard against the floor. An anguished scream rose up, but Death sealed my lips before it could free itself. What fresh hell was this? A broken wrist or ankle when shifting was one thing, but every bone in your body shattering at once?

I'd only ever wish such agony on my worst enemies. I sucked in breaths through my nose, but any semblance of calm denied me as I thrashed, my torso caving in on itself one rib at a time. Seconds turned to minutes with no relief in sight. How much *longer*? But I knew better. Shifting into some*one* required incredible restructuring—clear down to the marrow—in order to rebuild the body in a new image it wasn't accustomed to. Lyvias's teeth shoved their way into place as my own fell out into my palm, one by one, before clinking to the ground. The edges of my vision brushed black, and suddenly, dying didn't sound like the worst thing. Peace. Nothingness. Oblivion.

Darkness devoured me.

I awoke sometime later to Suri's worried stare and her hand on my cheek. "Gods, are you okay?"

I sat up, my hands drenched in dried blood. "Did it work?"

"See for yourself," Cadagon said.

I crawled towards the mirror, my stomach souring. Sure as shit, the eyes peering back at me were not my own but rather crimson and ravenous. I pulled my cheek aside to reveal long, pointed canines, and inky vines twisted up my throat. It'd worked. I'd done it.

"Incredible," Suri whispered from behind.

"Undoubtedly." Death turned to her. "You are excused, dear one. But do heed my call. I will require your assistance with a matter soon."

Cadagon turned, pressing his fingertips together. Suri met my gaze in the mirror briefly—her eyebrow raised in question—and mouthed, "Dear one?" Such an odd kindness on the king's tongue. Regardless, she bowed and made her exit.

Death set a black-stained hand on my shoulder. "I will meet you in the royal graveyard at precisely three o'clock this morning. Ensure you bring the corpse. Do not be late."

With a final glance, he evaporated into thin air. I lingered on the ground, transfixed on the stranger reflected in the looking glass. I'd become a wraith, a silhouette of my former self, and yet I was more determined than ever. This newfound form—steeped in secrets and sinister energy—would see my goals achieved. Monsters would die by these hands. Sins would be purged. I'd become a blade, a weapon to be wielded by *her* alone. How fitting that with the very hands that'd sowed chaos and debauchery in the kingdom, I would undo it. Deliver vengeance. But first, I had to infiltrate Lyvias's life, discover what he'd been up to behind the scenes. My fleshy mask grinned back at me in the mirror. Yes. I would eradicate anyone who sought to dismantle Anathema's return to balance. And in doing so?

Lady Death would reign in all her vicious glory.

CHAPTER SIX

ONE BALLROOM, ONE BODY, ONE CROTCHETY OLD MAN

S uit tailored to perfection, I straightened my collar in the floor-length mirror and sighed. I'd never understand why the Gods saw fit to bless assholes with such beauty. Whether I liked to admit it or not—which I abso-fucking-lutely did not—Lyvias looked damn sexy reflected back at me. Did that make *me* a monster? To find him pleasing to the eye? I mean, come on. Broad shoulders, cut jawline, dark ink that popped off his ivory skin. Such an odd sensation. One that both sickened and intrigued me at the same time, given that *my* consciousness resided behind those eyes.

Enough ogling.

I stalked through the halls towards my first face-to-face glimpse of true beauty since my arrival in Anathema. Of her. My queen. Anticipation buzzed in my veins. We'd hardly gone a day without seeing each other, let alone *days*. I let myself wonder. Did she long for me as I did for her? Did she find herself considering what could have been if we'd never left our simple, mortal lives? My chest tightened at the thought of her knelt over the coffin Death had procured for me with tears streaming down her beautiful face. How I wished I could tell her the truth and reveal myself before she ended up in yet another impossible situation on my account, but I'd bet a crisp, hundred-dollar bill she'd already made at least one new enemy in her hunt to cure me.

Such a stubborn, fierce heart she had.

I bit my cheek, my leather shoes skidding against the carpet as I paused to reset my jaw. I shoved a finger into my mouth, and it came back shiny red. *Again.* Thanks to my new teeth—pointed, bulky, and foreign—I'd already managed to chew my cheeks to a consistency resembling ground beef, though that wasn't the worst of it. I'd expected changes would arise to accompany the new face I wore, but I'd underestimated how demanding those changes would be. How difficult to ignore. I swallowed hard, my throat burning. *Gods,* I was thirsty.

Upon approaching the ballroom doors, a strange throb settled in the base of my skull, like a tiny creature crawling around inside, its legs tickling my brain.

Hello, Lyvias. Death's voice mocked but...not audibly.

I turned, expecting to find Cadagon's frame slinking about; but the halls were empty aside from guards positioned every ten feet at their posts. "Uhh...hello?"

Don't bother; I am already seated inside. I come with a warning. Malachi, Lord of the demon court, has decided to grace us with his presence this evening. Do not, under any circumstances, allow my daughter to be alone with him. Do you understand me?

Great. My research of modern leadership in the demon court provided little information aside from references to Lord Malachi being permanently shrouded in shadows. The demons, it seemed, cherished privacy. Or maybe the dude was ugly as hell, hence the hiding. Either way, I knew one thing for sure: Kim was safest by my side. I cinched up my tie, pushed my shoulders back, and glared at the ballroom doors encased in gold leaf.

"You have my word," I whispered.

Good. And in case you weren't aware, the door handle won't, in fact, bite you. Get in here.

Golden candlelight encompassed the room, but its beauty paled in comparison to the guest of honor. An absolute vision in her floor-length gown, Kim's smile hit home like a sucker punch. My stomach jumped as her eyes fell on me. Her sweet smile dissipated, replaced by an even deadlier loveliness. So menacing. She tore her gaze from mine, but I continued to study her from the dimly lit sidelines, fighting to settle my rising heartbeat. What a knockout. The things I'd do for this woman would sicken others. To die for one's love is easy, expected. But to kill? To topple kingdoms in her name and rip apart her adversaries inch by inch? That called for true dedication, and I'd take pleasure in such atrocities if it meant her happiness. After a push from Death, she started my way.

"You will dance with me," she demanded.

I quirked a brow. "Will I?"

"Yes. And you will respect me. Do I make myself clear?"

Holy hell, did she. How I *yearned* to be at her mercy in that moment, to submit to her beck and call. My desire caught fire like gasoline on a spark. What *was* it about her that set me ablaze so easily?

I grinned, taking her hand in mine. "Indeed."

The scrutinous sights of society descended on us as I tucked my hand around Kimber's hip and twirled her about the dance floor, words evading me. I craved the ease our relationship had always allotted, but I reminded myself that I was, well, not myself. I was Lyvias Kraven: royal dickhead of Anathema. Conversation proved far more difficult than I'd anticipated. If I was too kind right away, it would arouse suspicion; but to be foul and cruel like Lyvias wasn't something I could stomach, let alone muster. Despite the awkward energy, I couldn't help but smile at her hand in mine. Yet she seemed so far away, lost in a distant thought.

"Princess," I said, spinning her out and back in, "you seem distracted."

She shook the fog away. "Not at all, I was simply...remembering. Forgive me."

Oh, how I *burned* to know what that meant. To dig into that beautiful mind of hers and help her sort through her troubles. But such sentiments wouldn't fare well coming from the rival she'd already resorted to hating.

Maybe if I just break the tension a little...

"That depends. What will you give me in return for my forgiveness?" I asked with a wink.

She raised a brow. "What's up with you tonight?"

Too flirty. Reel it in!

I dipped her back, frantic for a way out. "I'm not sure I know what you mean."

"You verbally attacked me earlier, made me feel like absolute shit. And what, now you're suddenly playing nice?"

She didn't buy the act, not for a second. I should have known Kim would have none of my cheap attempts to deceive her. Clever girl.

"Why be kind now?" She finally asked, her cool demeanor giving me a chill. "Is it because we're surrounded by people? Or is it because I put you in your place back at the training grounds?"

I fought a laugh as the memory swept over me in vivid color. *Lyvias wouldn't laugh at his own humiliation, idiot.* I cleared my throat. "Hardly. I would simply be a fool not to have the most beautiful woman in the room on my arm tonight, would I not?"

"And there you have it." She shoved from my hold, a cynical chuckle on her red lips.

Anddddd…wrong move. Again. "Have what, exactly?"

"The insult I was waiting for. You're getting better at this. Really shaking it up on me."

"What are you talking about, Kim?"

She froze. "That's 'Princess' to you."

"Fine, Princess, I meant no harm. I—"

"Save it." She snatched my arm, moving us out of the public eye. "I don't care what you were trying to say; your meaning was clear. I'm sure you have been able to use that little smirk of yours to get what you wanted in the past, but you can save it. The only company you'll have in bed tonight is your hand."

My stomach dropped, the awkward tension choking me. "That's not what I— Look, I was clearly an asshole before, but this marriage is going to happen whether we like it or not. Can't we be civil?"

"Civil? After everything you've said to me, you have the audacity to ask me to be *civil*?"

What he *said to you*, I nearly responded, but the Lord's prior cruelty forced me to play a harsh role I'd never wanted to embody. "I'm sorry, alright? What do you want from me?"

"To admit this is shit! That we don't love each other and that...sucks."

Every muscle in my body tensed, because I—*I* did. I loved her more than I'd ever loved anyone, and even though I understood her words were aimed at Lyvias, they stung the same as if they'd been intended for me.

"I have feelings for someone else, okay?" She sighed.

June. Of course that's where her head had been at earlier. While I couldn't do anything in regards to their relationship, I *could* give her a safe space to feel. "You do?"

"Is that so hard to believe?"

"Of course not." I dodged her gaze. "I didn't expect such an honest answer is all."

"Honesty: it's my curse."

She sauntered out onto the veranda overlooking the gardens—rosy perfume seemingly calming her flames—and I retrieved champagne, returning to extend her a glass. "It's not a curse you know. Honesty, I mean. That's actually a very noble trait."

"Think so, huh? Seems to get me into trouble more than not."

I saw it plain on her face: she was questioning her worth; and I couldn't allow that. "I do. I believe it to be crucial in a ruler. Unforeseen situations are bound to come along. A straightforward stance in the route to a decisive solution. It unites."

Her confidence returned, and she rested a hand on my arm, the simple touch sending lightning through me. Crazy, how such a small comfort could reset an entire evening.

One sarcastic jest later, and we were back on the dance floor. The night blew past like fog on the wind, an eerie presence taking root in me as the night progressed. I searched the crowd time and again, but found nothing out of sorts until, that is, he *wanted* to be seen. Hidden in the ballroom's recesses, the fabled demon Lord lingered. Our sight lines clashed into one another, and from there, I couldn't shake him. I pulled Kim close to me, heeding Death's warning. I tried to pay Malachi no mind, but his fixed attention burrowed into my skin, his rogue shadows twisting around my ankle on occasion. Probing. Searching. His desire for Lyvias's attention was clear. But why?

By the ball's conclusion, I'd lost track of the ominous shadow wielder but had managed to keep Kimber away from him at least. Questions plagued me as I ensured her safe return to her suite. Whatever Lyvias and Malachi had going on...it rattled me. Deeply. I should have reveled in my newfound lead, celebrated the fact that, with some digging, I might be able to draw out the details of Lyvias's dark past through Malachi. Instead, reality reared its ugly head once again.

My standing appointment with Death loomed.

I checked the time, my sore head and muscles throbbing in tandem. Well past two o'clock. *Awesome, no sleep for me.* By the time I found some miraculous way to drag Lyvias's now swollen corpse to the castle graveyard, Death would have had ample time to formulate a lecture about tardiness and living by one's word or whatever the crotchety, old bastard thought I needed to hear. Between the thirst making my mouth drier than the Sahara Desert and the remnants of champagne wearing off, I didn't have the patience to hear any of it. Better to get it over with. Quickly.

I started cleanup duty. First, mopping up more blood than I'd seen in one place at any given time. Second, sealing and taping the dead Lord's throat shut—couldn't have him leaking all over the place—and third, stripping and tossing his soaked clothes in a bag to burn in the nearest hearth when possible. I couldn't risk leaving a blood trail as I dragged him through the halls. Murder was a damn chore, I swear.

Turns out, I'd severely underestimated the muscle the dude was packing. While I'd received the brunt of Lyvias's strength during our little murder dance, it became apparent how much iron the asshole lifted in my attempt to haul his lifeless frame down the stairs. Even dead, he managed to vex me. Figured.

Here I'd expected his vampiric strength to transfer to me—maybe lend a helping hand—but it appeared not. Though something told me the ever-growing thirst in me coincided with the onset of weakness. The hunger. As much as I hated to admit it, I'd have to feed eventually, but not yet. Not until I absolutely had to.

Approaching footsteps sent me into a panic. *Shit, shit, shit!*

Because *that's* what I needed: for someone to walk up and see Lyvias carting his doppelganger through the halls. Imagine explaining that! *Oh, hi there! It's me, the vampire Lord. A body, you say? I've no idea what you're talking about, good sir.* Right. Straight to the dungeon for me. Despite my frantic attempts to keep quiet, Lyvias's head *thunked* against one step after the other, his tongue falling out as I neared the last stair. Lovely.

I dragged him to ground level and landed on my sole option: an alcove cut into the stone wall. Frantic, I shoved Lyvias's corpse behind the reaper statue within the recess. His stiff feet and hands jutted out around the sides like a mannequin perched for a jump scare. Albeit a tad hilarious to behold, it was also visible to anyone who passed. Far too visible. But I was out of time, footsteps rounding the corner.

Nasheesh crashed into me. "Oh!"

I smoothed my suit, acutely aware of the blood droplet on the lapel. Perks of wearing a vampire's face? Unexplained blood stains were to be expected, though my heart rate still climbed.

"My apologies, Lord Lyvias. I didn't expect company in the halls this late."

"It appears neither of us did." I laughed a little too hard, my pent-up nervous energy peeking through. *Get yourself together, man.*

Nasheesh's forehead tensed. "Are you alright, Sire? You appear to be out of sorts tonight."

"Fine. Just taking a walk to clear the mind."

"Mmhmm." Nasheesh looked me over. "Might I lend an ear? I've not much time, but my next meeting can wait should you require my services."

Next meeting? Who would he be meeting at such a late hour? Clearly not Death, as he and I had a standing appointment that I grew increasingly late for by the second. Curiosity peaked, I bit my lip and logged the info away for future consideration. The haunting scene unfolding an arm's reach away stole my focus. From the corner of my eye, I caught a glimpse of Lyvias's dead frame slowly sliding down the wall, ready to plop out on the floor in plain view. Naturally, the dude would be an attention whore even in death.

The advisor turned, following my sight line, and I snatched him by the shoulder. "That's quite alright. Some fresh air is all I require."

"If you say so, Your Highness."

He tried for another look, but I stepped forward to cut off his view. All the while, my new, hyper-focused ears honed in on the drag of skin rubbing against stone. My palms grew sweaty. I needed Nasheesh gone. Stat. I wrapped my arm around his shoulders and guided him away. "I insist, really. Go have your meeting. I'll be fine, I assure you."

His feline eyes lingered on me, his lips pursed. "As you wish. Goodnight, Sire."

"Goodnight, Nasheesh."

My heartbeat echoed in my head as I watched him disappear down the hall.

That'd been *way* too close for comfort. Returning to a now fully visible corpse, I scoured the scene one last time before dragging him back out into the open. Time to ditch this loser. It took me a minute to hit my stride—what with Lyvias's bulbous head catching a corner or two in transit to the southernmost kitchen. The staff had hunkered down for the night, leaving the space free for us to sneak out undetected. Fantastic news for me.

Fog enveloped the hillside, its moist touch on my cheeks a welcome reprieve. Momentarily, anyway. Death had, once again, left details to be desired. I'd thought transporting a bag of bones *down* stairs was rough, but lugging him *up* the graveyard's steep incline? Far worse. As if my muscles weren't screaming enough already after having changed my entire anatomy mere hours before. No biggie. Seething, I pulled and pushed to the top.

"They should really post some guards in the kitchen between shifts," I grumbled, dropping Lyvias at Death's feet. "Somebody could easily sneak into the castle."

"A fact I think you'll find will fare well for you, boy," he responded.

True. But still. "So what are we doing back at the family crypt? You think this prick deserves a royal burial?"

"Oh, there is no chance of that." Death shook his head. "But considering we can't have anyone finding him, I had an idea that suits ours as well as Kimber's needs."

"That doesn't sound ominous or anything. What exactly are we talking about here?"

Cadagon turned and placed a hand over an ancient placard. "Come. I'll show you."

The ground rumbled, opening up beneath us. Per Death's request, I dragged Lyvias down the windy steps, my lungs laboring. Steady drips echoed about the space as I stumbled through the pitch black in the crypt's depths, falling flat on my face. "Dude, I just can't catch a fucking break tonight!"

A chuckle from Death, and every candle lining the room erupted to life.

"Couldn't have lit those any sooner, huh?" I asked, dropping Lyvias like a sack of potatoes.

"And put an end to such an entertaining sight? Certainly not."

Glad *somebody* got a kick out of my suffering. Cadagon snapped once, and the coffin meant to hold my rotting flesh flew open.

"Drop him in," he ordered.

"Care to lend a hand, or you going to stare at me all night?" I hunched over my knees. "I mean, I know I'm pretty to look at, Death, but you're not my type."

He rolled his eyes. "A king is wise to not involve himself in matters such as these."

I grunted, flinging Lyvias's legs over the casket's side. "What does that make you then? A fool? You're already involved, so why not help?"

"Bad back."

"Right." *Jerk.*

Lyvias rolled back out with a thud. Dear *gods*, this *guy*! Placing his left arm and left leg in this time, I managed to shove him over the coffin wall; he landed face down, ass to the heavens. I snickered. *Good riddance, douche bag.* I found a stone near the stairwell and hammered the nails into the coffin's smooth wood.

Finally, I melted onto the ground, my sweaty locks plastered to my forehead. Done.

I leaned my head back against the stone wall, turning to Death. "Wait...how does this make any sense? Kim will be able to see it's not me in there. You know she'll come to visit."

"Ah, but if I put a glamour over the casket window to say...make it always misty and *appear* as if you are the one inside? Would that suffice, you think?"

I pursed my lips. "Smart."

"Yes, I am."

"Certainly not humble," I whispered under my breath.

"Watch it, boy," he warned, though his lips fought a grin.

He ushered for me to stand, and we parted ways without another word. Fine by me. Time for some damn sleep.

After stripping off my clothes, I crawled into bed. The cool, silky sheets soothed the throb in my, well...my everything. At last, a chance to close my eyes. To turn off my mind, reset, and—

"Lord Lyvias," a dainty voice called through the door.

I clapped my hands over my face. And no sleep for Coop. Silly of me to have hoped for even a teensy, tiny, little catnap. Dragging my hands down my cheeks, I stared at the ceiling a second longer before donning clean clothes and cracking the door. "Lana? Everything okay?"

"He sent me," she said, and extended a rather large black box tied up with a bow.

"Wait...who sent you?"

She blinked and shook her head; sworn to secrecy it seemed.

"I must go. But I will return tomorrow to attend to your needs, Lord Lyvias. Or wait..."

"Ah, Suri told you then."

"She did, but I swear your secret is safe with me," she rushed. "I would never betray your trust or—"

"Hey, hey, it's okay. I believe you," I said gently. "You can call me Cooper. And don't worry, you need not attend to me, child. You are free."

She quirked an eyebrow. "But Nasheesh will grow suspicious if I do not come, will he not?"

She had a point. Smart kid. I shifted on my feet. "I'll tell you what: on occasion, when you so choose, you can come visit me, okay?"

"And if you aren't here?"

"Then consider my space yours. Breathe. Read. Take a long nap if you like."

Lana picked at her fingers. "And if you *are* here? What will we do then?"

The heartache written across her face killed me. This poor girl. I leaned down. "We will do whatever you want to do. I promise I am not your enemy. You are safe with me."

I could tell she didn't believe me, but I decided right then and there that I would do everything in my power to prove it to her. If undoing wicked men's actions at her expense wasn't an option, maybe helping her towards a kinder future could be.

"Okay," she whispered. "Just...be careful tonight."

"You too." I placed a gentle pat on her head and sent her on her way.

In the seclusion, I placed the package on my bed and looked it over. Considering others *surely* hated Lyvias as much as I did, I pondered for a moment if the box might contain a bomb or noxious gas. But in the end, curiosity won out. With a slight tug on the ribbon, the box unfolded like magic. Inside lay a red suit complete with pinstripe tie and an ornate black mask: a permanently grinning skull with deep-set eye sockets. A wax-sealed note lay beneath.

I require your attendance at the club this night, dear friend. It has finally happened. Our dreams have come to fruition.

- Malachi

Oh, unholy fuck.

Chapter Seven

VIP IN THE DEVIL'S LAIR

Seeing the demon court in my winged form was nothing compared to witnessing it as intended from the streets below. Glass buildings in bright gem tones jutted towards the sky. Trains and cars and trolleys honked and skidded on metal tracks, sending sparks across the busy streets. I adjusted my tie with sweaty palms. Now...what road to take? I dug in my pocket, referencing Malachi's invitation again. No address. No hints on where to meet him. And why would there be? Lyvias would have known where he was going. Me? Hopelessly lost, naturally.

Like a beacon summoning me into the city depths, the tallest tower—carved from emerald stone—disappeared into the clouds. There. I'd start there. Get a vantage point or a hint or...something. My shoes clicked against the sandstone sidewalk as my sights bounced here and there. The farther in I got, the more enamored I became, intoxicated by the liveliness of it all. How amazing: to realize you're so small yet feel like a cog in a vast, thriving machine. Simultaneously insignificant and somehow irreplaceable.

The scent of cured meat stole my attention, and my stomach growled in response. I waded into the bustling crowd. My nose led me to a food cart with speakers bumping behind an eccentric cook covered in glitter. I watched him take stock of a woman—shaking and dirty—on the sidewalk ahead. Without a second thought, he grabbed a bottled water alongside a charcoal-colored pastry and brought them to her. She tried to push back his gift, insisting she had no money. But his response? Food was a natural-born right, not a privilege; and her smile was payment enough. Her joy was contagious, putting a bounce in my step as I met the chef back at the cart's counter.

"My, my, that's quite a smile you got there, dollface," he said with a wink.

"And that's quite a heart you have. I saw what you did for that woman. That was very kind."

A blush dusted his freckled cheeks. "Ah, that was nothing. Just paying it forward. Now, what can I get for you?"

"Chef's favorite, please." I leaned over the counter, my throat on fire. This thirst: it'd be the death of me. But at least food satiated the worst of it. For now.

"You got it, love."

He got to work, dancing about his small space like a stage. My grin widened as he threw down a red, chunky mixture onto the flattop and swirled the bubbly dough. The way he carried himself...so full of life. I envied him. Such passion. But more so, I felt a sense of responsibility to him. Anathema's imbalance threatened his way of life. Threatened all lives. He'd played no part in society's decent into chaos, the same way Kim had inherited a crumbling kingdom she herself hadn't broken, and yet they reaped the consequences. It wasn't right. He was innocent, wholesome, and kind.

The glittering man rolled the cooked dough into a funnel, stuffed it in crunchy wax paper, and extended it to me. "Ta-da! One blood crepe for the handsome vampire."

The iron perfume settled around me, and my mouth watered. I grabbed the delicacy and took a hefty bite, the dough soothing my singed throat like a balm as it slid down. Divine. I'd had fine dining experiences that paled to his creation. Digging in my inner coat pocket, I pulled five silver coins out—courtesy of Lyvias—and laid them on the counter. "Thank you. Have a nice night."

"Wait!" He rounded the counter and tried to hand back four coins. "This is way too much."

"Just paying it forward." I winked and closed his fingers back over the coins.

He thanked me and returned to his dance floor when two men in bright red suits caught my eye. I looked down at my own attire. Perfect match. There was my lead. With quick steps, I fell in line behind them, scarfing down the last bites of my crepe and ditching the wrapper in the nearest trash can. The second the paper dropped inside, a *poof* of flame devoured it, making me jump. Talk about resourceful. We left the city streets behind, heading towards the rural outskirts.

Plavin Park had an eerie beauty to it—one that both calmed and unsettled the soul. Crumbled stone and droves of demons littered the scene, kicking my heartbeat up a notch as I donned my mask, securing the silk tie in a firm knot. This was it. No turning back now. I found my place in line, and not a second later, a woman in a leather corset stepped out to greet me. She shuffled me away from the main door.

"Come. You are to use the VIP entrance, my Lord."

She led me down and around the shed's backside to a padlocked cellar hidden behind a thistle bush. With one swipe of her wristwatch over the lock, it burst free, allowing access to the heavy metal doors. She struggled to gain a good grip, and I instinctively stepped in to help. Wrong move. Her lips puckered below her half-mask as she gently moved my hand away, explaining that Malachi's personal guests were not to attend to anything on their own. That she was to "serve my every need." My jaw clenched, the notion giving me pause. The way she'd said it...like she had no choice in the matter. Like she feared repercussions if she didn't obey. I should have known better. Lyvias would never have offered to help. Awesome. I'd shown kindness which—based on her scrutiny during our decent down the blacklight-lit steps—aroused suspicion. *Stay in character, dumbass. WWLD: What Would Lyvias Do?*

"Through there, my Lord. Malachi awaits you in the meat market."

My stomach knotted. *Meat market?* As in... Oh, hell no! If she meant what I thought she meant, I'd rip that shithead's throat out right here and— Nope. Don't show compassion. Think like a monster. Plot. Plan. Win. *WWLD?* She turned to leave, and I summoned my inner prick, placing a hard smack on her ass. "Come find me later, love. I have something else you can service."

With a nod and a "Yes, sir," she was on her way. I could only hope I'd been douchey enough to convince her that I was, in fact, the piece-of-shit vampire Lord.

The dark hall taunted me, bass echoing through the door ahead. Whatever waited on the other side would test my patience, invoke my rage and challenge me to keep my murderous urges to myself. My body tensed. If I had any hope of getting to the bottom of Lyvias and Malachi's seeming alliance, I'd have to fake it. Stonewall my morals. Deny my conscience. I took a deep breath, pushed into the room, and found a scene more reminiscent of a horror movie than real life.

Flashing lights gleamed over leather chairs encompassing the round space—chairs which held perfect sight lines to glass-paned rooms the size of small closets. Inside each stood a pedestal connected to a pole and a girl with chains jangling around her ankles as she danced. Blank stares, bumpy rib cages, visible collar bones, sunken cheeks; and yet their bodies were acutely in tune with the booming music. Almost robotic, like they had no choice. Hands shaking, I waded deeper into the abyss of men barking like rabid dogs.

A click caught my attention, and I paused my stroll. Upon the lavish armrests sat a small interface with three buttons: up, down, or out. Studying the nearest man's fervent press of the up button, I watched the number on a screen behind the closest dancer increase. Four thousand. Another man came to stand beside the first, his own device aimed at the screen like a remote. The gin in his cup tinged the air with a sharp aroma as he tapped away. Five thousand. Six. Seven. My fists tightened. This was no strip club.

These girls were being fucking sold!

"There you are," a gravelly voice said as a shadow curled around my left shoulder. "I'd feared my messenger might have abandoned her duty. I'd hate to have to punish Lana. She'll turn a pretty penny in a year or so."

Malachi.

Speaking about a child in such a way—or anyone for that matter—sent my pulse into overdrive. *Don't snap, don't snap. Do. Not. Snap.* I cleared my throat, turning to find Malachi cloaked in darkness, but I could sense it: the smirk he boasted beneath. He was proud of his creation. Of this horrendous place. My fingers twitched, begging to wrap around his throat and end him. But not here. Too many witnesses. Not to mention an organization of this scale no doubt had more people backing it. I needed to bide my time, discover his investors and business partners. Only then could I put a stop to it all and come like a thief in the night to claim their lives. Every. Last. One of them.

Sly and slow in his touch, Malachi traced a finger down my wrist. Seductive. Intentional. Chills burst to life on contact—nausea rising up—the sensation hearkening me back to when Lyvias attempted to help himself to my body. The fuck? Were they...together?

"Come. I have something special to show you." He swirled his finger in my palm and tugged at my sleeve to follow.

We wrapped down a winding hall—a door to the left letting out into the front of the club where non-VIP guests gathered in droves on a dance floor—and entered a small, soundproof office. Malachi motioned for me to enter first, locking the door behind us. The voices silenced and the bass evaporated, replaced by a haunting string quartet projected through small speakers at the room's edges. My sights carried about. Above the demon Lord's desk, a grand oil painting hung. Within it, a blue-skinned beast stared back with x-ed out irises and inch-long talons protruding from inhumanly long fingers.

"Do you like it?" Malachi busied himself at a small bar in the corner, returning to my side with two crystal glasses of iced bourbon. "I had it imported from the mortal world just yesterday."

Wait, imported from the mortal world? But Death had sealed the gates between worlds long before. Only *he* held the power to travel between planes...

I waited for Malachi to sip first before taking a drink to calm my overworked nerves. Couldn't go getting myself poisoned on my first night. "What is it?"

"Not what, *who*. The Ancient Lore of Chaos. It is through our deal with him that this became possible." He motioned about the space. "But what matters more is the treasure it conceals."

Reaching for a small remote on the oak desk, he clicked once, and the painting shifted away from the wall. It rolled ever upwards to reveal a viewing station similar to what I'd seen upon my arrival. Only this time, the woman within it had no pole or pedestal. Instead, she had a bed. A nightstand. But there was no comfort, for it wasn't intended to be a home.

It was a prison cell.

I bit down hard, fangs digging into my lip to spill blood across my tongue. I focused on the taste. The smell of whiskey in my glass and the sheer suit fibers between my pinched fingers grounded me. I had to hold it together. Breathe.

Malachi drifted towards the glass prison, and the young woman—no older than eighteen if I were to guess—receded into the far corner. Fear so palpable I could taste it emanated from her, and the sight alone crushed me. Chewed me up and spit me out. I swallowed every curse crawling up my throat as Malachi latched onto the back of her neck, guiding her towards me.

He flung her at my feet like discarded trash, and she bowed her head in false reverence. A beautiful, broken thing with tan skin, striking green eyes, and silky red hair tangled and plastered to her sweaty brow. Stunning. To think, the damning quality that'd landed her here was one she had no control over. Her beauty. Her youth.

"On your feet, girl. Shoulders back, eyes forward. Present yourself like the gem you are." When she refused to look up, Malachi *tsked*, wagging a finger. "Oh come now, little one. Smile! You're worth a fortune, you know. How many young women can say such a thing?"

Her gaze crashed into mine, reflecting a thousand unspoken pains. I reached for her, taking her chin in my hand, and my blood ran cold. The young woman's energy sang to me a sad, lamenting song of betrayal. She'd fought: done all in her power to avoid her fate; but they'd broken her. Body and soul, they'd broken her. How could the Old Goddess allow such torment to befall one who hadn't even lived yet? Abandoned her own child in her hour of need? Fine. If the Gods gave zero shits about their own, then I would fight for them. My life might hold little value in the world, but I vowed to do what I could to make my time worth it. To protect the ones forgotten by their own creators.

Malachi hyper-fixated on my clenched fists, and I forced myself to relax. To ruin him, I had to play along. Let him believe me an ally. So, though it tore me up, I swallowed hard and shoved the woman away. "Am I to believe that this scrawny thing will turn a profit, Malachi?"

"Clearly, you are not looking hard enough." His shadows laced around her, forcing her face up once again. "She is special. Look closer."

I studied her, circling. Look closer, but for what? Starting at her feet, I noticed nothing of note; but as my sights wandered upward, it hit me one blow after the other. No black-stained hands of a reaper. No bright, feline eyes of a demon. No pointed teeth of a vampire. And no sharp cheekbones of a shapeshifter. My stomach dropped. This young woman, she was... "Human."

To this, Malachi chuckled. "Indeed, my friend. Go on then: have a taste."

My heartbeat accelerated as the woman shrank under the weight of his offer, but Malachi would have none of it. He snatched her wrist, thrust it towards me, and before I could object or prepare myself, dragged a pointed nail across her wrist, opening her vein. My gums began to throb, hunger setting in. Her scent was otherworldly, like honey drizzled over perfectly smoked meat. Blood dripped on the hardwood floor, each droplet like a gavel crashing in judgment. I couldn't reject his offer, not without sending up red flags in his mind. I had to do this. There was no other way. I pressed my lips to her wrist. Just a sip to appease him. One. I sank my fangs into her supple skin, my eyes rolling into the back of my head. Another gulp. One more. Maybe another—

She hissed in pain, and I retracted my bite immediately. My chest heaved with heated breath. *Gods*, that felt good. I hated the thought, but didn't deny it. She recoiled, and I caught a glimpse of myself in the glass door. Fangs bared, blood spilling down my chin, pupils dilated to pinpricks. A monster. I was a damned monster! I wanted to apologize to her. To tell her it wasn't *her* that pleased me so, but rather her blood.

Instead, I wiped my mouth with my sleeve and turned to Malachi. "Delectable."

"A rare commodity not seen on the market in centuries: human blood. This girl alone will see us living lavishly as kings. And there are more to come."

More? "But how?"

"How?" he called over his shoulder, returning her to her cell.

I squeezed my eyes shut as she banged on the glass, pleading for her freedom. Desperate and alone. The disturbing painting slid back into place to hide her away from the outside world despite her fight. I ground my teeth. I had to betray my morals. Again.

"How," he continued, "is this."

He gestured to the painting again. Death had told me about Fate and Death's attempts to build a family at the beginning of time, and I'd heard tales about their supposed children in my youth, but the Ancient Lores' existence wasn't fact. It was fable. While the Old Gods' existence couldn't be argued, there had been no proof they'd borne offspring.

"The Ancient Lores are a myth," I said. "They're a bedtime story meant to scare naughty children into believing that if they don't obey their parents, they'll be locked away like Fate and Death did to their own children."

"Ah, but that is where you are wrong. The Ancient Lores are quite real." He downed the remaining whiskey in his glass. "And ravenous. The Shroud is a barren place. And with appetites like theirs? Well, let's just say they are *dying* to make deals with anyone offering them a means to fill their bellies."

The world rattled beneath me. If what he said was true, then the imbalance in Anathema ran deeper than I'd ever imagined. To strike a blood pact with creatures in another realm went against the laws of the cosmos. "You made a deal then, I take it?"

"Me? Hardly. But I may or may not have convinced a certain baneful witch bound to the Shroud to assist me in my endeavors."

"Convinced how?"

His glass *clacked* against the desk. "Someone is suddenly *quite* interested in the inner workings of things. I thought we'd agreed—by your request might I add—that I run the business while you secure our future? Or has your position changed, my friend?"

Business. Future. What fresh hell had Lyvias gotten me into?

I donned a playful smile. "My apologies. It's an accomplishment what you've done here, and I am simply curious as to how your clever mind works. My position has not changed."

"Good," he said, a threat lingering beneath. "How is your part going then? Does she trust you yet?"

Trust...Kim. Shit. "She's beginning to."

"And was I right? She has a thing for men with sharp tongues?"

The threat I'd overheard Lyvias hurl on the castle steps...had that really been an attempt to woo her? A challenge for her rage to reveal itself, sure. But these two were absolute imbeciles if they believed she would have come crawling back with affection. "It appears a balance is necessary there. Sharp tongue, yes, but she reacts quite well to kindness in turn."

Malachi scoffed as his swirling shadows stilled for a moment. "Atrocious."

"Agreed. But fear not, I'll have her exactly where we want her in due time."

"I certainly hope so. Without her, I will never reach my full potential." He drifted towards me and, to my utter surprise and disgust, placed a kiss on my lips. "Now be a good boy and return to the castle. We don't need anyone discovering the future king is mixed up in the skin trade, now do we? I'll have my hounds attend to you."

Vomit reared up, and I swallowed it down. "No need. The night is quiet. I can attend to myself."

"If you so desire. I will send for you when the final pieces are in order. Until then, keep Kimberly distracted. We can't have her sticking her nose in places it doesn't belong."

Careful not to appear too eager to rid myself of his presence, I stepped out into the hall with a final glance over my shoulder. My mind cycled through the cryptic details. Full potential...what had he meant by that? He was already a Lord. Maybe he vied for the throne? Intended to overtake it? But he'd willingly referred to Lyvias as the future king, which unraveled that theory. And though he'd admitted to a deal with a baneful witch, it didn't explain the physical technicalities surrounding human girls entering Anathema. What the hell was going on?

I started a slow amble back towards the club's entrance. Death had to know more about all this than he'd let on. Maybe if I asked the right questions, I could get around the parameters of the blood pact that bound him to secrecy and—

A hard crack echoed down the hall. "Fuck, Odin! That's Death's girl!"

I peeked around the corner to find my absolute worst fear, and my entire being seized, locking me in place. There—trapped in a corner surrounded by five men—lay Kim. A fresh split in her lip dripped crimson down her chin, the smell making me salivate. I started towards her, and an unpleasant aroma replaced Kimber's sweet scent the closer I got. Wet dog. These were no mere men; they were hellhounds in human form. In a horrific turn of events, the largest man knelt down with the obvious intent to shove his dick in a place it didn't belong or deserve to be. Wrong. Fucking. Move.

I relinquished control, giving myself over to the monster.

A rabid grin spread across my face, and I cracked my knuckles, ready to sever heads from bodies. The hound nearest Kim lurched backward on my approach, but not in regards to me. I caught a glimpse just as Kim spit the man's severed dick at his feet, and a proud chuckle rolled through me. *That's my girl.*

And now, it was my turn.

I let my instincts take over. One after the other, I ripped hearts from rib cages; hot, torn flesh buried itself beneath my nails. The urge to feed—awoken by my recent taste—coursed through me. Why I hadn't expected Lyvias's needs to coincide with his identity and eventually take over, I wasn't sure. But they were there, and they were adamant as my fangs buried themselves in the third hound's neck. I sucked in heaving mouthfuls, aware of how the sensation *should* have sickened me, yet it did anything but. The blood on my taste buds rivaled the sweetest wine, and the ache in my muscles subsided the more I drank, the sleepless brain fog finally lifting. Before I knew it, I was straight-up high, rolling like I'd taken molly or ecstasy or some mind-altering drug that gave people a god complex. I...I loved it.

I sent the final, dickless hound running back to Malachi to keep up my façade. After all, he had said to keep Kimber from sticking her nose where it didn't belong, right? Something told me he wouldn't give two shits about me killing off a few mindless grunts if it meant not blowing his cover.

The haze cleared, my chest rising and falling in heavy breaths. Then I saw her. Broken and scared. I reached for her, but she shied away from my touch; and my chest tightened. While I'd known heartache before, it'd never cut so deep. She knew my face as an enemy. I couldn't comfort her, hold her, tell her everything was going to be okay. And that fucking shattered me. She tried to stand, but her legs bowed beneath her. I gave her space until she crumbled again. Carefully, I coaxed her to my chest. She resigned herself to her enemy's arms, spilling fresh tears on our return to the castle grounds.

Water rushed into the porcelain tub, the rose oil I'd added calming my frayed nerves as I considered the night's turn of events. Despite how much I wanted to make it all go away—for Kim to smile and stand proud again—I knew Odin had tarnished a part of her soul. A part I'd likely never be able to fix. But that wouldn't stop me from trying. I returned to her suite, tapped on her door, and peeked my head inside. "I've drawn you a bath."

"You..." She swallowed a sob. "You what?"

"A bath. Can you walk, or shall I carry you?"

"I can do it myself."

She stood, crashing to the floor a second later, a frustrated scream on her lips. I fought the urge to take her in my arms, but me touching her was on *her* terms. I needed her to know that.

I settled at her side. "Maybe, just for tonight, we could put aside our hatred and get you into a warm bath, hmm?"

A moment passed, and her face softened. "Just for tonight?"

"Of course. We can go back to planning each other's murders tomorrow, when you've had time to rest."

"...Fine."

I took her in my arms and started down the stairs. All the while, I pictured flaying Malachi and his hounds into bits with a cheese grater, savoring their screams of agony.

Chapter Eight

NEW EYES

"You don't understand!" I slammed my fist into the nearest bookshelf, sending tomes crashing to the ground. "Malachi is selling mortals. *Humans*, Death, are being trafficked through the Shroud somehow. If he's willing to do something that sadistic, and his own hounds don't know better than to attack their future queen, you can't seriously stand there prepared to do nothing!"

"I. Am. Bound!" Shadows slipped from Cadagon's fingers in plumes, filling the moonlit space with incredible darkness. The spiral staircase leading to the topmost shelves rattled under the weight of his projected energy. "You speak to me as if I haven't known true suffering in my sacrifices to protect my daughter. As if I wouldn't do *anything* in my power to see to her safety! But I cannot intervene here."

"If you wanted her safe, you'd tell me what you know!" My nails dug into my palms. "Someone threatened her."

"Threatened her? Who? What did they say, precisely? Do not skip any detail."

Whatever had been in that box had scared the living shit out of Kimber. So much so, she'd almost let the details slip to me—her supposed mortal enemy—but in the end, she'd kept it close to the chest. My guess? She was trying to piece together if I—Lyvias—had something to do with it all. I sucked in a heavy breath. "I...I don't know. She received a package, and whatever was inside riled her."

Death sighed and interlocked his hands in front of him. "Cooper, while I understand your concern, without accurate details I cannot do anything to help in this matter."

"You've got to be kidding me! You're the Reigning Reaper. What happened to the 'I have eyes everywhere' bullshit? Find out!"

"Do not order me to do anything! And who is to say I have the means or the resources to provide the answers you seek?"

"You do. You're just too much of a coward to risk anything on her behalf!"

Cadagon's sights narrowed. "You are treading on thin ice, boy."

If he couldn't intervene like he claimed, it meant whatever deal he'd made somehow touched Malachi or the club or the hounds or...fuck! Whose sins was he hiding? I pointed a finger at him and pushed my shoulders back. "Don't play coy with me. I saw the way your brow twitched when I mentioned Malachi's true potential. What are we up against here? Give me a hint, a lead, something—"

An invisible hold locked around my throat, the burn of hunger minimal compared to the severe pressure. I fought for words, but they refused me. I'd never had the unpleasant experience of being claustrophobic in my own damn body, and yet here I stood. Panicked. Trapped. Sinking deeper into my own crippling fear. The stained glass window began to blur into an amalgamation of color, all borders lost. I clawed at my skin, but still the candlelight from the overhead chandelier dimmed. Stop. I needed it to *stop*!

"You are wasting your time," Cadagon snarled. "I cannot give you the insight you seek. End of story. And while you stand here demanding things of me, your charge wanders the halls alone. Unprotected. A breach of contract, some would say."

He released me. My breath returned, but the throb—the pressure—remained. I studied him closer, my expression hardening. "You're torturing me now?"

Cadagon didn't bother to respond but raised his hands, palms out. Magic no longer leached from him, but my breath wouldn't steady; my body wouldn't relax. Thick, acidic vomit rose up my throat, burning like fresh slices of a razor blade. What the hell was going on? He'd hexed me! Cursed me! Something, because...the *burn*. I fell to my knees—sludgy, black tar projecting from my lips—and the all-too-familiar tug of soul and body severing apart sent my heart into overdrive. The sourness of rot sat heavy on my tongue. Seriously, how many times could one person approach death's door before losing their ever-loving mind?

"What is this?" I choked out.

"That," Cadagon said calmly, "is what it means to retract on one's blood pact. As I am bound to another, so too are you to me. To her. Or do you wish to leave her to the wolves?"

"Never!"

Tar dribbled down my chin in chunks, but it solidified suddenly, blocking my airway like I'd swallowed gravel. Pure torture. If there truly was a hell on another plane, this sensation hailed from it. My lungs labored for a modicum of air to sustain me.

"Make it stop," I barely pushed out.

"Our arrangement remains intact then?"

"Yes," I forced.

"Good." All at once, the torment fell away in a heartbeat. Gone. An eerie, unsettling sensation. The room spun as Cadagon leaned down, offering me a fresh cloth from his inner robe. "Clean yourself up. You look a mess."

I crawled to the nearest chair, slithered into it, and focused on evening my breath. In and out. One, two, three. Once I'd regained control—my shirt ruined by whatever matter had poured out of me—I looked Death straight in his burning irises. "That's what happens when you break a blood pact?"

"Yes. The steeper the terms, the worse the consequences. Your deal with me will allot you no kindness should you breach our agreement; do not forget that."

"Fuck..." I sighed, thankful to be in control again. But he still hadn't given me what I needed. I considered another angle. A safer one. "Can you tell me *anything*?"

"Now *that* is a better question. I can tell you that the past holds the key to the present."

A cynical laugh passed my lips. "Because *that's* super helpful."

"The family crypt. You will find your answers and Kimber there. Look for the final resting place of Ivy Bitters, counterpart to Reigning Reaper Shadra. Now, if you will excuse me, I have some business to attend to."

"How will I know where to find her grave?" I called after him.

"You'll know."

"Right."

He started towards the door. "It might not have occurred to you in your emotional fit, but have you considered simply asking Kimberly what resided in that box? Considered she might need a shoulder to lean on?"

The realization hit me hard. I hadn't. I'd been too wrapped up in my own feelings. My own rage. "I guess I could try that..."

"I suggest you do. The weight of our kingdom rests on her shoulders, and I would go so far as to say she could use a friend right now. Even one who bears the face of her enemy."

Death paused at the door but didn't turn back to me, his next words carrying through my head for me alone to hear. *And one final thing. I need you to promise me something.*

I narrowed my gaze. "Promise you what?"

His shoulders slouched as his head came to rest on the door frame. The sight—vulnerable and out of character for the king of Death—shook me. *You must agree.*

"You don't want to bind me in another pact first? Make sure I can't get out of it?"

He forced a laugh. *No. This promise will be an easy one to fulfill, because her life depends on it.*

"Name it." I stood and stepped closer.

When the time comes, you must end my life.

Cadagon's words haunted me on my trudge to the royal graveyard. He'd uttered no other words. Explained nothing. But I knew in agreeing to his request, I would never get a straight answer. Why would anyone seek their own murder? The only reason I could come up with was that his pacts had gotten away from him. That he'd bound himself so impossibly tight in his attempt to protect Kimber—which I was becoming increasingly convinced was his true desire—he'd decided death would be an easier solution than reaping the consequences of a broken pact. His desperation had practically flowed off of him, the conviction in his request bone-chilling. Almost like he feared something...or someone. Whoever had the ability to rattle the Reigning Reaper's cage in such a way was surely an enemy of the crown—and Kim. Another mystery to add to my research list. Whoever the hell they were, I would find them, and I *would* kill them.

For the time being, I had a standing date with the future queen.

Finding Ivy Bitters' final resting place and her personal accounts of the shapeshifter massacre wasn't nearly as difficult as expected. Seeing Kimber weep over the coffin housing my supposed body, however? Quite possibly the hardest thing I've ever had to do. Her tears, her loneliness: they made my chest ache.

She ran a finger across the coffin. "I think I have a target on my back. And that's not even the sickest part. Bet you can't guess what was in that damn box."

I stiffened.

"His dick, dude." She laughed. "How sick is that? Guess the hounds really have it out for me now. But don't worry; I'll find a way to take them out somehow...for you."

What a sick bastard! Who in their right mind *did* that kind of thing? Her words disturbed me, but what rattled me more was how in the midst of chaos, she was still thinking of me. Suddenly, I understood Cadagon, because I too was bound. Despite the overwhelming desire to pull her to me and kiss the tears from her face, I hid instead, donning yet another mask. While she loved Poe, her affections toward my alternate form were not the same. Nonetheless, I savored the small smile she gifted me on approach. At least my growing bloodlust curbed slightly when in my winged form, though Kimber's scent tempted me regardless. Red wine and citrus: intoxicating as hell.

I spent some time helping her find answers, her usual stubbornness shining through. Regrettably, I had to bite her to steer the dang woman in the right direction, but I'd be lying if her shock hadn't made me chuckle. Following her back to her room, I fell asleep in her arms. Well, Poe did anyway, but that didn't stop me from soaking up her peace. The quiet. The contentment.

My tranquility was short-lived, of course. Restless and hungry for answers, Kim slipped out in the night with her sights set on *The Book of Shade*.

I rushed through my transition—breaking my body to meld back into Lyvias's form—determined not to waste precious time. A decision I knew I'd pay for later. Knife pricks stabbed at my temples—a migraine already setting in—but I followed. My hands quivered. I wouldn't lose her, not with the frantic energy I'd picked up in her leaving. Something was wrong. Very wrong.

She snuck through the halls, her silk gown swaying in the wake of her hurried steps. Wrapped in moonlight from the overhead, domed windows, she paused on the main staircase, searching. Naturally, I couldn't waste a perfectly good opportunity to scare the living shit out of her. After all, that's what friends are for, right?

"Where are you going?" I called from the shadows.

She jumped, grasping her chest and cursing my name. "Lower your damn voice."

I smiled and stepped out from the hallway. After some persistence on my part, she accepted my help, but not before denying me time and time again. Commendable, really: her wariness of me, given whose face I wore. But I couldn't let her go, not when my gut told me to be vigilant. Warned me that trouble lingered nearby. Right on cue, said trouble presented itself at precisely the most inopportune moment.

Nasheesh.

He emerged from a nearby corridor. The way he slunk about looking over his shoulder at every turn made the hairs on the back of my neck stand up. He was up to something. I grabbed Kim, sweeping her up the stairs into the dark hall and pinning her to the wall.

She shoved against my chest. "Get off!"

Shock waves raced down my limbs as I drank her in up close. Those lips, that sharp tongue. Gods, how I wanted to devour her. To kiss my way down the supple skin of her neck and sink my teeth into the dip above her shoulder. A reckless desire. One that threatened to undue everything I'd done to secure my secret and remain by her side. Yet I leaned closer. My gaze dropped to her lips; her own eyes mirrored mine. Her pounding heartbeat echoed in my ears. Wait, did she *want* me? But as quickly as the thought came, it passed. Honestly, maybe I'd imagined it all together.

When Nasheesh disappeared from view, I released her, and she was off like a shot. Raw emotion had always fueled Kim, but this was different. Insistent.

I reached for her. "I bid to extend our truce."

"What?" She pulled from my hold.

"Let me come with you."

"Why do you even care?"

"Because I can see the fear in your eyes." I stepped closer. "And if the contents of that box scared the woman who pinned me to the ground with an axe upon our first meeting, it's clearly something I should know about."

She argued until blue in the face, but finally she caved, presenting a note written by Odin. He wanted war. And hell, if I wasn't more than pleased to give it to him.

By the time we found Death's quarters and managed to sneak past his personal bodyguard—a sandman far from home and possessed by his duty to protect the king—Kimber's energy had grown static, nearly flustered, which struck me as odd considering her usual demeanor. Her hands trembled as she attempted to get the centuries' old Reigning Reaper tome to obey her.

"It doesn't react to my blood," she snapped. "It won't open."

I leaned closer. "It's *The Book of Shade*, right? So use your shadows."

Her magic streamed from her fingertips like billowing smoke, slithering across the pages; and the book fluttered open, stopping on a specific page.

She squinted at the words, and her brow crinkled. "This doesn't make any sense. This passage is about hybrids."

"Hybrids don't exist."

"Right..."

She flipped the pages, the flutter of paper a serene whisper. But the scream on her lips as the book seemingly nipped her finger? Not so much. The sandman rushed in with a hiss, taking Kimber to the ground before I could blink. Goosebumps crawled up my neck as I attempted to pry the being off her, but its ironclad grip held firm. Convinced things couldn't *possibly* get any worse, my stomach dropped as Cadagon's presence shook the room. *Awesome.* He snapped, and the sandman released his hold.

Death glared at Kim. "Of all the infuriating things you've done since your arrival, this is the worst yet."

"I won't apologize," she bit back. "I will find out what you're hiding, and you can't—"

"Silence! You have outdone yourself this time, my foolish daughter."

They sniped back and forth, but what caught my attention wasn't their harsh words for one another, but rather the strange pauses between Kim's responses. It was as if something, somewhere, had tapped into her brain, like an incoming call on a nonexistent headset. Without warning, she hurled her shadows at Death, which he dodged with minimal effort.

"You made an oath to fulfill your role," he snarled, pinning her in place. "You will remain here in Anathema, even if that means I have to sever your connection to the astral."

It hit me the same moment her pleading glance did: the fear, the distraction, the urgency. June. *That's* who'd been calling to her.

"Help me. Please, Lyvias," she begged.

I flashed her a grin. "You fucking owe me."

Though I knew it might be the death of me, I tackled Cadagon. Kim seized her opportunity, launching into the astral to find her lover. It was just me and good ol' daddy Death now. He rocketed me off him, slamming me into the nearest wall.

"You absolute fool!" He knotted his fingers in his hair. "Do you realize what you've done?"

I jumped to my feet—my attention bouncing between Death and the sandman—and slowly circled the room. "You mean, having a heart and allowing her to check on Juniper? Yeah, I stand by my decision, old man."

While I'd always envied June and the connection she shared with Kim, there was no choice when it came to giving them the chance to be near one another. My girl's needs were mine, even if her affections might never be.

"Her lover is no mere being!" Death boomed.

"What does that *mean*? I don't—"

"She's the embodiment of Fate, Cooper!" Cadagon's anger slipped away to reveal raw, palpable fear. "What you have done risks Kimber's life more than any shortsighted decision you have made to date! The knowledge hidden within the Reigning Reaper's tome causes a rapid acceleration in one's cosmic path if read before their ascension to power. Do you understand?"

Fate. Kim was in love with the incarnation of *Fate*? *Holy...* I shook my head, forgetting to breathe. "I didn't know."

"That is because you do not *think*, and now Kimberly's destiny has awoken before its time. The sliver of astral space created by their connection in order to meet each other in the Shroud is a temporary place, and the door to access it is closing by the second—with her *in* it!" Death's face grew eerily still. "Not only is her life in grave danger, but should she survive, her heart will be shattered. In helping yourselves to that book, you severed the connection between the future Fate and Death before the Goddess intended."

No. I thought...I...damn it!

"I'll go after her. I'll help her undo it. I'll find Juniper and—"

"No, you have done enough damage for one night. I will see to her care." Death snapped his fingers, and his disturbing pet floated to his side, fixing its hollow, expressionless face on me. "For what it is worth, part of me wishes I could spare you the consequences of your actions, but the laws of the cosmos are inevitable."

"What is that supposed to mean?"

And then the sandman opened its gaping maw, smoke pouring out to consume me whole.

Energy zapped across my skull. The sensation mimicked what I imagined it might feel like to shove a fork in a light socket. Then…nothing. I looked around, but there was only darkness. Pitch black. Wait, were my eyes actually open? I brought my hand to my face and twiddled my fingers about, but again…nothing. Where the hell was I?

"You defied the natural order of things, shapeshifter," something whispered in the blackness. "You defied Fate's wishes. For this, you must be punished."

The words opened up a cavern in the darkness, and I saw it: the sandman. Emotionless. Reaching.

Suddenly, I felt *everything* in a devastating rush. Wherever I'd landed, I didn't belong. The frost accumulating on my skin told me I was somewhere other: a place never intended for the living or anything warm. Beastly visions cascaded through me: gnashing teeth, the sky torn in half by taloned fingers. All the while, the sandman punched and drained me. Each strike of the creature's hand brought its smoke closer, surrounding me in a gut-wrenching loneliness and an aching throb. A delicacy for the sandman, it appeared. The monster devoured my fear in mouthfuls, its rabid thirst eager to break me for stepping outside the universal fabric laid out by the Old Gods. On and on it went, but for how long I couldn't decipher. Had it been hours? Days?

The cloaked figure landed another hard crack to my jaw, splitting my bottom lip and crashing me back to the present. "Where have you taken me?"

A hollow laugh slipped past the sandman's emotionless lips. "Where all go to be punished for their crimes against the Old Gods. A place of nightmares. A place of forgotten children. A place of destitution and foul magic. Look, and behold your fate."

The smoke parted, and my swollen eyes managed to make out a shred of the world around me. Monstrous cries lifted into the violet sky, solidifying the all-consuming sense that I was being hunted. Forgotten children...Old Gods...destitution...

"The Shroud," I whispered.

The sandman hissed. "How do you know of the in-between?"

A tinge of relief flitted through me. If I'd made it into the Shroud, then likely Kim had too. Maybe she'd found Juniper and gotten to say her goodbyes. If so, then I'd succeeded in my promise to the woman I loved and ensured her right to attend to the woman *she* loved. I'd upheld my word. But on the other hand, I'd failed. A toxic mix of gratitude and guilt swept through me. It'd never been my intention to put Kim in harm's way, let alone seal her heartbreak in the same breath. My chest tightened. Maybe there was still time to change this. If I could figure out a way to escape this nightmarish creature and find Kim, I'd have a chance to redeem myself, save her, and get her home.

"You've grown too thirsty in your search for knowledge, false Lord. Such untamed thirst must be quenched and repaid for its wicked reach. Broken down and made to yield."

My wrist rose to my lips of its own volition, sliding between my teeth as the sandman smiled for the first and only time.

"Drink, and be purged of your sins."

Drink? My *own* blood? A punishment like that was dealt to the worst offenders in Anathema's rankings. Murderers and treasonous filth. Not me. Not— It hit me as my teeth sank into the thick blue veins of my wrist. To the sandman, I *was* a traitor. I'd defied the king's orders and put the future queen in danger. This monster perceived me as one far worse. Maybe it was right.

Frigid, salty blood spilled across my tongue, pooled in my cheeks, and clawed its way down my throat. Blisters and boils burst forth in its wake, paralyzing me. I accepted my fate. I deserved it: the torture, the punishment. There would be no escape or freedom from this prison. And you know what? Fair enough. I'd failed, and every burning sip reminded me of that failure. So despite how I *yearned* to call out for Kim, I denied myself as I always did; because the sole person who'd stuck by my side, who'd truly seen me, I'd abandoned. I didn't deserve her.

"Go on then," I called out into the void. "Finish me!"

Blinding light ripped through the darkness, sending the sandman cowering into the distance. Sunlight trailed its warm touch across my skin, instantly lifting the layer of frost and soothing the burn in my chest. What in the actual fuck? A hand gripped my elbow and pulled me to my feet.

"Who are you?" a silky voice asked.

The light she wielded; her rich, dark skin; the peace she carried…I knew her, if only in the context of Kimber's words. Juniper. *Fate.*

I struggled to stay on my feet. "Did you find her? Kim? She needs you. You must go to her before it's too late!"

"Too late?" June's brow crumpled as her grasp on me tensed. "How do you know Kimber? How do you know *me*?"

I struggled to find the words, to lessen the blow, but fact was fact. "You don't have much time. You have to go!"

"I do not bend to Time's will; he bends to mine," she scoffed.

With the flick of her wrist, the scene around us pivoted on its axis, coming to rest back over us in a strange, sloth-like tone. The clouds above no longer swirled violently but rather spun, slow and steady. The ripping wind settled into a gentle breeze. *No. Way.*

"Did you just slow time? That's incredible!"

"One of the many perks of being Fate incarnate. Now take a breath, and tell me what I need to know."

I did as she said, and my panic dropped down a notch. "Kim…she opened *The Book of Shade.*"

"What?" Light billowed in her hands. "How could Death have let this happen? The insolence!"

"It wasn't his fault; it was mine. Kim sought answers regarding her enemies, and I encouraged her."

"Her enemies are closing in? But…I didn't foresee it. How can this be?"

"Look, I know it doesn't make any sense, and you don't owe me anything, but you have to trust me. If you don't go now, you may never get a chance to…"

Her sights danced across my face expectantly, but my tongue turned to lead, unwilling to spew the heartbreak on the tip of my tongue.

"Never get a chance to—" Her words stopped short as her golden eyes fell to her feet. "I…I have to say goodbye. This explains why our connection felt so weak when I called out to her. Why I landed here with you and not her. Our bond is severing."

"I'm so sorry," I muttered.

"I knew this day would come, but selfishly I had hoped to hold onto her a little while longer. To love her as if she was destined to be mine, though I knew. I *knew*."

I grabbed her hands. "I know how much you two mean to each other, and I can't bear the thought of her moving forward without a chance to be near you one last time. Or you to her."

She smirked, studying me closely. "You're Cooper, aren't you?"

"How did you know that?"

"Kim has told me much about you and how you've always taken great care of her. That, and glamours peel away under Fate's gaze, even clever ones such as yours. Why do you wear the vampire Lord's face when you're of shapeshifter decent?"

"I am whatever Kim needs me to be," I said, stern in my conviction.

She pursed her lips. "Even if it means wearing the mask of her enemy?"

"Without question."

"You can stand her hating you? Blaming you?" June squinted as the world around us sped up a click.

I swallowed hard. "If that's what it takes to ensure her victory, then yes."

"Because you're in love with her, aren't you?"

Oh, shit. I hadn't expected to get into a pissing contest—especially one I would one hundred percent *lose*—with the personification of a goddess. Regardless, I knew better than to lie to Fate, no matter how much I wanted to avoid being reduced to a pile of ash.

"Yes, but I do not expect her returned affection. I just want to keep her safe."

The understanding reflected in June's stare told me she was quite familiar with that sentiment.

"Honorable." She smirked. "I will go to her, but first there is something I must do."

Ethereal light dripped from her hand, encasing me in pure euphoria and sinking into my veins. My blood. My very life force. An angelic song echoed through my head in a tongue I'd never heard and somehow knew. A lost language.

"You have a strong heart. You will need it for the path laid before you. For your efforts in protecting the one I love, I honor you with the gift of unrivaled sight." She tapped a single fingertip on my forehead, and the entire scene pulsed around her. "And do remember: the desires of *her* heart are not all that matters. Be true to your hopes lest you fall victim to another's destiny and abandon your own. Now, see with your new eyes and fix your gaze upon those who wish our queen harm."

I bowed before her. "Thank you, Fate."

"My friends call me June." With a wink, she was gone.

I stood there as time reshaped itself. The sky spun, and the wind whipped once more, a symphony of cries and moans erupting around me. Monstrous cries. But one stood out above the rest, carrying closer. Though my vision remained fuzzy, I spun around to face the incoming threat.

My heart sank.

There at the meadow's edge sat a creature so foul it locked my knees in place. My palms grew clammy under the weight of its stare. Eerily motionless, head tilted, a disturbed grin twisting clear up to the beast's temples. *Holy fucking shit.* Blue skin, long talons. I'd seen that face before...mounted on Malachi's wall. Chaos: the amalgamated child of the original Fate and Death. Great. Just what I needed.

A strange mist radiated from it—thick and seeping—and wafted to me on the breeze. Dark, baneful magic. Wait, how did I know that? I brushed a hand across my face. Right, unrivaled sight. But had Fate gifted me the means to see *all* magical affinities? Or was this unique to the creature before me?

"Come to me, oh mighty vampire Lord, so I may feast upon your bones," Chaos called with a sinister laugh.

Oh, gods. I smacked my cheeks. *Wake up!* Or was I even asleep? The Shroud was one confusing-ass plane. Did I need to click my heels together three times like Dorothy? Recite, "There's no place like home"?

Chaos charged, and I about pissed my pants before taking off at a sprint. Winding through thorn bushes sharp as razors, I tried my best to ignore the clomping steps drawing closer and closer. Run. I had to run, and then I'd be safe. Right?

Too bad I didn't notice the low-hanging branch about to knock my damn lights out.

CHAPTER NINE

INSATIABLE THIRST

Humid air affronted me. I coughed as I sat up straight, the world around me spinning and taking shape slowly. No more beasts. No violet sky. Actually, no sky at all, just stone and bars.

The castle dungeon.

I'd have taken the time to wonder what had earned me yet another cruel punishment if it weren't for the *magnitude of life* demanding my attention. Colors on the light spectrum I'd no name for refracted in the torch light, and a shuffle of silk and flesh rang out. Upon inspection, I narrowed the sound down to the spider weaving her web in the cell's corner, a green mist radiating from the eight-legged beauty. Somehow, I knew it held an affinity for nature. It wasn't imbued with supernatural gifts itself, but an unquestionable connection to elemental magic coursed through it.

So Fate *had* gifted me with oracle sight...

The steady thump of boots echoed from the floor above. It drew closer and closer, but I didn't need to look up to know whose footsteps they were. Her unique perfume needed no introduction.

She came into view, and my body stilled. I'd thought her beautiful before. But watching the red and black mist sweeping about her ashen hair? Otherworldly.

Her magic was dark, vengeful, impulsive even, but not evil like what I'd witnessed in Chaos. No, hers was powerful: the Old Gods' magic in a fleshy vessel.

My queen had come for me.

Kim surveyed my wounds with wide-eyed horror, lingering on the torn and bruised skin at my wrists. Shadows slithered from her fingertips: her growing rage personified.

"What did he do to you?"

"They're bite marks..."

"Death *bit* you?"

I didn't have the heart to tell her of the sandman's attempt to break me or the horrors brewing in the Shroud. She already worried for her kingdom and her people enough. Desperately so. To confirm that unbalance was spreading to adjacent realms would only cause her unnecessary concern with little information to go off of in regards to action. I pushed to stand, met her gaze, and fought the rising sense of betrayal in keeping such a secret from her. We never hid *anything* from one another. Chaos's guttural growl replayed in my memory; the image of its sunken shoulders hunched over as it barreled towards me constricted my thigh muscles, causing my flight instinct to kick in all over again. In the right time, I'd tell her. I'd tell her everything. But not until I knew more about what we faced. For now, half-truths would have to do.

"No, this is courtesy of Cadagon's personal torture master. He made me drink my own blood."

She reached for me, but I pulled away on impulse, attempting to keep my omission close to the chest. Or maybe, if I were being honest, I did it more because I grew increasingly tired of pretending. Of being Lyvias. I craved to peel away his face and be me again. Funny, how I'd wanted to be anyone but myself for so long; and yet here I was, once again forcing myself to consider "*What would Lyvias do?*" with gritted teeth. She was standing right in front of me, but I missed her...missed us.

On our conversation went; her argumentative tone and rage festered the closer we drew to the conclusion on both our minds. If there were any hopes of saving Anathema, it meant striking down the one actively decimating it. The one whose pacts locked us into our only option. A dark chuckle rolled through me as it clicked.

"I'll handle it. Cadagon shall die by my hand."

She went rigid. "You want him dead?"

In the end, this wasn't about my wish to kill him, but rather the feral, primal urge to protect Kim at all costs. Whatever trouble Death had landed himself in, he knew well enough that he himself had to die to burn his sins away with his own blood. I watched Kim's magic twist about—draping around her chest like a breastplate over her heart—and it became apparent that maybe, just maybe, she didn't need me to protect her anymore. Her true nature had awoken. And gods, how I wanted to taste her fury.

"His blood belongs on my hands," she said, stern.

Hearing her mirror Death's wish for his end only inspired me to lend her my blade further. A crooked smile overcame me as I drew a stone down my palm, flaying it wide open, and extended it to her. "Together?"

She mirrored my smile and offered her hand. "Together."

Pinpricks swept up my arms as our blood intermingled, her magic seeping into me to explore my body. My new sight locked onto the deep burgundy mist swirling beneath my skin. Not her magic. Not mine. Ours. With a sharp jolt, it shot into the open air above, broke in two, and seeped into our severed palms. The deal with Lady Death had been struck.

We were bound to one another.

Her hand tightened around mine in a bloody hold, and my body reacted as if I'd injected every aphrodisiac known to man straight into my bloodstream. I could *feel* her shadows inside me, coiling around my heart like a vice. I thought I'd loved her before. But now? I'd never wanted her more. Never craved to lay her out, trail my kiss across every inch of her skin, and feel her writhe beneath me *more*. Pure devotion. I'd lend myself to her, to bend or break—it didn't matter which one.

Because I was hers *alone*.

Her sights dropped to my mouth. Our shared magic danced on her tongue as she licked her bottom lip. "Damn, I'm thirsty..."

Bloodlust: courtesy of my magic. Or rather, Lyvias's extended to me. Kim looked up at me with hooded eyes, a mischievous gleam within them. Oh, the fun we could have with that. My cock throbbed at the vision of her teeth sinking into me, bending me to her will like she'd done long ago. Claiming me. I stepped closer, ready to take her right then and there on the floor, but stopped short.

Not in this body.

When, or *if* ever, I had the honor of burying myself inside her, it would be my name on her lips as she cried out in pleasure, not Lyvias's. I forced my eyes shut, simmered my need, and with a final glance, I walked away. Even though the magical cord now tying us together called me back to her.

Three hard knocks battered the door. I crossed my room and opened it to find Lana with a box tucked under her arm. I waved her in, shutting the door behind her.

"Well, hello. And what, might I ask, do you have there?"

She smiled, setting the box on the table in front of the hearth. "It's a chessboard."

"Ah, chess. I've never been very good at it."

"Me either, but..." Her face fell.

"But what?"

"I thought maybe...maybe we could learn together?"

I grinned. "You know what? That sounds like a great idea."

Good thing Lyvias's abilities included a minimal need for sleep, because apparently the realm of eternal night wasn't about to let me have any. But a giddy giggle from Lana as she divided out the marble chess pieces made it worthwhile.

My internal clock woke me at precisely the right time: midnight. The moonlight cast shadows about my new suite—courtesy of Kim—and illuminated the scene as I readied myself for the night's events. I needed to return to the club, not only for my own investigative needs but to keep up appearances with Malachi. What I'd seen in the Shroud disturbed me to my core and had kept me tossing and turning in my attempt to sleep. If a monster like Chaos had the ability to make deals, and the demon Lord had willingly entered into such atrocities, I feared for Anathema's future. For every person at the demon Lord's mercy as he strove to pack his precious meat market.

Red suit and mask donned, I crept from my room. Tonight was an information grab. Finding out who Malachi worked with and how they operated was pivotal in learning how to unwind the web he'd spun. Since that first glimpse, the girl he'd tucked away behind the painting had plagued me. Her soulless eyes. Her desperation. I longed to free her, to see her returned to those she loved and given a chance at a life outside those soundproof walls. Nobody deserved such cruelty.

I clicked the lock on my door and turned to descend when I met an unmovable force.

"And just where do you think you're going at such an ungodly hour?" Suri asked, hand on her hip.

"You stalking me now?" I teased. "Look, I've already told you I'm spoken for."

"Yeah, yeah. Very funny. Kim told me she moved you into the south tower. Why?"

I raised an eyebrow. "What, don't want to share her attention? I know I'd be jealous if someone as handsome as me moved in next door too."

"Gods, you're full of yourself." She cinched up the tie on her silk night robe.

"It's a defense mechanism. Helps me cope with my unprocessed mommy issues." *Oof, that was a little too real...*

She smacked my shoulder with a limp wrist. Her blood sang to me, my gums pulsing in response. I really needed to curb this rising hunger before I hauled off and…I don't know, ate Nasheesh in a fit of annoyance or something. I swallowed against the burn in my throat.

"Don't you think things will be harder this way?" she asked. "Sneaking about with the future queen one floor above you?"

I demonstrated the speed Lyvias's heart had lent me, sweeping to the winding staircase's end and back in a heartbeat. "Not a problem."

Why was Suri's pulse so *strong*? It throbbed in my ears, carrying through me.

She followed my line of sight where it lingered on her throat. "But that thirst will be if you don't get it in check."

"I'm fine."

"No, you're not. You're practically drooling."

I started down the stairs. Suri was right, but I refused to allow my weakness to rule me. I'd fight it. I'd eat a raw steak or a stray animal before I let myself take from an unwilling party. Unless of course they were a complete piece of shit, but I digress. And really, who would *want* to be fed upon? Although something told me Kim might get off on such a thing. Damn, the thought of it— *No. Focus.*

My senses flooded, overwhelmed by a sudden, crippling perfume. Suri extended her hand, a pool of fresh crimson in the center. "Drink."

Fuck. I stepped away from her, my mouth watering. "No."

"If you don't drink, then what use are you to the girls you're trying to help free? I assume that's why you're dressed up, is it not? To return to the club?"

I bit my cheek, hard. "If I give in, I— It's getting harder to control, Suri."

"If you don't get your urges under control, you risk blowing everything. Something tells me you would become a lamenting mess, hiding out in a dark room for eternity if you allowed yourself to harm anyone because of your bloodlust."

She thrust her hand closer, a crimson droplet rolling off the side to *splat* at my feet. Such a waste.

I pinched the bridge of my nose, but the smell lingered. "I don't want to hurt you."

"I have worked too hard for this: to free them. And I am no stranger to pain. Stop being dramatic and drink!"

She shoved her hand between my lips, and the sensation was nothing short of orgasmic. Stepping closer, I backed her against the wall, and a whimper escaped her, sending a charge rolling through my veins. How easy she'd be to drain. To devour. To consume completely. I savored mouthful after mouthful until finally, she set a gentle hand on my cheek.

"That's enough," she whispered, her eyes locking onto me.

But I didn't stop. Couldn't. This feeling—this god-like bliss—dominated every rational thought. I sank my teeth deeper into her palm, parting her supple skin like warm butter; and she winced at my bite, her heartbeat accelerating. She was afraid, but I liked it. Why did I *like* it? The sensation drove me mad, encouraging the violence simmering in my mind. How easily I could rip open her jugular and drink until I saw stars. Worse still, I held no guilt in that moment. Just desire. Overwhelming, primal desire.

"Please," she begged. "Know your limits, Cooper."

My name on her tongue broke the spell but not my hold. Her thumb caressed my jaw, and in the fuchsia mist emanating from her, peace took root in me. The light pricked a hole in the darkness, and I found myself again.

"Thank you." I rested my forehead in her hand.

She wrapped her bleeding palm in the hem of her shirt and grasped my hand with the other, leading me to her room without another word. Her calm rattled me. I'd almost lost myself in the urge to end her life, and yet she remained gentle. Understanding. How? I didn't deserve such kindness.

She sat on her bed, patting for me to join her. "I can think of one way you can repay me for helping with your little hunger problem."

My palms grew slick and clammy. Oh...no. No, no, no. She was stunning and strong and everything a man would be lucky to call his own, but not *this* man. "I'm sorry, I can't—"

"Calm down. I am not asking you to make sensual, life-changing love to me." Again, she tapped for me to sit, and I did, leaving a foot between us. "Lana, she told me about the summons you received. I need to know: what did you see in the club's underbelly?"

I released my held breath as my shoulders relaxed. Thank the damned. My concern quickly gave way to the weight of her question, my fury renewed and charged by my recent feed. I told her the disturbing details about girls being auctioned off and the countless men ready to snatch them up to serve their own selfish desires. She sat in stunned horror—face pale—but upon my account of Malachi's supposed deal with the Ancient Lore, she shot to her feet.

"Humans?" She paced about the room. "They're trafficking *humans* through the Shroud? Into this realm? That imbalance will see us wiped into the void faster than anything Anathema has faced before!"

"I know."

"We have to do something! We have to tell Kim, immediately!"

She started for the door, but I cut off her exit. Kim had enough on her plate—what with planning her own father's murder and trying to get to the bottom of Odin's threats. Not to mention, I wanted to be the one to deal with this. To put an end to Malachi. The realization gave me pause. Wait, I *wanted* to...for me. Juniper's words about finding my own destiny replayed in my mind. Was this to be my path? My fate? Suri pulled at my arm, attempting to move me aside, and snapped me out of my potential epiphany.

"No, leave her out of this, please," I said, stern.

"She deserves to know what is going on in her own kingdom—"

"And she will. Just not yet."

"Fine." Her magic sparked about her. "Then we will go."

"Thank you. I don't want—wait, we?"

"Yes, *we*." She flitted to her closet, facing the wall to peel off her clothes with zero concern for my presence.

"Whoa, there!" I averted my eyes, catching a glimpse of the intricate galaxy inked across her shoulder blades.

"Relax. I have no intention of showing you the goods, so don't go all honorable and righteous on me. I can't very well wander into the club in my servant's outfit."

"You're seriously coming? Won't that risk our cover?"

"I work there. How would that blow our cover? I mean, sure, the dancers and staff aren't permitted in the lower levels; but with Lord Lyvias accompanying me, it should work."

"Should? That's promising." I rubbed my face, a series of *what-ifs* flooding in. "You want to risk both our lives on a maybe. Awesome."

"I saw the way Lyvias looked at me. The man practically rubbed one out in the corner when I danced for Malachi once. Repulsive prick. My point is I can sell it, and this might be the only chance I have to get a lay of the land down there." She pulled a purple corset over her head. "When it comes to getting those girls out—which I can already tell you have resigned yourself to doing—you are going to need me."

The stubborn woman reminded me of someone a little too keenly, but she wasn't wrong. Still, I tried. "I can't be worried about watching out for your safety while we're down there. I have to dig for answers."

Having access to Lyvias's abilities and appearance didn't provide insights into his former thoughts and actions, unfortunately. Would Malachi question me bringing Suri? Challenge me? Not to mention, with an ego as big as Malachi's, jealousy could play a huge role. What if he didn't want to share his precious dancer?

"It's too risky," I said, my conviction waning.

"Yeah, well, without risk there is no reward. I can handle my own. Accept it, pretty boy. I'm coming. Now, lace me up?"

She swept her hair over her shoulder to reveal the crisscrossed back. Reluctantly, I obliged. It seemed there would be no changing her mind regardless of how hard I pleaded, which meant I'd have to be even more on top of my game. Sharp and attentive. *Great.*

After Suri cinched up a pair of knee-high boots and snagged a bunny-eared mask, out the door we went. Whatever came next, I had to hand it to the spitfire: the chick did, in fact, know how to handle her own. And while the concern for her safety entering the meat market loomed in my mind, she was right: without risk, there would be no reward.

Her self-assured stride as we entered the demon realm further confirmed my confidence. She'd handle herself. All I needed to do was sell it. Suri remained a safe distance ahead of me to ensure nobody saw us together until we wanted them to. We couldn't risk a hound bringing back any information that might tip off Malachi.

As I drifted through the bustling streets and onto the nearest train, I wove the story together in my head. Lyvias had taken the train to Plavin Park, and on said train, he'd noticed a certain fuchsia-eyed demon. He'd gotten the wily idea that Malachi might enjoy some decompression time: a fun romp with his favorite dancer. Maybe Lyvias could even present the idea of Suri waiting on the VIP members in the meat market in the future, considering her dedicated service. Yeah, a business endeavor. That could work.

From there, I'd have to wing it. Whether Malachi would believe the lie or not remained to be seen. But add some liquor plus a dash of lust, and my gut told me the plan would go off without a hitch. That is, until I entered the booming club to find an obscene number of guests and dancers.

And one fucking furious demon Lord.

Chapter Ten

RADIUM

"What in the damned were you thinking?" Malachi slammed his office door behind Suri and me. "Are you an absolute fool or too drunk to function, Lyvias?"

Oh shit. Okay, so *not* the right move bringing her here. But drunk...*that* I could work with. I added a sway to my step as I helped myself to brandy from the minibar, sloppily pouring us both a glass. "Come now, can you blame me? Look at her. She is sensational! You truly have exquisite taste, my friend."

Suri took stock of the scenario and leaned into my placation with ease. Donning a saunter and a pair of innocent doe-eyes beneath her mask, she laid a hand on Malachi's chest. "Daddy, please don't be mad. I missed you, that's all."

Malachi stepped from her reach. "Do not toy with me, girl. You know you are not permitted down here. You *both* have forced me to make a decision I never intended to make involving your fate."

He walked to his desk and downed the entirety of his whiskey in one go. The air grew thick. Tense. His shadows thrashed around him as he tapped a finger on his shiny wooden desk, deep in thought. Seconds ticked by, until I realized what would be required to ease his troubled mind. What would force him to remove his business hat and put on one of sin and debauchery, thus loosening him up to share a secret or two that could lend a hand in ending this nightmare. I ran my fingers through my hair. *Just for show*, I reminded myself. A role. A performance. For one night, I'd lean into it: become Lyvias, body and soul. For

the restoration of the kingdom, I'd become a monster to ensnare another. One.
Night.

Kim, forgive me.

"Let's have some fun, yes?" I called to Malachi playfully. "Everyone deserves
a break now and then. Especially someone as devoted to his life's work as you."

Appealing to his massive ego, I wrapped a hand around Suri's shoulders,
backing her up against me. My sights locked onto Malachi as I set my lips against
her neck and trailed kisses up to her jawline, pausing near her ear to murmur
words meant for only her to hear. "It's just a game, nothing more."

"Anything for you, my Lord," Suri said. The underlying sharpness in her
tone let me know she understood.

The way she melted beneath my touch would send any other man over the
edge—her arching back, the depth of her breath—but I knew my place and to
whom my heart belonged. I had to hand it to her though: she knew what she
was doing. Good. It'd make selling this easier.

"Come play with us," I begged Malachi.

He froze.

More. I had to push him more. Give him a show he couldn't say "no" to.
Without warning, I sank my teeth into Suri, and her moan rattled through
the room, her blood sending me into a frenzy. My fingers curled into tighter
and tighter fists with each mouthful of her essence. *Don't lose your shit. Hold
it together.* But to my surprise, she egged me on—much to Malachi's pleasure
it appeared, based on the change in his churning shadows. They crept closer,
curious.

"Does my taste please you?" Suri whispered.

To that, Malachi sat up straighter. At attention, he watched with sinister
intent and made his way to the sound system adjacent the ominous depiction
of Chaos. Flashes of the poor girl hidden behind it snaked across my memory.
That broken smile. Her visible loneliness. My skin crawled, pleading to peel
from my bones and escape the character I portrayed, but I had no choice but
to continue our ruse. Malachi had to trust me. He had to believe I was, in fact,
his sordid business partner if I had any hope of saving the mortal girl and all the

others in the market. I pinched my eyes shut, curbed my racing thoughts, and feigned pleasure at Suri's touch. Rage wouldn't—couldn't—fuel this situation. It'd blow our cover. *Focus, Cooper.*

The music rose, filling the room with a lusty beat. Malachi perched himself on the desk's edge and crossed his legs at the ankles. "Go on then, Lyvias. Convince me that you breaking our sacred rule was for good reason."

Blood spilled across my tongue. I tried to let the thrill of Suri's soft skin direct me as I slipped a hand across her stomach, careful to avoid any intimate places, and she guided my touch lower. I fought her hold. Fuck, I was blowing our cover, but this all felt wrong. Like a betrayal. I removed my lips from Suri's throat and clutched it instead—gentle but with purpose—spinning her around to face me.

I buried my face in her neck and murmured, "I can't do this."

"Relax and let me take control. I know what you crave."

The gleam in her eyes held a promise as she danced to block off Malachi's line of sight. Her hand drifted down my chest but stopped before it strayed too far, although it surely appeared seductive from the demon Lord's view. I instinctually stepped back, but Suri's finger hooked my belt loop to keep me in place.

"I fear you are being selfish, my Lord," she projected with a wink. "I am to be shared."

She flipped to turn her attention to Malachi. A perfect segue. I downed my drink, eager to assuage the growing thirst onset by Suri's blood. Her scent floated away from me. The way Malachi melted under her touch soothed my fears. He was taking the bait, buying into the illusion. Maybe we really could get him to spill his secrets in a drunken stupor and gain insight—

"Stop," Malachi demanded abruptly.

My heart sank into my toes. *Or not.*

He removed Suri from his lap and made his way to me. Before I could react or prepare myself, he forced me against the wall, his tongue jutting into my mouth and swirling about with vicious, demanding motions. My lungs shrank. Malachi's frenzied touch brought back the searing memory of Lyvias's assault in vivid color. The way these men took what they wanted with zero remorse or consideration sickened me. My vision went red. The urge to rip his heart out right then and there clouded my senses, but I pushed my sights past him, catching a glimpse of empathy in Suri's gaze. She felt the same: despised his touch. While our mission and what was required to accomplish it remained clear, I'd be damned if I let Malachi take advantage of us. I was in control. *I* decided, and he'd sing whether he liked it or not.

I flipped him around, pinning him against the wall. Forcefully, I laid my weight against him. "Even now, you refuse to lift your shadows for me?"

He chuckled darkly. "You know only my mate is allotted such luxuries. Though you tempt me with this newfound dominance. It suits you."

His mouth busied itself at my neck, and I let my mind drift away from his touch, distancing my senses. Wait...he had a mate? Fated mates were rare, almost unheard of these days. A tie like that was unbreakable. It merged two hearts, two beings, two destinies into one. Whoever his counterpart was, they surely played a heavy hand in the club's dealings. The potential for leverage made my fingers tingle. I had to know who it was.

I forced a moan I didn't mean in the slightest and pulled back to behold his shadows. "Then bring your mate to me. Let us broaden our fun."

My gut twisted as Malachi raised a shrouded hand and waved it once, a sickening mist lifting in its wake: baneful magic. But also something else. An opalescent sheen shimmered beneath the vapor. Mated magic maybe? It had to be, considering the way two distinct affinities melded into one before my eyes. My intuition told me two things: one, he had summoned his mate; and two, he had done as he'd said and dabbled in black magic in the Shroud. My soul quivered. His aura matched Chaos's to a tee.

Stay sharp. One step at a time.

I wrapped an arm around his shoulders. "Will she share? Your precious mate?"

"She?" Malachi backed away.

My mouth went dry. I'd just assumed, and... *Idiot!* The fact that I hadn't considered Lyvias knew the demon Lord's partner—most likely very well—was a serious mistake on my part.

"What do you mean 'she'—"

"Of course I will," Suri stepped in.

Thank the Gods. Woman knew how to read a room. This seemed to explain away my fraudulent slip enough for Malachi to ease up.

"My love has made it clear that he fancies you, Lyvias," Malachi said. "And I make it a point to do whatever I can to ensure his pleasure. However, I must say, I never thought I'd see the day where you shared *me*."

Oh. Ohhhhhh. Okay, *now* I was getting it. A love lost situation. Lyvias wanted Malachi, but his heart was already bound to another. The closest the two could get was business partners with benefits. Interesting.

Malachi busied himself in his desk, pens clicking together as he rummaged. He waved a hand for Suri and me to come closer and extended two of four bright red pills. "For stamina. The four of us shall need it, seeing as we'll be spending the night together, don't you think?"

"Radium..." Suri's brows lifted.

I wanted to ask what it was. What it did. But given my supposed line of work, I couldn't. Lyvias surely knew what it was. Anything lending stamina in the bedroom was bound to be a trick of the trade. I looked to Suri, pleading for a hint. What exactly was I in for? Shit, this night was not going as planned.

"Last time I dabbled in R, I swear I saw the Old Gods themselves," Suri offered, downing her pill dry. "The sensation is otherworldly."

"Indeed. There truly is no sweeter feeling," Malachi agreed.

Suri's conviction and ease in accepting Malachi's offering gave me hope that I would survive this. If she'd thought it unwise, her quick mind would have come up with some solution or exit strategy. I stared at the pill. For Kim. All of this was for her. To cast down her enemies and drain the filth from her kingdom, I'd burn these bastards alive—even if it meant I burned with them.

Suri rounded Malachi's chair, began massaging his shoulders, and met my gaze.

"Information," she mouthed.

Even the tightest vaults tended to unlock—spilling their secrets—when under the influence of euphoric substances. Lucky for me, I'd had many a dalliance with ecstasy back in the mortal world. Partying was no stranger to me. Forgiving myself after whatever debauchery the night might bring? That would be a different story. A bridge for future Coop to cross. I tossed the pill back, chasing it with a sip from the whiskey bottle to my left.

Malachi's shadows lightened a shade, revealing his wicked grin in greater detail. His defenses were lowering. Perfect.

"Odin and I frequently dabble in the thralls of the devil's drug. It keeps things fresh and exciting. Wouldn't you agree, Lyvias?"

My muscles tensed. Odin? As in...

"You called, my love?" a deep voice rang from behind me.

Oh, *hell* no! Shrimp dick? The man who'd put hands on Kim? Who'd planned to wickedly help himself to her innocence? I should have taken the prick out when I had the chance. Now—amped up on booze and looming drugs—who knew how long I could keep the murderous urges at bay? My hold on my whiskey glass tightened, a crack splitting across it. How the fuck was I going to survive this without ripping his heart out? Suri took notice, removed the glass from my hand, and laced hers through mine. The kind touch dulled my flames slightly. She rested her head on my shoulder while Odin and Malachi ravaged each other in greeting.

"It's one night. I am right here. My best recommendation? Let your body take over and keep your mind focused on the real mission. I'll make sure you don't have to engage in anything you do not wish."

I sighed into her hair. "This is going to be hard."

"As long as they believe *you* are hard, that's all that matters," she teased. "I'm good at sleight of hand. Don't worry."

And so the party began. Hands, tongues, bodies, and moans meshed together; but Suri and I kept close to each other, upholding our clever ruse. She truly was a master of distraction; her manipulation of angles and appearances sold it. Not once did I enter her. Not a single time did I have to betray my own body. In turn, neither did she. We were in this together, reminding each other in stolen moments why we were doing this in the first place. Although to the two monsters whose heads I couldn't stop picturing stabbed on the ends of spikes, it appeared we were having the time of our lives. Every time they'd approach me, Suri would redirect. Another drink or pill. For them—always for them—as we'd stash our radium in a pocket or leave our drinks to warm in a forgotten corner. Anything to skew their senses further, giving us the upper hand. Suri evaded their clutches with effortless poise. She offered them a meaningless touch here and there, sure, but the two men had wound themselves up in each other so deep that we truly weren't much of a factor aside from a sleight-of-hand show. Which fared well for us and our attempts in getting them to believe we'd bought into their dream. Lust. Sex. The business of pleasure. Excellent. We'd infiltrate their ranks. Convince them we were on their side. And then?

Then we'd slaughter them. Every. Last. One.

I steered clear of Odin until I couldn't any longer. Being close to the man who'd hurt the woman I loved was damn near impossible. It rotted me from the inside out, made my skin crawl like spiders skittering across my skin. Even meeting his gaze made my hands shake as everything in me hungered to destroy him in slow, calculated moves. That fantasy fortified me. First, I'd pry his fingernails off with a pair of rusty pliers. Then I'd peel his fingers like carrots. Maybe pluck out an eye. Or both. But as he stepped to me—ready to partake in whatever disgusting desires he'd wrapped up in his mind regarding Lyvias—I vied for an escape. I *would* kill him. Soon.

"I thirst," I boomed, Suri's head bobbing against my bare chest.

"I can help with that." She offered me her wrist.

But I had other plans: insight for the little demon resting against me. "I crave a different flavor. Malachi, would you be so kind as to offer me another sample of your top-shelf gem?"

Malachi pulled his tongue from Odin's mouth, considering my request. He looked Suri over. "I am not sure it's wise considering tonight's unexpected guest."

"If you aren't convinced of her loyalty by now," I said, "then I have half a mind to take her off your hands permanently. She'd warm my bed nicely. Don't you think, doll?"

"I could get used to that." She kissed my arm circled around her.

"You both know I only share when I'm involved." Malachi chuckled, hopping to his feet. "A quick drink, then we switch. Yes?"

Like hell we would! I tapped Suri's arm in hopes of conveying a need for escape, and she sighed, assuring me she was working on it. Despite the night's overall foulness, I smiled. We made a good team.

Malachi walked to the desk and removed the remote I'd seen previously.

"Watch him closely," I whispered into Suri's ear.

She hopped up, made her way over to Odin, and wrapped her arms around his waist. The display seemed to please Malachi, the drugged-up fog of his desires lowering his shadows a touch more. Enough that Suri had a direct sight line to his finger typing in the security code. Chaos's portrait rolled up to reveal the young woman tucked away in her glass prison, and I felt Suri's shock from across the room. Her magic plumed about her, pointing like arrows ready to strike through Malachi's chest. But to the naked eye? One could only imagine how she felt. Imagine, because she didn't so much as flinch. Quite the skilled actress. A deadly talent if applied during certain interactions, I'd dare say.

I ambled over to the weary young woman, now a step outside the makeshift cell. I hesitated long enough to lock eyes with her—hoping to convey my hidden remorse—before gently sinking my fangs into her neck. I drank. And drank. And drank. The monster within me took control faster than anticipated, pushing me well past my moral limit in an instant. Zero to sixty. My thirst overcame me. I didn't stop. Couldn't. Malachi drifted into my sight line—his words inaudible in the hazy bloodlust—but still I continued, addicted to the high pounding in my veins. Why wasn't I *stopping*? Then it hit me: the radium didn't only heighten sexual pleasure; it intensified desires of all sorts. Demanded they be fulfilled.

"I said, 'Enough!'" Malachi ripped my head back.

A plan began to form in the bliss-filled fog. I licked the blood off my teeth as a maniacal laugh tore through me. "She is the sweetest thing I've ever tasted. We must share her with the world!"

"Is she?" Malachi asked with genuine interest. "I feared her slight frame might affect her potency."

I clapped a hand on his shoulder. Time to go in for the kill. "She is sweeter than cherry wine, my friend. Tell me, do our investors know about her?"

"Not yet. I had hoped for a soft launch on the market's new product soon."

I didn't fight the blood frenzy rising up inside me, instead letting the high take hold and thrash through me like a crashing wave. He needed to see what the woman's blood could do. Needed to believe that this was something he simply couldn't keep hidden any longer. I grabbed Odin and spun him about while reminding myself not to squeeze too hard and break his spine...yet. Odin's laugh pleased his mate just as I'd hoped. "This is a gift far too precious to conceal! Would you not agree, Odin?"

He twirled from my hold to wrap his arms around Malachi.

"You *have* been sitting on this for some time," he agreed. "It would bring me such pleasure to see you finally revel in the fruits of your labor, my love."

That's it. Take the bait, assholes.

Odin sighed, and their mated magic laced itself around Malachi's shoulder.

Malachi buckled. "I suppose a quaint viewing might be acceptable."

"Quaint? We must celebrate this monumental feat!" I yelled like a drunken fool. "We shall throw a grand party in your honor where our brethren can sample a taste of heaven itself. Be it blood or flesh, we will have them eating out of the palms of our hands!"

Careful to not truly hurt myself, but to sell the fact that Lyvias was done for the night, I crashed into the liquor cart, sending glasses crashing and brandy splashing. Malachi merely chuckled, charmed in his drunken stupor.

He yanked me to my feet. "Alright, alright, you have convinced me. I shall see it done."

"Soon," I slurred, and licked my lips. "Or I fear there may be none of her left to share."

"You, my friend, are far too drunk for your own good." Malachi patted my shoulder. "Suri, see to his safe return to the castle."

Suri nodded. "Yes, my Lord."

"I shall send word when the final plan is in place. Go get some rest." Malachi placed a kiss on my cheek and promptly returned to his partner's embrace.

Suri and I walked arm in arm, silent in our approach towards the demon gate. Once in the clear, far from the club in the now quiet city streets, she turned to me.

"What the hell was that?" she asked.

"That," I said, standing up straighter, "was our ticket to success."

"Throwing that poor girl to the wolves is your idea of success?"

"Of course not. But every investor being summoned to the same place on the same night..."

"I don't see how—" It clicked into place. "Oh. Oh my!"

This was our chance to end things, once and for all.

I wrapped a hand around her shoulders, staring up at the stars. "When they arrive, blood hungry and unguarded, you and I will burn that motherfucker to the ground."

CHAPTER ELEVEN

A LESSON IN FORGOTTEN MEMORIES

Sleep evaded me. My mind reeled, twisting and combing over every potential outcome in what Suri was now calling "the plan." Unoriginal, sure, but her eyes lit up like twinkle lights on Christmas morning each time she got to use the phrase. So naturally I didn't fight her. It was strange. Somehow, despite my best attempts to remain neutral, I found her slithering into my heart and playing a vital role in my life that I hadn't intended for her or anyone else to claim. The term rattled around in my head like loose gravel: *friend.*

I didn't have the heart to ask her how long she'd been searching for a means to free those girls. Girls she'd come to love whose names rolled off her tongue on multiple occasions. Discovering these women's names, identities, and family histories broke me more and more with each new story. But I had listened, because nobody had lent an ear to the painful secrets Suri kept locked in her vault, forcing her to fight on her own. Well, not anymore.

She spoke of Anesda: seven years in service to the club, two in the meat market. She had exactly one sister—younger—whom Anesda had become guardian over after their parents' untimely deaths. A year after her forced entry into the market, her sister, Adawna, had become the newest addition to the club scene. Adawna was a dancer for the time being, but based on Suri's uncanny ability to sniff out information, it'd be mere months before Malachi would transition the eighteen-year-old to the club's insidious underbelly.

The way the demon Lord watched the club staff was nothing short of stalker status. He'd take personal interest in the girls who became favorites—falsely love bombing them to make sure they felt irreplaceable and important—while taking stock of how many returning clients would ask them for private dances or side services. Then, to ensure his precious VIP lounge remained intact, he'd dig into the girl's background. Who would miss her? If she were to drop off the face of the earth, become dead to the outside world, would it raise suspicion? Suri told me that had been her only saving grace: her ties to the castle. Her absence would bring too much attention to the club. A simple, fortunate fact. I'd let her spill the poison she'd held inside until there was no more to share before encouraging her to get some rest.

My stomach in knots, I wandered about the halls and shut my brain off, focusing on life's more easily digestible details. Death's castle was truly a marvel. The intricate, colorful stained-glass detailing in the main corridor held my attention for the better half of an hour. Such craftsmanship: the way the inlays swept about curved panes, allowing pale light in through crescent-shaped panels. Moonbeams hit precious oil paintings just right, as if they'd been placed on those particular walls for that very reason. A portrait of Reigning Reaper Shadra hung in the north hall and Valhalla in the south, but the most intriguing one of all had to be Cadagon's.

Its prominent placement on the main stairwell was surely intended to intimidate passersby, though his hollow stare and clutched scythes had the adverse effect, enticing me. I ran a finger across the smooth, dark stain of the frame. Who was this man, really? What manner of sin had he gotten himself wound up in? The way he looked out for Kim behind her back but refused to give her even a modicum of affection in her presence had become a noticeable trend. Why? I saw the way he blinked back pain when she'd jab at him. My best guess was that he believed the further away he kept her, the safer she was from the vipers in his corner. His request for his own death became a little clearer in light of that thought. Or quite possibly, it could be pure deception. Making me believe him a martyr in all this.

Candlelight swept through the study hallway, dragging me back to reality. Curious. I edged closer, my steps quickening. I'd know that smell anywhere: Kim. Up to her usual mischief no doubt. Her honeyed perfume lingered in her wake, driving me mad, and that was *before* I laid eyes on her deep-cut, lacy nightgown.

"What are you doing, Princess?" I whispered into the still study.

She jumped at my approach, and a snicker escaped me. Her visible fear—a rare treasure—was downright adorable. Those wide eyes. Her slightly parted lips. The flush on her cheeks. I swear, this woman could step on my throat, and I would *thank* her for it. Gods, why did I have to choose silk pajamas? Damn things made it nearly impossible to hide my growing arousal. I sank into the nearest chair, carefully tucking my hardened cock into my waistband.

Calm down, Cooper. She doesn't want you. Not like that.

And yet, I couldn't help but picture drawing out her fear in the dark, pinning her against the nearest bookshelf, and sinking my teeth into her neck. Kissing my way ever downward. Oh, how her heart would race. How her blood would pump into her most private of places and throb for me. I'd demolish the lacy little number she wore—tearing it from her skin to reveal those perfect, round breasts—and waste no time sucking a pebbled nipple into my mouth. I would nip at her peak with my front teeth as she squirmed beneath me, her breathy moans in my ear and her hands knotting in my hair. She'd edge closer to her release.

But I'd deny her.

Heaving her into my arms, I'd set her tight ass on the edge of the table and do what I'd craved since our one delicious night together: get on my knees for my queen. Oh, the way I'd savor every stroke of my tongue against her swollen clit: heady and sweet and weeping for me. Bringing her to the verge, I would pull back just in time to see the heat flare in her gaze. She'd beg, and I would let her until she laid claim to me. Until that one precious word spilled from her plump lips: *Mine.*

Ripping me from my fantasy, she extended a worn tome to me. I cleared my throat, my face hot. The tattered book spoke of past treasons during Valhalla's rule. One in specific mirrored our current situation too much to dismiss as happenstance. It clicked suddenly: if Death had the ability to manipulate and read energy, then perhaps Kim did too. "You could read the shifter realm."

Kim looked me over as her nose wrinkled. "You know, for someone who wanted me dead upon arrival, it seems strange you're suddenly so...cheer-leader-ish. Why?"

Shit. Too nice. Too helpful. Damn Lyvias; why did the dude have to be such a dick? I stood, feigning indifference.

"Maybe that sharp tongue of yours finally won me over. Or maybe, just maybe, I changed my mind about your heathen upbringing." I lowered myself into her sight line and savored the bob in her throat at my proximity. She didn't shy away but held my gaze, setting me ablaze all over again. "Regardless, I now know where my loyalties lie. We're in this together, remember?"

Her expression softened. "You'll come with me then?"

"Anywhere."

Despite me insisting on waiting for a less ungodly hour to go wandering in the forbidden shifter realm, she'd made up her mind. We were going. Now. She was such a reckless thing. But who was I to deny her? Of course, nothing in Anathema came easy. Nasheesh—always lurking somewhere he was not want-ed—cut off our exit to the main foyer. Dude had a serious creep factor that bordered on stalker status. Did he even sleep? I cracked my knuckles, ready to play my part yet again: distracting him so my girl could make her escape. "Nas, my good sir, how might you be this fine morning?"

"You," Nasheesh greeted coldly. "What are you doing here?"

He drifted about with interlocked hands, stealing glances down the halls as baneful magic billowed from his mouth. Not only did he have a wicked, lying tongue, but he was paranoid to boot. What was he hiding? He offered me a wink, and my jaw locked. Right. This was for show, to convince any potential onlookers that he and I had nothing tying us to one another.

He offered me a playful grin and shouted, "You should be rotting in a cell until the end of time!"

Play along, Coop. Don't snap his neck.

"Oh, you haven't heard of the queen's pardon then?" I leaned against a carved pillar.

With one final survey of the halls, his shoulders relaxed, finally satisfied that we were alone.

"A little late to be exploring the castle, don't you think, my Lord? People might get suspicious."

"I was about to ask you the same thing. Wandering about the halls at such an hour could get a person into trouble."

His brow furrowed. "Precisely my thoughts. Keeping the company of the future queen...I fear you might be getting too close to your charge, seeing as this façade is merely a means to an end after all."

Kim. An end. Malachi's words about cozying up to her in order to secure whatever future he hid from me came roaring back to life. Coincidence? Unlikely. Nasheesh knew more than he'd led me to believe: that much was clear. I extended an air of calm about me, though I was anything but.

"Ah, so even you believe it? I would say I have been doing my job well then."

"Careful, Highness. Those of the Reigning Reaper lineage have a way of manipulating a person's very soul. Demanding loyalty." His condescending smile faltered. "We wouldn't want you getting mixed up with the wrong side now, would we?"

Sides. Okay, so this fucker really *did* have dealings with Malachi then.

"I can't say I know what you mean. Trust is a hard-earned thing, especially for someone with a mortal upbringing."

He shivered. "Mortals are vile creatures. Whatever undertaking she has coerced you into at such an hour is nothing worth the future king's time. Would you like me to intervene?"

Hell no. For him to intervene meant a potential blow out; and with my returned thirst, I didn't have much faith in my ability to keep my hands to myself. Dude had to go. ASAP.

"She is far more suspicious than most, which requires dedication on my part. You stepping in would ruin the progress I've made. No, I will attend to her. Get her to trust me further."

"If you are sure?"

"I am. By the end of this, I'll have her eating out of the palm of my hand."

More like I'd have *him* eating out of my hand before I used it to sucker punch the shit-eating grin plastered to his face. Based on his smug parting nod, I knew I'd gotten through to him. Perfect. Let him think me a treasonous beast. It would make his shock when I stabbed him in the back that much richer. The thought alone had me salivating. What a slow death his would be.

With him gone, I found Kim in the courtyard.

"Nasheesh?" she asked.

I cracked my knuckles in jest. "Handled."

She rolled her eyes, and we found our way to the shapeshifter gate.

Fate can be as cruel as she is kind. For example? The shifter gate required royal blood to open; and given neither of us had come prepared at such a late hour, we had one option. Me. *I* had to break Kimber's delicate skin despite the hunger ravaging me from the inside. Cruel, indeed. I brushed my lips against her soft wrist—the urge to tear her wide open thrumming in my head—and she shivered under my touch. The sensation splayed tingles up my arms. *Control yourself. Not too deep.*

Her heavy-lidded stare burrowed into my bones as I sank my fangs in, gently. *Holy. Shit.* Suri's blood had been sweet—delicious even—but Kim's? Cosmic. Notes of iron, honey, and wine rushed over my tongue as magic leached from her open wound, caressing my lips upon its escape. But not her magic. Ours. The magic born from our agreement traced a touch down her neck, leaving goosebumps in its wake, though she didn't seem to notice. It turned to me, offering a similar caress, before separating into two misty orbs and disappearing into our chests. *The hell?*

Her heartbeat picked up, the thrum of excitement in her veins rushing between her legs; and I stole a glance to find her bottom lip pinched in her teeth like...like she— Wait, was she *enjoying* this? Oh, fuck yes. The world around us fell away as she flooded my senses until all I could smell, feel, hear, and see was her. Her taste coiled around my mind, burrowing down into my soul. Everything in me cried out to pull her into my arms. Ravage her until thirst and passion were satiated, though I doubted either would be fulfilled in a timely fashion. Days wouldn't appease me.

To my dismay, she pulled her wrist away a second later, an embarrassed smile on her face. Whether her reluctance was a blessing or a curse, I wasn't sure. But there was one thing I knew with deafening certainty: my addiction to her had amped up ten notches—her magnetism once again flexing the white-knuckle hold she had on me. Whatever had happened between us, it had changed something, and not just for me. I could sense it in her. Feel it in my own chest: magic churning about as if two heartbeats rattled inside me. What the damned *was* that?

I met her gaze, searching for signs that she'd sensed it too, but she gave me nothing. The air grew tense. "Did I hurt you?"

"No. Let's just go," she dismissed coolly.

We started towards the gate, my ego bruised and heart hammering.

The realm paths were nothing short of mind-bending. Suspended over an endless void below, I struggled to connect what I was seeing with reality. They defied rationality, but I suppose many things did in Anathema. Movement in the black abyss caught my eye as a stream of violet fog rose from the pit. One by one, more plumes followed suit, each dingy and thick. Magic, but different. Tainted somehow. Violent in nature, they jerked about to battle their neighboring billows, but not like the misty magics I'd seen since Fate had gifted me new eyes. These were solid and greedy in their reach for the sky above. Snarls, moans, and cries carried from the depths, intermingling in the chaos; and my palms grew clammy.

Chaos...

The brief glimpses I'd gotten as the beast hunted me in the Shroud...this magic looked incredibly similar. I stood frozen, watching the feral clouds creep too close for comfort, only for each plume to bash against an invisible ceiling at my feet. The nearest hissed and moaned, slamming again and again for release, but to no avail. I swallowed hard. Did the void surrounding Anathema belong to the in-between? Was *this* how Malachi had managed to make his deal with the Old Gods' child? It didn't make any sense. He couldn't very well jump into the void and return...could he?

I looked towards Kim, eager to see if her expression mirrored my own, but she'd already disappeared through the gate. With hurried steps, I caught up to her, ready to tell her my suspicions; but all thoughts fell from my mind the second I stepped through that gate. Catastrophic destruction greeted me. Sure, I'd seen it in my winged form during Kim and Suri's tour through Anathema; but witnessing it in first person on ground level—smoke and ash tangling in my nose—lodged a knot in my throat.

The seaside realm had once held such beauty. While my memories were few, the town's skeletal remains still sang of its once peaceful charm. I pictured mothers flying kites near the cliffs and a father's booming laughter as he watched his child reel in their first fish. This place had thrived on promise and joy: truly alive in every way.

Until it wasn't.

Turmoil and loss and grief replaced any semblance of happiness my child-hood home once contained, reducing it to nothing more than a horrific ener-getic imprint. As if that wasn't enough, I had no choice but to watch Kimber's heart break in tandem. The more she saw, the more she felt. She took the shifters' pain into herself, and their torment became hers, her rage building alongside mine.

Kim wandered close by, wrapped in her own thoughts, when a shrill cry pricked my ears. My blood ran cold. Why did I know that cry? It rang out again, taunting me towards the town outskirts like a specter luring their victim into a darkened forest. Much the same, the sound possessed me, and I doubt my feet would have listened if I'd ordered them to stop. But I didn't.

I found the source, or rather *her* hunched down behind a bush at eye level with a young boy, his back to me. I sank to my knees—my fingers fiddling with the loose gravel—bewitched by her kind eyes.

Panic showed on the woman's face. "Mama has to go, but I've sent for help; and I need you to go with her when she arrives. No matter *what*, you go with her. Do you understand?"

"Why can't I stay with you?" the child argued.

"Because I have to go help your father. That is what we do for those we love: we protect them. Right?"

"Yes, but—"

A blast shook the ground, and the three of us jumped in time as the windows in a nearby house blew out, flames engulfing the roof. Two screams echoed from inside but were quickly silenced when the home crumbled in on itself. The woman shuddered.

"I need you to be brave. Protect Amelia and her daughter, yes?"

"I'm scared," he sobbed.

"I know baby, but fear is how we stay alert in the face of danger. It is how our body keeps us safe." She took his face in her hands, bowing his head to place a kiss atop it. "I'm sure her little girl is probably quite frightened too. I bet she could use a good, strong friend right now to hold her hand and help her feel better."

"But...don't you need me?"

"Always. But you, my dear sweet boy, have a destiny to fulfill. A grand one full of adventure and love and wonder."

Another boom carried in the distance, and he dove into her arms.

"I won't leave you!" the boy cried.

"Leave? Why, of course not. Do you want to know how I am sure we will never be apart?"

He nodded against her chest.

"Because I will always be right here." She forced a smile beneath misty eyes and placed a gentle touch over the boy's heart. "While that big heart in your chest grew in my womb, Fate smiled upon you, gave you a special gift. You see, she took part of that big heart of yours, and she gave a piece of it to another. It is your job to go out there and find it."

Fire tore through the Evermoor Woods, drawing closer to the building atop the hill—the same one her attention kept gravitating towards. It became clear in an instant that this was more than a means to soothe the boy. It was a goodbye.

"I don't want to go. I want to stay here with you, forever."

"I am so sorry." She stood, prying his hands from her tattered gown and placing them in his lap. "I promise, one day this will all make sense. Now stay here. Wait for Queen Amelia."

After a final smattering of kisses and one tight hug, she tucked him away in the bush, fluffing the branches to conceal him. She turned towards the heart of the terror surrounding us. Her frame silhouetted against the raging flames, she whispered into the night, "I love you always, Copernicus."

My heart seized.

I circled the crying boy to find my own childish reflection staring back. *That can't be...*

"Mother?" I whispered.

I reached for her, but my hand slipped through the vision like vapor as she ran headfirst into her own destruction. Gone. My fists tightened and shook. I wanted to grab her, hold her tight, weep with her; but no. Instead I got to relive a torturous, long-forgotten memory. And memories could never be flesh and bone, no matter how much they clawed at one's soul, begging to be real again. Tears fell freely, only this time I wasn't alone. I had the company of a young boy whose life had been irrevocably changed that day, and together we mourned. My mother's bravery, her love for me...I owed her everything. I could have stayed there lost in my own brokenness for eternity. Drowning in my own sorrow.

But Kim's bloodcurdling scream sent me crashing back to the present.

Chapter Twelve

TO SEVER A BLOODLINE

For days I tried to coax Kimber from her depression cave, but she remained firm in shutting me out. Her door never opened. Footsteps never haunted her tower's halls. Finally, I grew desperate in my concern and requested an audience with Death in hopes his stubborn ways could outweigh hers. If not, then I'd turn to my last resort: dragging her from that damn bed myself. Not that I didn't understand her pain or empathize with her. Someone aimed to end her bloodline. Actively. That knowledge compounded with her believing she'd lost me for good and *actually* losing June...hell, I'd be a mess too. But I wouldn't let her lay down and die. Her kingdom needed her. *I* needed her. More so, *she* needed *Anathema* to fulfill the true desires of her heart and restore balance.

Eager to avoid the churning emotions since our visit to the shifter realm, I'd kept myself busy. Distracted. Trying to forget. My younger mind had blocked out that memory for a reason, and yet here I was grown and bearing the weight of it. My mother's words plagued my thoughts: *Fate smiled upon you, gave you a special gift.* A cynical laugh tore through me. Right. I guess if you considered two dead parents, a life lived behind mile-thick internal walls, and a devouring, unrequited love a gift, then sure.

I sought refuge on the castle rooftop. Up here, the world seemed endless. New. A place where I could let go of my past to focus on the present instead. Galaxies lit up the sky, and the moon reached down her glowing touch, caressing my cheeks. In the quiet, my thoughts settled enough to weigh the facts of our current situation. Malachi and Odin controlled the meat market. Thanks to their selfish dealings, the Shroud and its monsters now haunted Anathema's doorstep. How they were getting the girls in wasn't clear, but that wouldn't matter after Suri and I burned their investors—and them—alive. And while I couldn't be one hundred percent certain, I'd bet my right nut that they were also the ones seeking to end Kimber's bloodline. I mean, it would make sense. They'd been vying for Lyvias to take the throne, encouraging him—well, me really—to cozy up to Kim "until the time was right." As if that wasn't some ominous shit. Why Malachi supported Lyvias's ascension to the throne when he clearly wanted control for himself remained a mystery.

The other wild card—the one I couldn't for the life of me figure out motive or reasoning—was Nasheesh. He had ties to Malachi. But how? Why? Part of me suspected he'd show at our little meeting slash murder party alongside the demon Lord's other business partners. Maybe with the two of them in the same room, I could finally connect the dots; but Malachi hadn't sent word yet. In fact, he hadn't made a peep or an appearance since our last meeting according to Suri. At least Nasheesh had seemed content with my explanation of cozying up to Kim, and he'd stayed out of my way.

But my gut told me our luck was quickly running out.

I spent the majority of my day digging through the castle studies with my attention fixated on how one might end a royal bloodline gifted by the Old Gods themselves. The idea alone seemed impossible; but if I'd learned anything in my time in Anathema so far, "impossible" was just a word. Anything could happen in the realm of night if you were willing to pay the price for it.

I'd burnt through not one but two candles on my hunt for answers; and *nothing*. Zilch. That is, aside from a beginner's guide to chess, which I grabbed for Lana's next visit. Turns out we were both pretty crap at the game, but it brought me joy to see her smile as we tried to make sense of it.

Prepared to call it quits for the night, I aimed to snuff out the remainder of my third candle when I saw it tucked away in the same small study where Kim had found the treason log: a disturbance in the otherwise untouched space. I crossed the room to the oak shelf to find a fresh drag line in the dust. Very fresh. Given Kimber hadn't left her room in days, this meant someone else had been digging about in here.

I pulled the stiff leather book from its spot on the middle shelf—the scent of old parchment heavy in the air—and cracked it open to reveal the first page. In bold, swirling penmanship, it read: *A Case Study in Modern Pureblood Ancestry* by Barges Frain. Interesting. The first entries were dry and factual, but halfway through the sixth I came across a line that piqued my interest.

Two shifting houses, one born of talon, the other bane of blood, deceived. One to blame, the other to pay. Beware the void-talker. I flipped the page. *For where he walks, Chaos shall come calling.*

The Bloodbanes and Talonborns. My lineage. I stole a look around the quiet space. To stumble upon a book so relevant to my research was a one in a million chance. Or...had someone intended for me to find this? Left a trail in the dust to lure me to it? I turned back to the book and ran a finger along the indented date scribbled on the inside cover. Fifteen years ago...which meant Barges Frain had been present during the massacre. Yeah, someone *defiantly* wanted me to find this.

"Hello, my Lord," Nasheesh greeted. "And what, might I ask, are we reading today?"

I startled at his sudden appearance, tucking the journal against my side, careful to keep his wandering eyes from straying where they didn't belong. Always there when you didn't want him. His robe squeaked against the leather chair as he sat, crossing his hands over his knee.

"Nothing of substance, I'm afraid," I said. "Quite drab, really."

"Pity. Though, considering the shelves you've chosen to pull from, not surprising." He rubbed his sleeve over a smudge on the armrest as his lip pulled back in disgust. "The king insists on keeping every tome he has read, despite whether he found enjoyment in it or not. This is the study where his least favorites come to die a lonely death."

"I can say with certainty that I understand why they've come here to rot."

Death's study... Was *he* the one leaving hints? If so, what a clever way to avoid a breach of blood pact. Maybe he really did want Kim to succeed as he claimed. Nasheesh shifted, a crinkle drawing my attention to the black envelope stuffed in his robe sleeve.

"What brings you here then?" I asked. "Have some business that requires my attention, I take it?"

"Indeed."

The advisor's smile grew vicious as he stood, extended the envelope to me, and positioned himself in the doorway, facing the hall to play lookout. This had to be serious. I cracked the wax seal with a pop.

Dearest Shareholder,

We have taken great pleasure in preparing a viewing party in your honor where we aim to showcase just how far your investment has gone. Please join us in celebrating this monumental moment in history where the elite shall take their rightful place above the lesser as the Old Gods intended. We look forward to seeing you in precisely a fortnight for our last *clandestine meeting to be held in the wee morning hours. The time has come to reclaim the night and restore Anathema to her former unholy glory! And please, do burn this memo after reading. We wouldn't want it to land in the wrong hands and spoil our fun, now would we?*

With pleasure, M&O

A fortnight, but that meant...

"They wish to do this so close to the future queen's crowning ceremony?"

Nasheesh stepped back into the room, keeping his voice low as he said, "It seems your encouragement lit a fire under Malachi to share the fruits of his labor. This allots him ample time to prepare a grand event as well as ensure our more reputable investors may attend."

Our, he'd said. So Nasheesh not only had ties to Malachi, but to the club itself. After seeing how he'd mistreated Lana upon my arrival to Anathema, I can't say it surprised me. Sick bastard. The thought of waiting two weeks to end him and the misogynistic pricks he brushed elbows with made me itch.

Keep it together. You need him a little longer.

I cleared my throat. "With your prestigious connections, I am sure a sooner date could have been secured without sacrificing the night's integrity, don't you think? I have seen how quickly others bend to your will."

"You flatter me, my Lord, truly, but even I have my limits," he explained, wringing his fingers. "Malachi is adamant that no corners are cut unnecessarily. This also ensures that those involved are given adequate time to acquire viable alibis should they need them, given the majority of our guests will be expected to partake in numerous pre-coronation festivities in the castle. You included, Your Highness."

Of course. If the guests weren't in attendance for Kimber's ceremonial proceedings—which was more a demand than an invitation—it could arouse suspicion, drawing unwanted attention, which was the one thing Malachi had made perfectly clear he wanted to avoid. Smart. Wicked, but smart. I snatched the candle from the table and swiped the letter through the flame. Crackling to a blaze, the invitation turned to ash and floated to the floor. I fought a smile. How fitting to burn the evidence, because that was precisely what I intended for each recipient.

To burn them to nothing more than ash.

I reeled from sleep, two prying hands at my shoulders shaking me back to the woken world. With the room barely illuminated by the new moon's amber light, I struggled to make sense of things. *The hell?* I rubbed my eyes, attempting to clear away the fog of my recent nightmare—my jaw raw and achy from gnashing my teeth together. I drifted between sleep and consciousness, the dream lingering: snarls, teeth, and rot. Countless sequences of my own death projected through my mind; but as my vision sharpened, I realized that nothing could be more terrifying than the reality staring me in the face.

Kim stood over me: her fists knotted in her nightgown and her chin trembling as fresh tears rolled down her cheeks. I shot up, reaching for her, but she shied away from my touch.

My chest clenched. "What is going on? Are you okay?"

"No," she whispered while searching the room. "I...I don't think I am."

Admitting such a thing didn't come easy for her. Even before she'd realized her birthright, she'd carried herself like a queen. Unshakable. Fierce. Whatever—no, *whoever*—had caused this reaction in the woman I loved would rue this day; but I curbed my rage, trying not to fuel her already charged energy.

"Come here." I tore a wool blanket from my bed, draped it around her, and guided her to sit.

Gods, her heart was racing. The terror reflected in her eyes frayed my composure, and I attempted once more to soothe her. I opened my arms, but didn't press or pressure. I would wait as long as she needed until she was comfortable. A sigh of relief passed my lips when she melted against my chest, her sweet scent encasing me. I rested my lips against her hair and hummed a soft tune to lull her split nerves.

"You're safe," I murmured.

She let go, her gentle sobs ripping at my soul. Countless, desperate comforts begged to roll off my tongue, but I let my presence speak the truth for me: *I'm not going anywhere.* Steadily, her heart rate evened out, and her shaking limbs settled. Still, I held her. I wanted her to know that this was on her terms. Her means. *Always.* Because I'd seen this version of her once before.

The night she'd cried over the man who had put his filthy hands on her as a child had altered me forever. A teacher: meant to mold the minds of his students towards a bright future. Yet he'd callously darkened hers behind closed doors. He'd cut out parts of her that—no matter how much she fought and healed and processed—would remain sore and scarred, festering under the surface for years to come. How anyone could commit such atrocities had shaken me to my core. Changed my world. My belief in humanity. Me.

I'd made it a mission to track the fucker down. For months I'd hunted him, determined to deliver his retribution. His punishment. After Kimber's "allegations"—as it was marked in the state records—he'd fled Cottage Grove for the sandy shores of California. Wrapped up in his new world, new wife, new life, he'd fallen into a false sense of security. Thought he had a chance at happiness again. How he could hold such shadows in his mind—knowing what he'd done—and attempt to remake himself as if a young girl's life hadn't been entirely changed by his actions remained a mystery to me. But his sins would not go unpunished.

When I'd finally caught his trail, I'd packed my bag, secured the first bus ticket out of town, and set off to end him. By the time I'd arrived on that humid summer afternoon, it became clear that Fate had beat me to him. He'd lain in a hospital room facing the backside of a dump site—the stench of burning trash hanging in the air—with cancer burrowing into his brain. Handcuffs bound him to his deathbed. Turned out his disturbed psyche was unchangeable, and he'd become a repeat offender of the innocent. Fate, it seemed, had known it all along. Planned for it. The Old Goddess had woven together a symphony of suffering for him alone, hand-delivering a blow far greater than immanent death: hope. She'd let him build up this grand, wonderful new existence. Allowed him to believe he'd evaded consequences, only to fall victim to his own depravity. A sinister justice.

Countless machines beeped, singing the man's final song as I'd waded into his room. I'd sat watching his chest rise and fall, studying the hands that'd nearly broken the strongest woman I'd ever known before she'd even had a chance at life. For a moment, I'd considered cutting those hands clean off, allowing him to bleed out while I muffled his screams with his own pillow. But he'd woken up. Lost and disoriented, he'd searched the room, unable to form words as his sights frantically danced over me. I'd known what he wanted to ask. Who was I? Where was he? What was happening? The sunset's orange light had streamed through the window, kissing my cheek, and I swear I'd heard Fate's gentle laugh. There was still a chance to cut him, deeply.

I'd leaned close and said two words: "Kimberly Bradshaw."

This? This he remembered. Not where or who he was...but her? Emphatically. With shame in his eyes, he'd begun to weep; but I hadn't averted my stare, letting it weigh heavy on him as I held up an invisible mirror to his depraved depths. When his tears had run dry, I'd dug into him again. "A child," I'd said. "Innocent," I'd reminded him.

I'd left him to choke on that memory.

He died the next morning alone; and I had peace in knowing that, in the end, there had been no get-out-of-jail-free card for him. No, he'd died with that little girl's face seared into his brain like a hot brand. As it should have been.

Kimber's heavy breaths finally steadied as I blinked back to the present. She looked up at me with red, puffy eyes.

"Thank you," she said in an almost embarrassed tone.

I fought the urge to caress her cheek and offered a gentle smile instead. "Even Lady Death needs comfort now and again."

Her entire being relaxed. From there, she told me about the hybrid she'd seen in the gardens and Nasheesh's appearance beforehand. Confirming a hybrid's existence was one thing, but her assertion that it'd been Odin gave me *another* rabbit trail to follow. It didn't add up. The embodiment of Death held sway over the realm entirely. What did her enemies even stand to gain? And who would be dumb enough to think a mixed bloodline could challenge a lineage imbued with the Old Gods' powers? No magic could match it. Kim and I were missing something; we both knew it. Some hidden agenda lingered right under our noses.

After hearing Kim's tales regarding Barges' journal—how he believed the missing shapeshifters were being sacrificed to create a hybrid capable of creating a new royal bloodline—we settled on our next course of action to study the Evermoor Woods. Maybe we'd find a lead there. You know, just one more item to tack onto my rapidly growing list of things to figure the hell out. *Awesome.*

With the night's adrenaline rush settling, Kimber turned to leave—her protective walls back in place—but I couldn't let her go. Or rather, wouldn't. Not when a war raged violently within me. My lungs shrank. I knew she was strong and capable, and yet the fear of losing her was so visceral, it buckled my knees. She drew nearer to the door as a glint of our shared magic shimmered in the dark like a rope tethering us to one another. I needed her with me. Close.

I snagged her wrist. "Stay with me."

"What?"

"You heard me. Let me watch over you tonight."

She pondered my offer—her internal battle showing through—until finally her soft lips curled up at the edges. "Alright, but you sleep on the floor."

"As you wish."

I felt her relief in my bones as if it were my own—despite her refusal to voice it aloud—and relished the sweetness of it. She *wanted* to stay. I smiled, sprawling out on the hard floor in contented bliss, the cold boards nipping at my back.

She'd stayed.

A few silent minutes passed before she shocked my system once again, inviting me to lay at her side.

"Fine," Kim groaned. "Come up here. Just keep your hands to yourself."

While we'd slept in the same bed numerous times before, the vulnerability woven into her request hit hard. Trust didn't come easy to either of us. We'd fought to get to where we were as best friends and confidants. Here I'd thought that in taking Lyvias's face, I'd never know that comfort again.

"Of course," I said, crawling into bed. "We'll figure this out, Kim. I promise."

Her tired breaths lulled me to rest; but just as I began to drift off to sleep, she stirred. I turned to find her eyes closed, lost in a dream.

"Cooper, don't go," she whispered into the cool night air.

At the sound of my name on her lips, the tears I'd fought in an effort to be brave for her rose up. I wrapped a hand around her cheek and uttered the words that'd been stuck in my throat for far too long. The words I knew her sleepy ears wouldn't truly hear or her worn mind remember.

"Never. I will *never* leave you, baby. Not even death could keep me from you."

CHAPTER THIRTEEN

LORE AND HEARTBREAK

The wind thrashed through the naked tree branches, their rustle competing with the click of my heels on the vampire court's cobblestone path. Answers held in the castle had run dry—no new hints left by my mysterious helper—and so I'd come to see what old wisdom might be tucked away in the notorious Immortal Library. Centuries of realm history, fable, and lore resided in those walls. I jittered with anticipation.

Rumor had it—based on an eerie children's book on nightmares I'd come across in Death's study—that a magical portal to the other realms had once lain hidden deep within the library's underground tunnels. A moving, living chamber overflowing with records and journals about the Ancient Lores and their origins. But the chamber hadn't returned to Anathema in centuries. It remained in the mortal world, save for dire times when multiple planes were at war. More curious still, one needed a key to enter it. A key supposedly lost to time. My inner child dreamed that I'd be the chosen one to discover such a room, to be found worthy in the Old Gods' eyes to uncover the vaulted secrets. A silly, ridiculous fantasy.

However, there were bound to be answers in regards to the sacrificial magic mentioned in Barges' case study. After all, the vampires were known for their ritualistic love affair with mortals. Had their bloodlust not consumed them, the vampires would be intermeshed with their beloved humans to this day. What an odd thought: to both love and crave to destroy in one breath. I licked my lips, hyper-focused on my own growing thirst. I was beginning to understand how one sensation could possess all of you. Hunger. And yet, food didn't fill that void or the hollow longing in my stomach. Honestly, I pitied the vampires. Perpetual thirst was a damned nightmare.

Tucked in the forest's shadows on the village outskirts loomed the Immortal Library. Brick towers jutted towards the starlit sky three stories tall. Darkened windows glared down, though the village below radiated life and celebration. The vampire court was notorious for fantastic parties, and they were currently enthralled in their weeks-long celebration of the mortal world's fall equinox. Which fared well for me, giving me the chance to roam the library's halls undisturbed. To be myself for a stolen moment: not Lyvias, but Cooper. Putting on a face for others, pretending to be someone you aren't...it wears on a person. Makes you question everything about yourself. How long had I worn the vampire Lord's face? I couldn't remember. Long enough for my own identity to begin to fade away though. I'd become this ravenous thing; and I knew if I let it, the beast inside would overcome me.

My sore muscles—thanks to Cadagon's insistence on me training now and again to keep up the warrior persona Lyvias flaunted—cried out alongside the screeching hinges of the library doors. I looked over to find a rack to my right boasting an aged, wooden plaque.

Please remove your shoes. You tread on sacred floors.

I kicked my boots off, placed them on the rack, and headed for the tall chest in the rounded entryway. Atop it sat multiple candle holders, and I grabbed one with a half-burnt, black candle inside, setting it aflame with a nearby match before starting down the curved stairs ahead. My body buzzed in the thick dark as I offered up a silent prayer. *Fate, guide me.*

A domed window above amplified the moonlight, a single beam reaching but narrowly missing a round mirror mounted on the staircase railing. I swiveled the mirror's base, giving it a turn to the left, and the room burst to life. The light bounced to a second mirror across the vast room, then to another, and on it went until the grand space filled with an amber glow. My breath caught. Bookcases crawled up the walls to the top story, a rolling ladder placed before each. The shelves easily stood thirty feet tall, and I arched my neck upwards. *Holy hell.* Good thing I wasn't afraid of heights.

"Now, where to begin..." I muttered to no one and leaned down to warm my hands near a central hearth.

It was a dry heat, but not fire somehow. The sensation tickled my fingers and brain as the metal contraption *whooshed*, expanding and retracting. I settled on my knees to look it over. Weird. It almost sounded like breathing. Maybe the stories were true. Maybe a giant really *did* slumber beneath the court, his breath heating the space and his blood filling the vampires' stomachs. Fascinating.

From there, I let intuition guide me as my socks shuffled over woven red and silver rugs on the marble floor. I spent hours wandering down this hall and that, up one ladder and the next. It took me a bit to figure out the library's sorting system, but once I did, I found the precise area I needed. Located on a shelf tucked between two large oil paintings depicting Fate and Death, a well-worn book sparked my interest. I slid the thick spine from its home and slammed it down on the nearest table, the thud echoing through the library chambers. A plume of dust wafted from the pages, and I fanned it away with a cough. "Shit, doesn't anybody keep up on this place?"

In great detail, the historical account chronicled the events leading to the gifts bestowed by the Old Gods at the birth of the new world. Bored in their eternal monotony—their makeshift children unable to fill the void in them as they'd hoped—Fate and Death had grown curious of the universe's developments and cast their sights on the mortal plane. What were these feeble beings? Such precious, fleeting lives they lived, full of love and heartbreak. During their creation of the Ancient Lores, Fate and Death hadn't given much consideration to such characteristics. Turned out they had granted the Lores consciousness and free will without concern for their ability to empathize or show compassion, which the Gods learned were crucial traits as they studied humanity. Little did they know, that oversight would ignite a global massacre.

The more the Gods' interest in mankind grew, the more their children had fought for their attention. Slaughtered and killed for it. Humanity had hung on the brink, hunted to near extinction by the God and Goddess's abominable creations. Fearing the cosmic ramifications, Fate and Death had wrapped their souls in mortal coils for one day and walked amongst the humans in search of a quick solution, but the damage had been too vast. Disgusted by her own children, Fate had acted.

She turned back time.

Unfortunately, the memories remained. Humanity's fears manifested the Ancient Lores in the mortal world through their nightmares, thereby forever solidifying the Lores' existence as multi-plane beings and weaving them into the universal fabric of all things. Fate's hands had been tied. She couldn't undo the Lores' existence, but she *could* lock them away. As an apology to the humans she had come to adore, Fate and her lover created the realms of Elysium and Anathema—as above, so below—bestowing a fraction of their powers to the new realms' leaders in order to uphold balance and maintain the prison realm created to hold the Ancient Lores: the Shroud. In doing so, the very first blood pact on any plane of existence had been struck: Fate and Death would never again reside in the same realm to ensure history wouldn't repeat itself.

And Death wept.

Legend claimed his eternal tears had birthed the ever-flowing waterfalls lining Anathema's borders. I'd never considered myself a religious man, but the tale hit home, inspiring a moment of silent reverence. My jaw tensed. Such pain. Such sacrifice. Some would kill for a love like that. *I* would kill for it. The idea that someone could be seen and desired so completely made my soul ache. Burn. I closed my eyes and released a slow, cleansing sigh. Love like that was only in fairy tales.

I refocused on the task at hand. The more I dug, the more infuriated I grew, but I couldn't leave without a lead. Determined, I searched the nooks and crannies, forsaking the main corridor to wander deeper into the sprawling veins of the library. Two floors down, I turned into a torch-lined hallway with large stone doors at the end, splayed wide open to reveal a solarium packed with willow trees and archaic bookshelves. Despite the room's position below ground level, a river cut through a dense forest outside the arched windows. Anathema: ever the mind-bender. In an ivy-covered cupboard tucked away from the rest, I found dozens of hand-written grimoires; and my sights snagged on one in specific entitled, *A Lesson in Baneful Magic,* written by Aisling O'Connell.

"Thank you, Fate," I whispered.

On page one, I began finding connections to the things mentioned in Barges' journal. The grimoire dove into the sacrificial magic he'd spent years trying to understand, yet there was no mention of hybrids. Not if they existed. Not how to create one. Nothing. By the end of my search, I'd acquired a crash-course bachelor's in how sacrificial magic had the power to do damn near anything as long as a mortal witch and multiple human lives were involved, but it left me with more questions than answers. Why would Malachi go through the trouble to imbue Odin with hybrid magic and not himself? He was clearly the power-hungry prick of a mastermind in their relationship. Unless...unless he'd made his mate a guinea pig. Baneful magic tended to have nasty side effects, cursing anyone who wielded it incorrectly.

Barges, please *be nothing more than an old kook.*

Because if he wasn't? If his claims about creating a hybrid powerful enough to overthrow the royal bloodline were true, and the demon Lord got his hands on such a spell, well...

We'd be royally screwed.

Turns out revels were more than a simple delicacy fit for a royal wedding. They were also quite possibly *the* most fucking terrifying things in existence.

Flower creatures sound fun and all until one sets upon you ready to gnaw off your face. But after collaborating with Kim and her baiting Cadagon into taking us on a trip into the shifter realm so we could investigate Barge's claims, the little bastards came with the territory. The farther into the trees we went, the clearer it became that the Evermoor Woods were sick. Diseased. Their knobby, peeling limbs arched over us like desperate, reaching hands begging for someone to take notice of their pain and suffering.

"If we split up, we'll cover more ground," Kimber said—Death safely out of earshot—and stalked towards the north side of the woods.

I fell in stride at her side, matching her step for step. "What, trying to get away from me so soon?"

"Am I that transparent?"

"I am afraid so. But don't worry, your secret is safe."

Her eyes crashed into mine. "Secret?"

"Oh, you know. That I'm growing on you. That you don't despise my company nearly as much as you pretend. In fact, I'd brave it to say that you quite enjoy me."

"Ha! You wish."

A playful grin tore across my face. "I do."

I didn't shy away from her defiant stare. Didn't shrink or wilt under her words. Because I could feel it: the spark igniting between us. And I was feral for it. Prepared to fan it into vicious flames.

"I urge you not to run from your feelings, Princess. They have a way of catching up when you least expect."

She scoffed. "I assure you, the only 'feelings' I have for you are that of annoyance."

"Given that a second ago you couldn't keep your hands off me, I like my odds."

"That was because I thought we were about to be eaten alive by a damn revel!"

"And I am pleased you turned to me for comfort." I leaned in closer, her warm breath sweeping across my face. "Please, do feel free to do it again. And again. And—"

"You truly are delusional, you know that?"

Her nose wrinkled—the tiny freckles dotting across it like stars in the midnight sky—and the air in my lungs thinned. How could one woman be so breathtaking? It was criminal. Our blood pact magic swirled about, knocking a weft of her hair loose as it circled.

"Delusion is merely a patient step away from reality, Kim. And I'll let you in on a little secret of my own." I tucked her hair back in place, my fingertips brushing the cusp of her ear. "I am *incredibly* patient. When I want something, I take my time. In *all* regards."

I ran the backs of my fingers down her neck, eliciting a shiver from her that she swallowed down.

"Well, for your sake," she bit, "I hope that's true. Because hell will cool and freeze over before I let you anywhere near me, Lyvias. Mark my words."

I smirked. "Before? So I *do* stand a chance then?"

"Ugh, you are impossible!"

She stepped around me; but in her passing, I saw it: the most exquisite shade of pink brushing across her cheeks.

I lost myself in that image as we split up in search of answers. Enveloped by the quiet of the forest floor, reality sought to steal my sliver of hope. I'd spent my young, most formidable years growing and learning here, surrounded by others who shared my same unique gifts. I'd had a home and a family to call my own. Support and community. I'd belonged. Wandering through these woods should have been magical. It should have been a chance to reconnect to my birth place, maybe even discover a lost piece of myself. Instead, I longed. Longed for a life and a sense of self I would never again have. My jaw flexed. I had nowhere to hide from the devastation or the stench of rot tangled in the decaying trees as the court's deadly history still seeped about in the charred soil. Time, it seemed, did not heal all wounds.

As if the hollow twinge in my chest wasn't enough, Barges' claims turned out to be infallible truth. After returning to Kimber's suite, she described the scene she'd stumbled on deep in the Evermoor: a rope reeking of sulfur.

"It didn't budge, no matter how hard I pulled." She shivered. "Let's just say it was dark."

I heaved a breath, unsure I wanted the answer to the question on my lips. "'Dark' as in sacrificial?"

The horror reflected on her face was proof enough, but she confirmed her energy reading had picked up on remnants of a baneful spell. Unabashed fear clouded her expression. A hexed rope. Great.

"I figured you'd want to see. I left you a marker."

"You tore your blouse?" I asked, looking over the tattered edge. "But it looks so lovely on you."

"Think so?"

Those eyes—pleading and frightened—summoned me closer. I knew that face like the back of my hand, had committed it to memory. She was overwhelmed. She needed a means to escape the mounting pressure and our inevitable, uncertain future. She wanted to shut everything off. Hell, I was right there with her.

I pushed off the wall, crossing the room. "Red is quite striking against your skin, and it makes your eyes glow."

The truth seeped between us like heavy smoke as I accepted what I had refused to before: there was a chance we might already be too late to fix this. Our enemies surrounded us, lurking in the shadows, always one step ahead. Enemies who wished Kim dead. What lengths were they willing to go to secure power? Shit, Malachi had already gone so far as to strike a deal with a creature locked in an eternal prison world by its *own mother*. On top of that, it was becoming increasingly difficult to deny that he'd used sacrificial magic to infuse Odin with hybrid abilities. My teeth clenched. If Malachi somehow succeeded in his quest to end the royal bloodline, Anathema would be doomed. Life as I knew it would be over. And hers—

No. I wouldn't let that happen.

The weight came crashing in, and the urge to push thought from mind in exchange for the simple peace of touch overcame me. I needed an escape. Something, anything else to focus on. Before I could stop myself, I reached for her—my heart hammering in my chest—and tucked a strand of loose hair behind her ear for the second time that day. Only this time I let my hand linger.

Just a touch.

I lifted her chin, and she shuttered under my caress.

"What are you doing?" she whispered, but didn't pull away.

Our eyes locked, and her gaze fell to my lips, the intensity in her stare making my stomach jump. What I'd seen earlier: the semblance of desire in her...it was true. There, plain as night and equally insatiable.

I slid a hand around her waist, pulling her to me. "What, you don't like it?"

"No..."

A grin caught my cheeks. Her lie hadn't even convinced herself. How I wanted to devour that lying tongue, take it between my teeth, and explore its sharpness. My length pulsed as her rapid heartbeat settled in my ears. So fucking sexy: the way her body yearned for me. Her dark, curious nature begged for release, and I would be a monster to deny her.

I licked my lips, the sweet aroma of her blood encompassing me. Gods, how I wanted to give in. To take her as her body wept for my attention. And why not? My thirst, well—it couldn't be satiated on blood alone. But did she truly want this? Me? Certainly, she must. If she didn't want to explore this...this hunger between us as bad as I did, she wouldn't hesitate to wield her power against me. No, she wanted this.

She wanted *me.*

Lyvias's mask be damned, I could *feel* she did, sense it. I towered over her, savoring the elation her poorly hidden smile lent me. "I never took you for a liar, Lady Death. Shall I wash your mouth out with soap or something more...substantial?"

The spark between us ignited.

Her hand slid along my hard cock, and chills raced up my spine. Her touch... *More.* I needed more, *now.* My mouth crashed into hers, a whimper rising in her throat to mix with my own. As my body tensed, I held back the urge to pin her to the wall, abandon restraint, and ravage her; but a woman like Kim was meant to be savored. Slow and steady. Teasing out her precious passion.

I nibbled her bottom lip, and her blood spilled over my tongue, the taste rivaling the finest wine. If heaven did exist, I imagined it would feel something like this. Like her. Like the way she melted in my arms, her heated breath brushing along my chest in kind. Absolutely divine. Her fingers teased the sensitive skin at my hip, tempting the beast within me to come out and play. She held my stare as she slid her hand into my pants. A moan tore through me.

Mine. My queen.

I freed the beast. Pinning her to the bed, I ripped her clothes off in frenzied motions and stood over her to behold her raw beauty. A gods-damned masterpiece. Her breasts were divine: full and round. I simply *had* to taste them. I kissed my way across her breasts, careful to skip over the pebbled peaks, and she writhed beneath me. Desperate. Pleading. I sank my teeth into her, nearly coming on contact, but I wasn't done with her. Not yet.

"Lower," she begged.

I sucked her nipple into my mouth, swirling my tongue, and her back arched. Her hips bucked, grinding against my throbbing length.

As she slid onto my lap, I knew without a shadow of a doubt that she would be my ruin. No other would or could compare to her. The power this woman had over me... I'd be whatever, become whatever, she needed me to be. I'd crush her enemies at her feet, make them bow before her, and—as she took their lives in her hands—worship her body, her soul. My dark temple. Every time I thought there was no way I could love her more, she wound her web tighter around me.

Her hand latched around my throat, and her fingertips dug into my flesh as she moved against me. The way she commanded me had me aching to fill her, over and over. A dark laugh rattled through me. "There she is."

But I still thirsted. Not for her blood, but her essence. I dragged her to the edge of the bed, pulled her lacy panties down, and parted her legs.

Holy hell...so wet.

I took her swollen clit into my mouth and nipped. Her gasp tickled my ears, encouraging me. Working her most sensitive spot in tight, firm circles, I felt her approaching release. Her knees shook as she neared the edge, and I clasped my mouth over hers as she came, devouring her unfettered cry of ecstasy.

Such a good girl.

Her hands dropped to my pants, frantic to free me. While I wanted nothing more than to bury myself inside her and see to her pleasure until the wee morning hours, a thought hit me suddenly. It wouldn't be my name she'd cry out in passion; it would be his: Lyvias. Everything in me pleaded to let her in, to let her near, but I couldn't. It would be unfair. A betrayal. She didn't know I lay beneath the mask. Had no idea who served her. She deserved to have all the cards on the table before making her decision on with whom she shared her most private desires. And so despite it fraying the very fiber of my being, I denied her.

"Did I...did I do something wrong?" she asked, her voice small.

I laced my hand in hers. "Absolutely not; you're incredible. But...but this isn't going to happen. Not tonight."

The embarrassment on her face pierced me straight in the heart. She believed I didn't want her, that I'd found her lacking. I don't know that I'd ever felt like a bigger piece of shit in my life. She'd opened herself up after losing Juniper, let me in, and I...I'd betrayed her trust. Not only that, I'd bred insecurity in her.

I grasped her shoulder. "I need you to hear me. It's not you; it's *me*."

"If I had a nickel for every time someone said that..." she murmured.

"But it's true. Before you give yourself to me, there are things you need to know. About my past." My hands flexed. "About who I am. Until then, I cannot in good conscience be with you."

"Then tell me."

I wanted to more than anything, but I was bound. Death would have my head—and Malachi hers—if I didn't keep this to myself. I had no choice, because her protection came first and foremost.

"It's not that simple."

"Yeah? Well, this is simple. You and me? We're business partners," she stabbed. "There is no 'us' or 'we.' So keep your secrets, Lyvias. Just know that if any of them put my people at risk, I'll do what I must."

I froze, my heart sinking in disbelief. Wait...she couldn't mean that. I dared a step closer, pleading for understanding, but her mind was made up. We were done before we even had a chance to start. How could I have been so careless? Allowed my selfish desires to overshadow her needs? Shit…I really was a monster.

With a cold and distant stare, she donned her crown and demanded my return to the shifter realm, extending me a vial of her blood to gain access. An order. This—all of this—was over.

"Yes, Your Majesty." I headed for the door but paused with my hand on the knob. "Even if today is the only taste of you I'll receive, everything I've done will have been worth it."

I stepped out into the hall, my self-deprecating thoughts threatening to swallow me whole.

I was alone. Again.

CHAPTER FOURTEEN

THE DAY THE WORLD BURNED

L ana glided her pawn up a square.

"Clever move, but if I do this..." I pushed my knight out, taking her pawn in one swoop.

"Ugh, I didn't see that coming. Mean!"

"Ha. Sounds like someone is jealous."

She laughed, but her smile quickly gave way, replaced by a furrowed brow and pinched lips. I turned the cool stone piece over in my hand.

"What's that face for?" I asked.

"I just...I never thought it could be like this."

"Like what?"

"Easy. Safe. I've...I've never really had that in my life. You're kind, Cooper."

My hand clenched around the pawn. As if I hadn't already been foaming at the mouth to end Malachi, seeing this sweet, kind, talented young girl shy away from my touch as I reached across the board—despite her knowing she was safe—made my gut drop.

"You know," I said gently, "there are far more kind people in this world than you think."

"Not in my experience. I suppose that's what I get for being out after dark when mama said not to, and now she's—" her words caught in her throat.

I knew that look: the echo of loss and misplaced guilt within it. "I am sorry the world has not been kind to you, Lana, but you do know that none of this is your fault, right?"

She huffed but didn't meet my gaze.

"Do you hear me? None of what you have been through is your fault. There are wicked people in this world who hurt others simply because they can." I leaned closer. "But want to know a little secret?"

Finally, she looked at me, her face flushed from rising tears.

"You," I said, "have an incredible future ahead of you. One filled with love and safety and every other good thing you deserve. You know why? Because Fate blesses those with kind hearts."

"Right."

"I think you forget that it was *you* who encouraged me when I arrived here. You told me to be safe and kept my secret. People with hearts like yours—who offer kindness to a stranger in need—are rewarded."

"You really think so?" she asked.

"I know so. One day, you're going to look back on all this, and it will be nothing but a speck in the grand story of your life. Now wipe those tears; we have a game to finish."

She sighed, but a smirk widened on her cheeks. Her eyes went wide as she looked over the board, and she shifted her knight with a giddy laugh.

"Checkmate!"

I grinned, knowing full well I'd left my queen wide open. "You got me."

For weeks Suri and I had waited for Malachi's grand viewing party, and finally our time had come. In the quiet morning hours while the rest of the world slept, my limbs buzzed with anticipation. I could almost *taste* the blood in the air. The time for vengeance was upon us. I'd end them all.

"How do we ensure they don't run?" Suri asked, smoothing her crimson mini skirt.

Ah, the question I'd mulled over for the past twenty-four hours. One, I admit, I was eager to answer. I turned to Suri, who stood before my full-length bedroom mirror tending to the sharpness of her eyeliner wings.

I shook a bottle of gin. "This is how."

"Booze?" Her brows creased, meeting my gaze in the reflection. "Surely they can't all be as easy to manipulate with substances as the Lord and his mate."

But a drunken stupor wasn't my aim. Not this time. I'd taken my winged form the night before—returning to the Evermoor Woods to confirm Kimber's findings—and solidified the horrifying truth of Malachi's ties to baneful magic. But to my surprise, I'd also stumbled on our saving grace: white oleander. Being that poisonous plants had always been a strange curiosity of mine—hence the floral tattoos winding up my arms—I knew the second I saw those star-shaped flowers tucked under a single, pointed moonbeam that Fate had smiled on us yet again. It seemed that although the future Fate and Death were torn from one another's arms, Juniper wouldn't let go so easily.

I'd lingered on that truth as I'd foraged the blooms. Even from realms away, Juniper's love for Kimber shone down, her helping hands guiding my steps. I wondered if the Old Goddess directed June, too. If the mother of Elysium had brought me to Anathema and instigated Suri's and my paths crossing. How else had Suri—in all her fierceness—ended up at Kimber's side? It couldn't have been happenstance. The future Death, a pureblood shapeshifter, and a demon seamstress fluent in tinctured magic: united in their efforts to see Anathema returned to balance. Could it?

What if we'd gotten it wrong? What if the Old Gods *did* still play a hand in divine intervention? I made a mental note to research further into the realm creators' history. Because if they truly did hold sway? I'd need to find a way to thank the Goddess for orchestrating these moments and granting me a chance at hope.

For a moment, I considered my own worth. If Fate in her divinity saw fit to bless those around me, then maybe I too was deserving. A strange, unusual thought. Maybe I had belonged somewhere all along: here in the realm of eternal night. Maybe...I'd always had a home.

One I was now called to protect.

Striking yet humble, the oleander flower hid a sinister secret in its seemingly harmless leaves and petals. If touched, you risked an irritating rash. But if ingested? It became a harbinger of death: blurred vision, vomiting, and heart palpitations. It was the perfect tool if you were trying to incapacitate a person to, say, trap them in a burning building. I'd ground the petals into a paste, mindful not to allow the mixture to touch any open scrapes or cuts. After an hour or so of reduction time, their hue grew pale and undetectable when mixed with triple-distilled gin. A silent killer.

"White oleander," I told Suri with a mischievous grin. "If the flames don't get them, the poison will. Which reminds me: when I raise a toast, don't drink."

"Noted."

"Gods, I hope this works."

The fiery demon walked towards me and placed her hands on either side of my face. On contact, her iridescent magic curled around me, settling my trembling shoulders. Together we took three deep breaths.

"It will work, Coop. Fate clearly has your back; and where she dispenses retribution, success follows. Trust yourself."

Her words brought my mother's back again: *Fate smiled upon you, gave you a special gift.*

For the first time, I think I actually believed it.

I rested my chin atop Suri's head and squeezed her tight. Crazy: how quickly someone could become an irreplaceable part in one's life. Her desires and thirst for revenge had not only fueled me; but if it weren't for her comfort and reassurance, I wouldn't have made it this far.

"I trust *us*. This." I stepped back to look down at her. "Our friendship. I hope you know how much I treasure it. How I appreciate you and all you've done for Kim and these girls. For me. You are one badass woman."

Tears welled in her eyes, and she slapped my chest. "You sap. You're going to ruin my makeup!"

"My apologies." I laughed.

"But really, you coming to Anathema, walking alongside me...I am forever grateful. I am in your debt."

Oh, absolutely not. I wiped her cheeks, lowering myself into her sight line. "You, Suri, do not owe *anyone* anything. You are a treasured part of this realm, and your loyalty will not go unnoticed."

She smirked and whispered, "Yes, my King."

Her words sucker-punched me in the gut. *King?* I was no king. Lyvias had been intended for the throne, sure. But me? No. An orphan estranged from his home could never hold such a title...could he?

The train to Plavin Park ground to a sparky stop. This was it: no turning back. The chips would fall where they may, and in the end, death would come. Though as I looked at the anticipation in the tinctured magic swirling above Suri's head, a sickening realization came over me: death might not come for those wicked men alone. The thought made my stomach turn. I'd been prepared to sacrifice my own life if it came to it, but I hadn't prepared to risk losing someone else. Again. We boarded, slid into the plastic seats—doors whooshing closed behind us—and Suri rested a hand on my knee.

"Deep breaths," she reminded me.

Right. I could do this. *Don't be a pussy, Cooper.*

Unlike our last visit, the club windows were dark on our approach. Nobody greeted us at the door as we entered. There were no flashing lights or booming bass. No men perched in the cushioned leather chairs, bidding on women trapped inside glass boxes. Instead, erected in the center of the round room was a long banquet table. Atop it, red candles flickered in ornate candelabras. Black bouquets lined the room's edges, and a stringed quartet filled the space with rich song that on any other occasion would have soothed me. More than a dozen heads turned as we stepped into the room, the guests' true identities concealed behind porcelain masks. A lion. A bear. A falcon. All predators set to devour the meal laid atop a silver platter in the table's center. Bile crept up my throat.

The young woman from behind the painting.

Her eyes were closed, but her chest rose and fell with steady breaths. Still alive. Time seemed to stop as I took in every little detail of the disturbing scene. Flowers peeked through the carefully curated waves in her hair, small braids splaying out around her like rays of sunlight. She almost appeared at rest, peaceful, if not for the rope that bound her like a pig strapped to a spit. My attention drifted to the needles inserted in various places on her body—wrists, neck, feet, and legs—each tapped straight into the vein. Connected tubes fed into multiple goblets positioned before the guests.

Drip, drip, drip.

The iron perfume threatened to undo me, but my growing rage squashed the selfish desire. I would have my fill of blood yet; it just wouldn't be hers. When I saw the blade at her side—encrusted in rubies and emeralds—the final piece clicked into place, and my fingers flexed at my side. This woman...she wasn't merely a meal; she was a sacrifice.

We'd walked into a damned ritual.

I glanced at Suri in my peripheral to find her jaw tight. Oh yeah, these fuckers would pay for their sins.

Malachi jumped from his seat at the head of the table. "Ah, there you are, Lyvias. We feared you might have lost your way."

I forced a smile in return. "Me? Never. Fashionably late is all."

He chuckled as a nearly nude woman collected our jackets. Shoulders back, he led us to our spots and introduced those already seated, one by one. Most guests were merely pompous businessmen and their giddy trophy wives, but one couple erected red flags in my mind instantly. Heavy, tar-like magic surrounded them, threatening to choke the air from my lungs.

"You remember Duke Jarlin and his beautiful bride, Duchess Nova," Malachi stated.

"Indeed. Thank you for joining us." I placed a kiss on the Duchess's hand.

"It is an honor, Your Highness," she replied. "As the house mother, I wouldn't dream of missing such a celebration."

House mother?

Malachi leaned in close. "Duchess Nova is the sole reason our girls are cultured and well-mannered, you see. She takes these broken, worthless things and creates beauty. A true artist."

A blush crossed her cheeks, and I fought the urge to rip her throat out. Appalling: to pride oneself on such an immoral duty. It riled me to my core, but I leaned into my character, eager to speed up the morning's imminent end.

What would a soulless vampire Lord do?

He would drink. I reached across the table, snatched the goblet laid out for me, and swirled the crimson liquid inside. My mouth watered despite my disgust, but I would need my strength if I hoped to save the poor girl. Turning to the Duchess, I raised the glass to my lips; my focus fixated on her as she sipped from her own.

"Delicious, is she not?" Nova asked.

While I'd tasted the young woman's blood on prior occasions, a new, sharp note I hadn't noticed before hung on my tongue. "Quite. Who knew humans could be so intoxicating?"

"Ah, but she is not just *any* human," she explained. "This, Your Highness, is the heir to the Nightshade coven. Her lineage ties back to the very first mortals blessed with power by Fate and Death as penance for their ravenous children pushing humanity to near extinction. Her magic and blood are uniquely endowed with cosmic energy."

Suri's hand tightened on my arm. *Not fucking good.*

The couples nearest us cheered at Nova's words, *clinking* their silverware against their goblets. Odin motioned for us to take our seats, and Malachi addressed his guests.

"My brethren, this morning we celebrate you and all you have accomplished. This club, as you well know, is my pride and joy. One I wish to see thrive—"

His words dissipated into the background as my sights traced along the crowd, settling on a lone man to my left. His cerulean eyes—like the sea on a clear sunny day—and round cheeks gave me pause. Familiar, but how? He offered me a wink, and it hit me. It was him: the man I'd met at the training grounds on my first day in Anathema.

"Two dukes sit amongst us," Malachi continued, "ready for change. Tell me, Duke Jarlin, Duke Adari, are you ready to claim your destinies and usher in this new era of power?"

The stranger I'd honed in on nodded once, his sights lingering on me. "Indeed, Lord Malachi. We shall serve tirelessly in our roles to uphold this new world order which you have graciously provided us."

Duke Adari. The more I studied him, the more confused I became. At first glance, the magic lingering around him appeared like the rest: imbued with sinister, baneful intent. But the closer I looked, the more it transformed, a strange light flickering underneath.

Malachi's voice intensified. "And a new world order we shall have! The Reigning Reaper lineage has become weak, watered down by mortal blood meant to sustain us, not rule us. It is time to forsake hiding and expand our way of life. It is time to stand, reclaim the night, and remake our world in *our* image. To denounce the Old Gods' vision since they insist on hiding away in their ivory towers allowing *filth* to infiltrate our courts."

Again, the table cheered. My stomach twisted, weighed down by the sheer panic on Suri's face. Whatever was about to happen had to be stopped immediately.

Malachi stepped up to the woman splayed out before us, took the knife in his hand, and placed it against her throat. "So my brethren, let us feast not only on her mortal blood, but on her power. Together, we shall reign. Let us lord our newfound strength over our adversaries at Death's precious ball tonight and show him the error of his ways before we strike down his heir."

Everything in me seized. Every muscle and joint. *Kim...*

Blade severed flesh, and the witch's life was forfeit. I watched her power—bestowed by Fate and Death—pour out, rich and dazzling, straight into Malachi's glass. My heart broke for her. This woman had known nothing but pain in her final hours. I considered the life she might have led before her abduction. Had she fallen in love? Built a home? Secured a future for her people? One she'd now never share in. As heir, her coven would spiral, mourning her for a millennia. What an absolute tragedy.

Intuition rattled in my bones, assuring me that if her blood made it into Malachi's system, Anathema would be doomed. There would be no way back. Her lifeblood slipped towards the demon Lord's lips as each person at the table raised their glasses and—

I jumped to my feet. "A toast!"

The room paused in tandem. I made my way to the drink cart, snatched the gin bottle I'd deposited upon our arrival, and grabbed as many glasses as I could carry—Suri following suit. We rounded opposite sides of the table, presenting each guest with their own glass, before returning to our places.

Malachi flashed a snide look. "Surely we can toast upon completion—"

"Certainly not," I responded, and poured into my own cup. "My friends, we are witnessing history here. Should we not celebrate our well-earned victory? Savor it?"

To my surprise, Odin nodded in agreement, swaying his partner and the rest of the guests in kind. Perfect. Malachi traded his bloody goblet for a new glass, and I poured freely. One by one, the attendees reached for their own fill, unknowingly walking straight into the trap set for them.

Good riddance.

I noticed Duke Adari's vibrant, frantic magic, and I lingered on him a second longer than the rest, warning him with a pointed stare.

I raised my glass. "To a new world order!"

"To a new world order!" everyone seconded, and downed the contents of their glasses.

But not me. Not Suri. And not Adari.

Malachi chuckled, setting a hand on my shoulder. "I've never seen you practice restraint when it comes to a bit of top-shelf liquor. Will you not join us in the toast?"

I grinned, my heartbeat in my ears. "Not when it's been poisoned."

"You jest too much."

He laughed again, but this time it didn't reach his eyes. I held his gaze as I poured my cup out on the floor, letting the empty glass fall and shatter at his feet. He referenced the shards, then me, then the rest of the now silent room.

"Lyvias, what have you done?"

"I have ensured that your treasonous vie for the throne ends here, secured freedom for those whose lives you have hijacked, and eradicated the monster whose shadow haunted my queen's throne. All in one fell swoop."

"You...fool..." he choked out, clenching a hand around his throat as the oleander took swift hold.

Like dominoes, the guests crashed to the floor one after another. Their bodies seized as they choked for air, crying out for help, but nobody would answer their calls. After all, they'd installed these soundproof walls themselves to hide their sins from the outside world, and those very same walls would serve as their crypt. Talk about cruel irony.

I turned to Suri. "Get the girls out, but be quick. I'll finish here."

"I don't know the back rooms. I—"

Adari stepped to her side. "I do. Let me help."

Suri and I shared a weary glance.

"Please," Adari whispered. "You saw my intention. I know you did. You are gifted in oracle sight, are you not?"

"How did you know that?" I hissed.

Panic gripped me, but the duke offered a gentle, genuine smile.

"Because I too have the sight," he said. "Please, I have suffered years in this place waiting for a moment to strike. Let me help you both."

I turned to Suri. "It's your call."

"Do you trust him?" she asked.

"His magic certainly isn't baneful. I can tell you that much."

She looked him over. "If he wiggled his way into the inner circle, then he'd know this place like the back of his hand. We need him."

"Then take him." I snagged Adari's sleeve as he turned to leave. "Do not make me regret this."

"I wouldn't dream of it, my King."

He bowed his head, and they disappeared into the club's depths—his final word hanging over me like an anvil dangling from a frayed rope: *king.*

Alone in the gasps and fevered screams, I drifted towards the table. Averting my gaze from the soulless witch, my bloodlust grabbed hold of me. It wasn't Lyvias's thirst this time though. It was mine. My thirst to end those who'd caused such pain and destruction. To make them feel the same way they'd made others feel. I leaned down over Odin as he writhed in pain, his hands clenched at his temples.

"You," I bit through my teeth. "I have been *dreaming* of the moment I'd get a second alone with *you.*"

I stepped on his chest, letting my full weight linger there for a second as he battled for breath. A glorious sight. But he needed to know, needed to *see* what damage he'd caused. I snagged his suit collar and ripped him to his feet. Oh, the enjoyment I'd get in his annihilation; I'd drink it in like a fine wine aged for decades in a dark cellar. He snarled, but his intimidation landed on deaf ears. He really believed himself menacing. A hound from hell. In truth? He was nothing more than a rabid dog. No problem; I'd put him down. Bend him. Break him.

As my sights bore into his, I imagined how Kimber must have felt that night at the club. Alone and cornered like prey, despite being the fiercest predator herself. My mind wandered to what could have been: the disgusting things Odin would have inflicted on her had I not stumbled across them in time. Fire burned in my gut, and I snatched him by the throat. What other atrocities had he committed? What rot had he spread within others?

I searched the room, locking onto the nearest viewing station, its glass panels gleaming in the candlelight. Empty save for the shackles of the woman who'd been forced to dance within it.

That'll work.

I dragged Odin—shrieking and kicking in a childish tantrum—towards it, slammed him against the wall, and secured the chains around his ankles. A chuckle shook my chest as I stepped back to behold him. I'd won. Despite the threats he hurled at me through foamy lips, terror refracted in his eyes.

"Killing us won't bring the bitch back," he screamed, his breaths labored.

I turned my back on him, strode over to the banquet table, and removed the bloody rope still binding the young woman. Her skin...already cold to the touch. I heaved a heavy sigh.

"Be at peace, little witch," I whispered, and straightened a wilting flower in her hair. "Rest knowing your life will be avenged this day."

Any traces of kindness I left there with her. I let my rage take full control. Fuel me. Cracking my neck, I studied Malachi's magic fading in and out in an effort to save him from the poison's clutches. Like he'd be so lucky. I ripped him off the floor, dragging him to the leather chair positioned before Odin; his screams were like music to my ears. With a hum in my throat, I bound the demon Lord to the chair with his own fucking rope.

Malachi lurched forward. "Don't...do this."

"What?" My frame cast a shadow over him. "I thought you liked to watch?"

I stepped aside, granting him an unobscured view of Odin.

"Sick...bastard..." he wheezed.

"Oh, I know you are, but don't worry. I'm about to put you out of your misery. I know, I'm too kind."

Suri appeared as if on cue, a long line of women between her and Adari. She paused, her attention bouncing about the room.

"Go," I said. "Get them to safety."

Suri stepped forward. "What about the upper level? Dancers and staff are known to stay overnight on occasion. There could be innocent people asleep up there."

"Adari, can you see to that?"

The duke nodded. "Yes, Sire."

Suri and her charges burst out the back door while Adari headed upstairs. Safe. Now, time to deliver on my promise and rid my kingdom of this filth. This festering disease of imbalance. Leaning down over Malachi, I ran a finger along his jawline. He lurched, but I didn't let him evade my touch.

I grabbed the candelabra nearest me—the candles still lit—returning to Odin's post to meet his gaze. "May the flames purge your cold, dead heart. Or not. Either way, you'll face Fate's wrath. And I doubt she will be as forgiving as me."

A single tap of the candle against the silk curtains, and the place ignited. Smoke billowed, tangling in my lungs. The few guests who hadn't yet succumbed to the poison pleaded for mercy the same way so many women had to them, but I offered no salvation. Instead I choked out a laugh, watching the flames jump from curtain to curtain and spread across the carpet.

Then the first body caught, engulfed in an instant.

The scent of charred meat settled in my nose. Thanks to the poison lulling him to sleep, the man didn't cry or wake. But Odin and Malachi? They were forced to watch. To beg. Seems the poison wasn't as forgiving to "more powerful beings," as they'd so deemed themselves. My lungs burned in the black smoke.

Time to go.

I stole one final look at Malachi, who sat motionless in acceptance of his fate, and made my way to the exit.

"May Fate grant you the same mercy you gave to others," I called with a wink, and sealed him away in his crypt.

I lingered, securing a vantage point atop a hill shrouded by trees. Adari and two dancers emerged just in time for the blaze to blow out the bottom windows like a shotgun blast behind them. Can't say I was surprised, given the amount of alcohol stockpiled within those walls. Flames reached for the waxing moon, unsatisfied until the entire building glowed and crackled. Whatever ties Malachi and Odin had made burned alongside their legacy of malevolence. Their sins: finally scorched from the earth.

The meat market was officially closed for business.

CHAPTER FIFTEEN

GHOSTS WILL HAUNT

The vision of Kim walking towards me—a bone tiara atop her head glistening in the candlelight—captivated my entire being. Power. She was power incarnate, ready to take her place as the new Death. Secure and confident in her ruthlessness. Her magic moved anew—surer of itself somehow—ebbing and flowing with intention to protect its wielder at any cost. There were still questions lingering in her evasive gaze, sure, but not about her worth or ability. She knew who she was now, and damn anyone who thought otherwise. Rightfully so, because only a fool would look upon this woman and see anything less than a goddess.

"You look ravishing," I said upon her approach, and attempted to catch my breath.

"I know I do." Her clipped words made my stomach twist.

"Spoken like a true queen."

Why I'd assumed she'd have softened towards me in such a short time, I don't know. Forgiveness never came easy to her; and even if it did, I'm not sure I deserved it. In her mind, I'd rejected her, left her wondering what she'd done wrong or how she'd lost my affections. But she couldn't have been further from the truth, because my affections were precisely what had kept me from laying with her. She was my home, my safe space. To sully a gift like that by allowing unspoken secrets to spill over onto her already full plate, to deceive her in her vulnerability…I would never forgive myself for such a betrayal. So I stood by my decision, despite it cutting me to the bone every time I glanced her way and she denied me. My sights fell to my feet.

In one stupid moment overshadowed by desire, I'd burned her trust in me to the ground. Idiot. I should have known better than to let feelings get involved. Winning her heart had never been my goal, even if deep down I would always long for it. Her security and protection remained my top priority.

I focused on the looming ballroom doors. "Are you ready for this?"

"You bet your ass I am."

I offered my arm to her, which she reluctantly took for appearance's sake in preparation for the night's event. She held her head high, but I caught the flinch in her fingers. She didn't want to touch me, and here we were about to parade ourselves around like lovers, arm in arm for hours on end. My toes curled in my shoes, squeaking against the leather, the silence between us deafening.

Here goes nothing.

Kimber's hold on my elbow tightened as the ballroom doors parted, revealing a vast sea of guests. All eyes turned to us, and her breath hitched.

I leaned in close. "Give them hell."

Though she fought it, a smirk showed through her steely resolve, and I took it as a win. A small glimmer of hope that maybe, somehow, she might find a way to trust me again. One day.

We took our places by Death, our thrones at his side decorated in cascading dead flowers and gemstones set alight by the chandeliers' soft glow. The castle's signature black roses littered the polished tabletops, their sweet scent filling the space. No expense had been spared this night. I watched the guests tilt their heads in attentive adoration of their coming queen and king, and I offered Cadagon a grateful nod. Solidifying allied partnerships—which I knew seconds after entering the room was the true intention behind the night—would be made much easier in a space so welcoming and decadent. The elite valued a lavish ball. Cadagon's quick smirk said it all: *For her, anything.*

Kim pushed her shoulders back, ready to address our people. "Honored guests, welcome! We are so fortunate to have such prestigious and influential minds in our presence this night. It is with great pleasure that we celebrate the coming change of an era."

Not an eye strayed from her, transfixed as if lured in by a siren song. She'd bewitched them, body and soul. Her shadows swayed, luring me in closer; and I stepped to her side, lacing my hand through hers like it belonged there.

"A change the future queen and I are excited to build with your help," I added. "We look forward to what is to come in the days ahead. Anathema, united."

Death stepped forward to speak, but his words dissipated the further my focus drifted. All I saw was her. *Us.* Our hands intertwined. I followed her line of sight, absorbing the shared mission we'd laid out taking root in our guests' minds. Chills carried up my arms as I pictured the future we could build together. That is...if she would have me. One truth remained firm in my mind regardless of whether or not she'd accept me as her partner: Anathema's enemies had fallen. The festering corruption had been purged by flames, giving the kingdom a chance to breed life anew. Who then, could touch her? Nobody.

Giddy satisfaction and genuine hope hung around me like a badge of honor as I watched Kimber demand my throne be raised at her side. *An equal*, she'd called me. While her heart may not have warmed to me in regards to our personal relationship, being considered an asset to the crown was a start.

We waded into the crowd. Conversation proved clunky at first, neither Kim nor I sure who should lead and who should follow. I gave her space to talk, to romance those in her courts, but she seemed adamant that I join in too. We approached the next group, the small tick in her brow conveying she wanted me to take the reins. *Right...no pressure or anything.* I turned my attention to the table, and my heart jumped. Gold bangles *clinked* on our next guest's wrist as he waved us over, his cerulean eyes heavy on me.

"You," I whispered before I could stop myself.

"Me." Adari smiled and squeezed his husband's knee, pulling him away from a side conversation. "Tovas, the future queen and king have graced us with their presence."

Tovas nodded but didn't say a word. Not at first. Instead, Adari's husband looked us over inquisitively. After a brief moment, Adari extended a hand to Kimber, the gold glitter on his rich brown skin shimmering. Without a second thought, she offered her hand to him in return, and he placed a quick peck on it.

"Kimberly," she introduced herself. "And you are?"

"Star-struck," he said with a grin spreading across his round cheeks. "Adari Melontin, beloved husband of Duke Tovas of Wentworth Manor. It is truly an honor to meet you, Your Highness. And might I just say, whoever your royal dresser is, I simply must meet them."

Kim's shoulders relaxed at his remark on the exquisite fabric of her gown, and the two fell into effortless conversation. With that, I took my seat at Tovas's side.

"So," he began, raising an eyebrow, "my husband tells me we owe you a great debt. Some might say a life debt."

Shit...

My throat tightened. "I beg your pardon?"

I fought to keep my expression even, my mind racing. How much did he know? How likely would this stranger be to, oh I don't know, turn in the person who burned a club down with prestigious members of society locked inside? My pulse climbed.

Duke Tovas rested a hand on mine. "Do not fear, Your Highness. Your secret is safe with me. Anyone who protects my most prized possession has my loyalty."

He looked over at Adari, mesmerized for a moment at the sight of his husband's effortless laughter in the queen's presence.

"Do tell me, *Lyvias*," he said, enunciating my name with intent, "how is it, you think, that you and I became so lucky in love?"

He took a sip from his glass, patient for my response.

"I can't say I have an explanation that would suffice."

"Indeed. The Goddess, even in her absence, holds divine control within our kingdom."

Kimber's giggle stole my attention, and I bit my lip. How I wish Fate deemed me fit enough to step out into the light, to be Kim's true partner in every sense, but letting hope in was a dangerous thing. That's how hearts were broken; and considering mine was already littered with fractures, I wasn't sure I could survive her rejection. Better to stay focused on my mission and accept that some were more worthy of Fate's luck than me. If the Old Goddess bestowed luck on all who wished for it, it wouldn't truly be luck at all. Would it?

Tovas shot me a knowing look and leaned in close. "The time will come when you can be your true self again; and when it does, I would bet a great deal that Kimberly will be pleased with your union."

My head whipped towards him. "I'm not sure I know what you mean..."

His mustache wiggled in time with his chuckle. "Oh yes, you do. Rest assured, the house of Wentworth will be here for whatever you may need, little raven."

He knew I was a shifter? But how? And when? And—

Again, he set a hand on mine, this time his thumb brushing against my wrist. A peace settled over me suddenly as I watched light tendrils curl out from Tovas's hand. The magical mist around him burst forth, but he never took his eyes off of me.

I studied the ethereal beams around his head. "You...but how?"

"Fate is the mother of all, not just those who belong in the light. Anathema was never intended to be a realm of solely Death's vision. Look closely, but do not simply look with your eyes; look with your heart."

He motioned about the room, and I turned towards the dance floor. The world around me opened up in droves of refracted light. Colors I'd never seen—even after receiving June's gift—swam together overhead. Each magic plume stayed near its wielder but ventured off in curious adventure. Some played nice with others; some did not. What was crystal clear was the sheer variety of the guests' abilities. Some wielded both ethereal and baneful magics, yin and yang united somehow in one being. Some leaned one way or the other, and some—like the strange haze in the backmost corner that made my gut turn—were pure darkness. I blinked, and the somber cloud disappeared.

"You'd be wise to use that gifted sight of yours more often," Tovas said low enough for my ears only. "And should you need help honing it, I know a certain couple who would be more than happy to help you do so. After all, our generation had a Fate too, and she was a gracious giver."

He twirled his finger above his glass—projected light whirling within it—and the stiffness in my limbs relaxed. I could trust him. My intuition confirmed it beyond a shadow of a doubt. I bowed my head once before offering my hand to him.

"I would be honored to accept your offer."

"Then please call on us if you are ever in need, Your Highness." He took my hand in a firm shake. "And thank you again. The house of Wentworth is at your service."

With the tension of the night easing, I retrieved two glasses of champagne and offered one to Kimber on the dance floor sidelines. She took a large sip, a contented smile gracing her face.

"You look happy," I said.

"I am," she replied. "How could I not be, when everything I've ever wanted is within reach? Even if..."

Her face fell. I wondered as I watched her study the fizz in her glass if she was thinking of me. Missing me. I had the honor of seeing her face every day while she assumed her best friend was locked away in a coffin forever. Gods, how I missed being *me* to her. I missed our dark humor, our roving ghost hunts in the woods, our friendship. Just...us.

I faced her. "You've sacrificed so much, Kim. I'm sorry you've had to give parts of your heart away in order to fulfill your duty."

"Thank you. It hasn't been easy, but..." A pained expression tainted her beautiful face. "I think, if I had the chance to do it all over again, I would do the same thing. They would have wanted it that way."

They: Juniper and me. Part of me ached at her admission, though the majority of me beamed with pride. Anathema had inherited a great leader. The way she gave and how she chose her people regardless of the hardships it inflicted showed just how deeply she cared for kingdom. If balance was to be restored, we'd need a guide like her.

A tear ran down her cheek, but she brushed it away as quickly as it came. I wanted to tell her how brave she was. Wanted to wrap her in my arms, and confirm that—at least on my part—I would have wanted her to do exactly as she'd done. Prioritize herself and her kingdom over me. Instead, I attempted to break the growing tension the best I could.

"Think it's time we meet them? The Lords?"

She downed her fizzy drink in one go. "I do."

A cute pucker on her lips, she wove her fingers through mine, sending goosebumps up my arm. I squeezed her hand like she was the gravity holding me to the earth, because in a sense, she was.

The corner of her mouth curved up. "Don't get cocky. I'm just trying to sell us as a united front."

"Right." I couldn't help but laugh.

Tovas's advice repeated in the back of my mind. I used my gifted sight to determine the intentions of those around us as Kim and I made our rounds. Lord Tarrant of the reaper court swept us up in talk of the future. Drenched in elemental magic—hence the reaper's connection to the earth—I found not a single red flag in his narrative. He voiced his concern for his people and the disruption in his court since the shapeshifters' absence. My knowledge of the deal struck between Malachi and the Old Gods' baneful offspring made the reaper Lord's words heavier, his words sinking like a stone in my gut. Such ruthlessness had leaked into the court of balance and kindness, but ease overcame me at the realization that the ones who were behind those atrocities were gone. Dead and buried. We could focus now on the solutions.

Lord Drystan of the vampire court—still new to his role after Lyvias had succeeded to his title of "Counterpart to the Future Reigning Reaper"—and his beautiful wife were no different. They aspired for a united Anathema just as we did, believed we could do it. In Drystan's eyes, the restoration of our people was just around the corner. We'd won.

"Come, our next meeting is on the veranda," Kim said, leading us away from the bustling dance floor.

Something in me shifted the closer we drew to those double doors. My palms grew clammy, realization cracking hard against my brain. We readied ourselves for another meeting, yet we'd already met the remaining Lords. All the dukes. My mouth turned to sandpaper. *Unless...* A shadow cast itself over my newfound hope like an eclipse blocking out the sun.

Duke Jarlin and Duchess Nova stood encompassed in the castle's shade. Very much alive.

And very fucking angry.

Kim's discomfort showed in her shadows, their tendrils latching around my arm. Her intuition was spot on, but running wasn't an option until I knew exactly what we were up against. Despite the dread coursing through me, I reassured Kimber. We'd make it quick, and the first second I had, I'd whisk her off to safety. Because if they had survived? Who knew who else had escaped that burning building.

Fuck, fuck, fuck.

"Greetings, children," Duke Jarlin bit out. "Finally, you grace us with your presence."

His sights drilled into me, the tension growing thick. *Wrong...this is all wrong.* A knot formed in my throat as Nova studied Kimber far too closely for my liking; the duchess's lip curled up in disgust the more she looked. My hands clenched at my sides. That look had broken many a woman in her lifetime no doubt, but Kim didn't break easily. Still, I fought the urge to hurl the bitch over the railing to her second death like a sack of rotten potatoes.

"We apologize for the wait. But the princess and I merely meant to save the best for last," I said through my teeth.

Jarlin snuffed his nose upward, turning his attention to Kimber. The weight of his stare on her made my gums throb, tempting me to satisfy my growing thirst by ripping his damn jugular clean out of his throat. How the hell had they escaped?

He pursed his lips before addressing her. "Tell me, does the princess speak through her lowly counterpart often, or does the girl speak for herself?"

Kimber's rage erupted, taking hold of her. Kim bit back—the situation escalating as Jarlin's snide comments baited her further—when the hair on the back of my neck stood up. Not on account of Jarlin or his sadistic wife though. Something lurked. Watched us intently. It burrowed under my skin, haunting me as I searched through the glass. I scoured the crowd. Shadows darted about, which I quickly dismissed since Kimber's shadows always reeled when she was upset. She stepped into the duke's face.

"See that your attitude is greatly improved upon our next meeting, Duke Jarlin, or I'll be forced to take much more," she cinched his tie hard against his throat, "aggressive measures. Do I make myself clear?"

That's my girl.

Jarlin drifted past as he excited the veranda, hurling his harsh, final words at Kim. But I knew his words were truly meant for me.

"I might urge you to pay better attention to those you aim to make an enemy," he said, tapping the rim of her glass once. "You never know when one might sneak up, hellbent on revenge."

His hand dipped into his pocket, reappearing to drop something on the marble floor. My pulse clapped in my ears—the scene around me slowing—and I stole a look at my feet to find my worst fear.

Oleander blooms.

Everything sped up tenfold, my eyes landing on Kim as she noticed the fizzing tablet in her drink a second too late. Why hadn't I seen it? Why hadn't I been more careful? *Fuck!*

I barely caught her before she hit the floor, her glass shattering.

"Death! Help me!"

I frantically searched the crowd. Anyone, everyone, *someone* had to help her! A shadow lifted my jaw, forcing my gaze to the ballroom's edge. Ice coursed through my veins as the crowd surged forward, running to catch a glimpse of what had happened. My target, however, stood eerily still.

Him.

Wrapped in darkness, Malachi offered me one gesture: a coin flipped high in the air. That night in the woods—back when Kim and I had thought reclaiming her throne would be simple—thrashed through my memory. We'd baited a demon in the forest for his blood, his hound primed to devour me. Damn it, I should have known! Should have seen the warning signs. *Of course* it'd been Malachi and Odin all along, their presence eclipsing our doorstep ever since. My throat tightened. I'd underestimated them.

Malachi referenced the coin in his hand, pointed to me, and shook his head, sealing my fate. I was a dead man. He wrapped an arm around Odin—fresh burns bubbling up on his throat—and they drifted out of view.

Kim began to seize in my arms, a buzz thrumming through my clenched teeth. I had one last chance to make this right. One. A horrible, awful, maybe impossible chance.

I'd have to bleed her out.

CHAPTER SIXTEEN

A CRUEL TWIST OF FATE

I will not kill the woman I love.

I bit her wrist, sucking hard.

I will not kill the woman I love.

Her thighs.

I will not kill the woman I love.

Her throat.

In the eerie silence of Kimber's suite, my gums blistered from the poison, my thirst threatening to overtake me. Still, I bit and drained and spit. Over and over. My last five mouthfuls were sweet, clean blood—the bitter notes of oleander undetectable—and yet she lay there motionless. I watched. Waited. Why wasn't it *working*? Another bite. Another drain.

"Come on, baby. Fight this! Come back to me."

A flinch in her fingertips caught my eye, and I sat up straight. *Thank the Gods.* She was alive. She was— Her shadows recoiled suddenly, her chest rising and falling with strained breaths. Then, all at once, she stilled. My stomach tied itself in knots.

No. No!

"Fate, don't you dare take her from me! Do you hear me?"

I pumped her chest between forced breaths into her mouth, but it was too late. I'd already lost her. The room began to spin, a sob ripping up my throat. No. This was *not* how it ended! She had so much life left in her: a bright future, a kingdom to rule. How the hell was I supposed to do life without her? There had to be another way. Something I hadn't thought of or considered or— *Fuck!*

I sank my teeth back into her throat, pulling straight from the jugular, but already her blood had cooled. A hollow ring settled in my ears. How? Why? Fate had guided our steps...and for what? To allow Kim to die a painful, cruel death? Gods, this wasn't possible! I stood and raked an arm across the mantle, sending everything atop it crashing to the ground. My home, my heart, my *world* was gone, and the only one to blame was myself. I fell to my knees—my hands tangled in my hair—and a bloodcurdling scream heaved past my lips.

My everything: fucking gone!

Cadagon appeared from the shadows, panic surging in his burning eyes. "What happened?"

"She's gone," I snarled.

My fist shattered the nearest stained glass window, and blood seeped down my knuckles, intermingling with the already gruesome scene.

"That is..." Death whispered, "that is impossible."

"I'm such an idiot! I never should have gone up against Malachi. I should have known he'd seek revenge on her!" I paused, a thought slipping through the madness. "Wait, you can save her!"

"I...I cannot."

"You are Death incarnate! You saved me. Now save her!"

"It's not that simple!" he burst. "I cannot return a member of my own bloodline to the land of the living. The Old Gods designed it so, to ensure no Reigning Reaper abused their years upon the throne."

"There has to be a way!"

The broken pieces of colored glass flickered in the candlelight. I froze, the passage I'd stumbled on in the Immortal Library coming back to me. Fate's power could alter time: turn back the clock in moments of grave danger where lives were at stake. Anathema's true ruler and the sole chance of restoring balance lay dead at my feet. Fate *had* to intervene. I snatched a broken piece, slicing my palm wide open, ready to bind my blood and my very life to whatever I must. I would save her; consequences be damned.

"What are you doing, boy?" Death asked.

"Fate, can you hear me?"

Moments passed. Nothing.

"Fate, I summon you!"

What if...what if she couldn't hear me? June had met with Kimber in the astral, in the world between, but I had no access to the Shroud. No way to get there and call out. Could a cry even manage to carry from one realm to the next?

"Juniper, answer me!"

Death grasped my shoulders. "I can summon her for you, but you will pay a great price."

"Do it! I don't care what happens to me. Just save her!"

He nodded once, and his shadows emerged from his sleeves, slithering across the floor to climb up the mirror's edge.

Cadagon raised his hands, a deep sigh on his lips as he looked over Kim's corpse. "By way of night and day reborn, I summon Fate in all her scorn."

A vision rippled in the floor-length mirror, and light shone through the surface.

Juniper appeared. "Who dares draw upon my power?"

"I do," I sobbed.

"Cooper?" She squinted. "What is going on?"

The pressure in my chest grew tighter, and I wondered for a brief second if a heart could truly break. Because, shit, it felt like it.

I extended my slit palm to her. "Make a pact with me! Turn back time! Kim...I—I couldn't save her. Please!"

June's sights drifted to the gory scene behind me, and she clapped a hand over her mouth, tears pooling in her eyes. "How did this happen?"

"It doesn't matter now. What matters is you turning back time and giving me another chance."

"I can't just turn back time. There are limits to what I am able to do. Rules I must abide by—"

"Then break them! Anathema will die without her!" My lip quivered. "*I* will die without her."

June's brow pinched. "In order to turn back time, I have to draw on raw energy."

"Anything! Name it!" I leaned closer.

"But—"

"Tell me what to do, damn it!"

"To turn back time, you would have to let me draw on your soul energy. For every minute passed since her..." She swallowed the word down. "For every minute, I require a year of your life."

Her words hit like a sledgehammer. How many minutes had passed? How many years would be cut off my life if I— Fuck, it didn't matter. I would save Kim. "Do it."

"Are you sure—"

"Stop wasting time and do it!" I wept.

"As you wish." Milky white seeped across her golden irises. "Repeat after me: 'Fate, restore the time that is lost. I offer my lifeblood to pay the cost.'"

"Fate, restore the time that is lost. I offer my lifeblood to pay the cost."

"Death, send me my libation," she ordered.

Cadagon took my hand, and a tendril of his magic bowed over the pooled blood in my palm, drinking it in. A shiver ran up my spine as the shadow wound down my leg and disappeared through the mirror, leaving a glassy ripple in its wake.

Please, let this work.

Juniper dipped down to collect it before swallowing the shadow whole. Strands of golden string appeared in her hands—their edges frayed—and piece by piece, she knit them back together. With each new stitch, my limbs grew heavier, the onset of severe brain fog clouding my vision. Slowly, I found myself slipping towards the floor. I pressed my forehead against the cool wooden boards as sleep summoned me, but I didn't dare close my eyes. It was working. The spell was actually working! A final pluck of her ethereal string, and my stomach dropped.

"It is done," Juniper said.

Body heavy, I dragged myself to Kimber's side just in time to see her heave in rhythmic breaths once again. I laid my ear against her chest, savoring her steady heartbeat; and relief coiled around me.

I turned towards the mirror, my cheeks hot. "Thank you."

"You did the correct thing in summoning me." Juniper forced a smile. "But you should know, the amount of time I had to drain from you—"

"It doesn't matter."

I ran my hand through Kim's bloody hair. She was alive. Anything else paled in comparison to that.

"Savor the time you have, Cooper. It will be precious. And please...remind her how much I love her?"

I gave June a sure nod. "Of course."

She choked back tears, and her reflection disappeared.

Cadagon settled on his knees at my side. "What you did was admirable, boy. She is lucky to have you."

"I'm the lucky one."

To my shock, Death wrapped his arms around me, tucking me to his chest.

"Thank you. I do not know what I would do if I lost her. My faith in you to protect her was not misplaced."

I relaxed into his embrace. No words. No explanation. Just acceptance. This man was no monster, though Anathema deemed him one. He didn't seek gratitude or recognition; his pride in protecting Kimber served him well enough, despite her hatred for him. In fact, part of me believed he'd *planned* for her to loathe him. Bred it purposefully. Because the further she was from him, the safer she'd be from the secrets that bound him. A tinge of jealousy wrapped around my mind.

What I would give to have had my own father love me in such a way.

I waded through the darkness in Death's wing of the castle. With Kim settled and resting for the night, the reality of my situation weighed on me. I'm not entirely sure where I aimed to go, but the pelting raindrops against the windows had lulled me into mindless wandering. There would be no running from my fate. Malachi would find me. And he would kill me.

A cynical laugh slipped past my lips, echoing around the quaint study I'd stumbled into. Even if I managed to find a way to evade the demon Lord and Odin, my deal with Juniper would come knocking long before I was ready to answer. I ran a finger along the bookshelf, suede bindings rough against my fingertip. How many minutes had Kim truly been dead? How many years had I sacrificed to bring her back? By the time I'd knelt at her side after her breath returned, her skin had brushed cold against my palms. Did I really want to know how much time I had left before Fate's bargain came due for collection?

No. Because given the chance, I'd have done it all again.

A clap of thunder and a flash of lightning filled the unlit space, and I noticed a winding staircase I hadn't previously. Curious and hungry for a distraction, I ascended the narrow hall. Bursting through the top door, I found myself on a landing overlooking Anathema in its entirety: a vast display made blurry by the heavy rainfall. As I squinted to make out my childhood home, a thought began to form. A dark, sickening thought. I looked to the ground, the downpour drenching my clothes. I still had a chance to make my death my own.

I could jump.

All this pain, all this guilt: it could simply...go away. My stomach twisted as I stepped up onto the stone ledge. A gust of wind would send me crashing to the castle steps below. Nobody could survive that. Sure, there was no guarantee I'd die on impact, but what Malachi had planned for me would surely be far more painful. I closed my eyes against the storm and extended my arms outward. Whatever would happen, would happen.

"Suicide is never the answer," Death's voice rang out.

I turned to find him ten feet down the wall, his feet dangling over the edge and shoulders hunched—a strange departure from the king's usual poised demeanor. Something told me he'd come to the rooftop to ponder his end just as I had. He tapped the empty space at his side, his face soaked and dripping. I glanced downward. He was right. Taking my own life would never solve the problems I faced or the ones I'd created; and while jumping might spare me torture, it would ensure Kimber's in the end. Heartache born of such grief never truly healed. I heaved a breath. I'd be wrong to bring more suffering to her door.

I stepped back off the ledge, the rain around me calming in time. Now only a light drizzle, I took my spot at Cadagon's side, and the true expanse of Anathema's beauty overcame me. I studied the way the kingdom defied gravity: the four courts suspended above a vast void of darkness. Waterfalls poured over the edges, their waters dissipating into mist and intermixing with the stars. I wondered if the story of the original Death's tears having created them was true. If he still wept for his lost love.

My sights swept farther to the paths leading to each court rounding along the borders of the realm. While their closest edges attached to nothing, I knew they came to rest at the castle courtyard somehow. A marvelous sight: one not many would get to see in their lifetimes. No matter how long or short.

"Amazing," I whispered.

"Truly," Death agreed, his gaze on the horizon. "You know, I used to come here often as a boy to clear my mind."

"Clear your mind of what?"

"My father's wrath mostly. I have a sense you are familiar with the sentiment?"

I hadn't let myself go to that dark place for years. I'd buried those memories behind an internal wall I had no intention of ever breaking down; but Death's words brought them all back, like a landslide careening down a mountain. My father had been a cruel man who'd spewed his wrath on many undeserving people, even his own wife. He'd demanded perfection. Strength. Emotion, to him, was simply a waste of time and energy.

I cleared my throat. "I don't think he cared much for my 'bleeding heart' as he called it."

"Mmm, that does sound like something Mathis would say."

"You knew him?"

"Of course. Quite well, in fact. I have always made it a habit to keep a keen eye on the Lords and Ladies of my land." He continued, "Your mother: she was quite a woman. I sincerely regret her having married your father. He was an arrogant man, full of vitriol; and though he carried himself like a man of honor—proud to uphold the Talonborn name—it did not take long to see through his façade. When you have suffered abuse at the hands of the one who is meant to protect you, it becomes second nature to pick up on such things in others, I suppose."

"I can see that."

"Indeed. You know, once I'd been so bold as to fight back. I believed maybe my father's rage was some sort of test of which I was unaware. A way to snuff out my weakness. 'A gentle hand is a weak hand,' he'd tell me. And 'a weak king is a dead king.'" Death smiled despite himself. "But there had been no test. Simply an angry man who never wished to be a father."

The night I'd lost my mother came back to me, but this time with the edges filled in. A part of me understood why she'd gone back for him. Love consumes. But in choosing him, she'd abandoned me. Him: the man who'd taken his anger out on his own son. Him: the one who had taken her with him in the end like he'd always said he would. I pinched my eyes shut, and quickly wiped away a stray tear. The bastard.

Death squeezed my shoulder. "For what it is worth, I do not see your tears as weakness. Not as our fathers did. Feeling one's pain is an exceptional strength. It purges out the old, enlightens us to the things that fuel our souls. A life void of suffering is impossible; but when you accept those dark, bleeding parts of yourself, it guides you to the things *worth* suffering for. Like your unwavering love for my daughter."

"Loving her came easy. She's the only one who ever cared." I tilted my head back towards the sky, the raindrops kissing my cheeks. "I never had a place, never belonged, until she made me part of her world."

"You belong right here. This kingdom, these people, need you just as much as they need Kimberly. Balance, dear one: that is what this realm was built upon. Her rage and your heart. Together, you will bring change to Anathema. Why else do you think I've watched over you all these years?"

His admission gave me pause. "Watched over *me*?"

"Yes, *you*. Or do you truly believe our first meeting was happenstance?" He smirked. "I heard your impending death call to me across realms. And so, I came."

"I...I had no idea."

"As I intended. While you may feel that you have never had a family to watch over you, and though I may not fit that role in your mind, I hope you know I have always cared greatly for you, Cooper."

The notion shook me. My past flashed before my eyes of when I'd fallen into the quarry, splitting my skull open. But even before then...the summer I'd gone to the river alone for solace but had waded too far in, and somehow washed up on shore amid the white-water rapids. Or the time I'd been so recklessly drunk that I'd tried to take on four men in an alley who'd cornered a woman. The beating I'd taken that night had been *brutal*, but I'd walked away. The nurses had called it a miracle. I'd never considered myself as someone with a death wish. But looking back, I'd pushed the boundaries over and over, believing I was simply lucky.

I cleared my throat. "All those times I should have died...that was you?"

"Indeed. I will say, you kept me quite busy. As did she."

A knot formed in my throat. He'd watched over me. For most of my life, I'd believed I mattered to no one. Believed I'd been forgotten by my people, abandoned by my family, had failed my father; and yet, Death himself had kept a watchful eye on my life. Words escaped me. So I let my feelings guide me and wrapped my arms around Cadagon. He didn't hesitate to fold his arms around me in return, a light chuckle rattling my jaw atop his shoulder.

His hold on me tightened. "My dear boy, you have always had a home."

"I—I don't know what to say."

"Then say nothing." He pulled back and smiled. "But you must know, everything I have done is for you two."

"But you let her hate you..."

"Her hatred I can live with. But her demise? That I would not suffer. Bear in mind, I've never had grandiose beliefs of reconciling with her or earning a place in her life, despite the desire. If I could do it over again, I would."

The living flame in his irises pulsed. I knew that pain: how loving someone, committing yourself to their success, was both lonely and fulfilling in one breath. A beautiful heartache.

As if reading my mind, he said, "My debts will come due as they do for all who dabble in dark dealings. I saved you because I knew the time would come when I could no longer protect her. Even in your youth, you were not afraid to make the difficult choices. You are willing to sacrifice for what you hold dear, and that is precisely why I chose you. Why *she* chose you."

"Chose me..." I chuckled. "If only she'd chosen me."

"You truly believe that?" His shoulders squared. "After watching her search for ways to free you from that coffin, after all those years of shared laughter and tears, you still believe she does not want you?"

"Not the way I want her."

"Secrets, even those concealed with the best intentions, deter a woman like Kimber. The time will come when you will be free to share your heart completely. And on that day?" He grinned. "On that day, I have no doubt the feelings she has for you will shine through."

I hopped back to my feet, my hands fisted at my sides. "And say you're right. Say she does want me. Then what? I tell her how our life together will end in me, once again, repaying a debt? How am I supposed to look her in the eyes and tell her I bartered years of my life away, Cadagon?"

"Perhaps you focus on what time you are allotted, not how much you have lost."

"How many years?" I asked under my breath, unable to meet his gaze. "I know you know. How many years do I have left?"

"Do you truly wish to know?"

I weighed his question. Considered what might come of knowing. On one hand, if I knew, I could better plan out my days. But on the other, I'd always have a gray cloud looming overhead, reminding me my happiness was finite.

"I...I don't know."

"Consider this," he said gently. "If I had given up—knowing my days were numbered as they are—Anathema would have fallen to ruin alongside me. Everything I have sacrificed would have been in vain."

My jaw clenched. "How did you do it? Go on when you knew death would come for you?"

"Death comes for us all. He cannot be bought or deceived or convinced. But I found peace in knowing that when my time comes, I made those choices of my own volition, and the consequences are worthwhile. In the end, my death will be on my own terms." His pained smile creased the corners of his eyes. "At the hands of a friend."

My body clenched. A friend...me.

When I'd made him that promise, things had been different. I'd believed his heart was twisted and depraved. That he'd forced others into unbreakable pacts. Hell, I'd blamed him for my people's destruction, pinning *every* awful thing in Anathema's recent history on him. Because why wouldn't I? He'd allowed me to believe it. Coaxed me. I'd thought him selfish, callused, and cruel. But now...

"You can't seriously expect me to kill you? After everything you've shared, I can't possibly—"

"You must. You made a promise. Are you not a man of your word?"

"I am, but this is different. You know that!" Weight spread across my chest. "How can you ask this of me? Tell me all these things and then expect me to end your life when I've barely gotten a chance to know you?"

"Because it is how it must be. One cycle ends for another to begin. Such is life."

The clouds overhead parted, and the moon shone down across his weathered face. For the first time, he looked upon me completely unguarded. Dark circles encased his eyes. He was so tired and worn and...afraid. But he didn't hide it away as he normally did. Instead, he let the character he'd been forced to play fade away. This was no longer Death. This was a father. A protector. A man.

"No," I muttered. "I won't do it."

"Do not mourn for me. I have lived. It is time for you two to do the same." He reached into his robe and returned with two wax-sealed envelopes, extending them to me. "For my children. When the time comes, and the dust of my reign has settled, you may open them, but not a second before. I will place them here for safekeeping."

For my children. I'd finally found my home, my family...maybe even a father. And now I held his life in my hands? What a cruel twist of fate. Cadagon made his way to the wall nearest the door, removed a loose brick, and stuffed the letters inside.

"Return for these when the deed is done. Feel your feelings, and then move on to the bright future laid out before you."

My vision blurred. "I can't. I won't—"

"I know you will uphold your promise, because you are aware of the hard truth we face in our realm."

"I don't understand how this is the only choice we have. There has to be another way."

A heavy sigh drifted through him. "In time, you will come to learn that the right choice is rarely the easiest one."

Like killing a man who doesn't deserve it...

"When one is bound, options have a tendency to evaporate. Vehement choices become reality, which is what makes this next part so difficult." he whispered.

"Next part?"

"Remember who you are. Fight. Win. I know you can."

He opened the door. With a final glance, Death disappeared down the shadowed stairwell. Nasheesh materialized in his wake.

"You. What are you doing here?" I hissed.

His fingers laced together before him, and he stepped out onto the roof. "Tying up some loose ends years in the making."

Loose ends? What did that mean? Wait a damn second...

The blood pact Cadagon was trapped in...the secrets and his inability to act...had his own *advisor* bound him to a life of silent agony? Why? What did Nasheesh stand to gain from it? Honestly, I didn't care to know. Whatever his reasons, they were the words of a traitor, and a lying tongue can't be used for blackmail once it's cut out. I was done with deception. Done with *him*.

"You really think you're a match for me, old man?" I laughed.

"Physically? I would never dream of it, *impostor*. But mentally? You are no match for me."

"Pompous as ever. Don't worry, Nassie, I'll make your death swift."

He shifted to the side with a laugh.

Odin emerged, chains in hand. "I am afraid you will have to get through me first."

Chapter Seventeen

THE OLD GODS ARE DEAD

Odin stepped towards me as the door skidded shut behind him and tightened his hold on the chains.

"Surprise," he snarled.

My nails dug into my palms. "You won't take me without a fight."

"Oh, I hope not. I would be disappointed if you didn't struggle to save that miserable little life of yours." He stepped closer. "By all means, fight. But know this: you will lose. And you will die."

Ha, right.

"You have no idea how much joy it will bring me to slay the last of the Talonborn line. Worthless, weak beings, the lot of you!"

"That's funny, because I was thinking the same about you, *dog*."

His grin widened. "May the best man win."

"Oh, I plan to."

I reached to my hip, my fingertips brushing the empty leather holster there, and my stomach dropped. Of *course*, because nothing—including defending my own damn life—could come easy, could it? Odin rattled the chains in his hand, taunting me. Cadagon's words cut through, hammering in the back of my mind.

Fight. Win. I know you can.

The simple fact was: I had to win. For my kingdom. For Kim. Hell, for *me*! Allowing a rabid dog to continue spreading disease, to breed filth, wasn't an option. Odin had to die. Period. I'd rip his throat out with my bare teeth if I had to. I rolled my shoulders, lowered my stance, and launched at him, nearly landing a blow; but he stepped to the side just in time. His elbow came down hard between my shoulders with a hard *thwack*, almost bringing me to my knees. *That speed…* I pivoted through the pain and managed to connect my next punch straight to his face.

"Good one." He laughed and spit a mouthful of blood at his feet. "But I am sure by now you are aware I can take a beating. Ask Kimberly; she knows."

Her name on his tongue made my entire body shake.

"You keep her name out of your fucking mouth!"

Again, I lunged, but his fist collided with my gut; and I keeled over, the wind knocked out of me. Shit, he was fast. The hybrid spell had easily doubled Odin's reaction speed, which didn't bode well for me, and I heaved for a full breath. I'd have to go at this from another angle. Study him and get out ahead somehow. I shuffled backwards to allow a few feet between us and focused on his footwork.

"Tired already? What a shame," he patronized.

"Fuck you!"

He stepped left foot over right, leaning back on his heels slightly as he did. I faked him out, his footwork repeating the same motions, step for step. *Bingo.* If I timed it right, I could counterbalance him, but there could be no room for hesitation. I darted, secured my hold around his waist, and slammed him against the rooftop railing. My hold cemented around his jaw. With a little more force, he'd tumble over, falling ninety feet to the thorny garden below. Hybrid or not, it'd take a miracle to survive a fall like that.

I pushed him farther over the open air. "Better make your amends to the Gods, Odin. You'll be seeing them very soon."

His chuckle rattled against my palm. "Fool."

I saw the magic curved over his shoulders a second too late. It sharpened to pointed tips arching above my head, and with a shrill whistle, it descended upon me. I was no match for its speed or force. Like a razor blade slicing through warm butter, Odin's amalgamated magic stabbed into my arm, my chest, my rib cage and flung me across the rooftop. My head cracked hard against stone—the magic pinning me in place—and though I fought, it held firm. Blood gushed and pooled around me as his magic buried itself deeper. I lifted my head, my neck bristling at the dizzying weight. I needed to get out from under him before he sank more hooks in me.

Odin straddled me. "I must say, I am disappointed. I expected more from you. Such a shame."

His magic retracted enough for him to collect my wrists, binding them in the rusty chains. No...no! This wasn't how I went! I told my arms to swing. Told my body to rise, but to no avail.

"I'll...kill...you..." I forced out.

Darkness tinged the edges of my vision as I lurched forward; the unnerving awareness of my scalp peeling open along the crack in my skull made me ill. *Damn it.* I turned my head to spill my guts. Not good. I'd resigned myself to Death claiming my life years ago—believed his hands would deliver my soul to the afterlife personally—but how wrong I'd been.

Forgive me, Kim.

Odin's boot crashed into my face, and my fight left me. Abandoned me. But as my consciousness began to fade, I made out Nasheesh's final words.

"Take him to the mines. Malachi wishes to end this himself."

My eyes fluttered open.

Throbbing temples.

Stabbing needles in my wrists.

Pitch black.

A steady *drip, drip, drip* in the distance.

The world spun, and the black void claimed me again.

I jerked back to consciousness—the sensation of falling making me catch my breath—and the room quivered. I shuffled to sit up, gain my bearings, but...nothing.

The hell...

My pulse hammered in my skull as I tried again. Chains rattled behind me as my vision sharpened, and it became clear exactly how far up shit's creek I was. Bound. I was fucking bound! My sights frantically searched the damp space, finding nothing but stone. Stalagmites stabbed down from the ceiling and jutted up from the floor, like a gaping mouth prepared to crush me in its jaws. Lovely. This would do wonders for my claustrophobia. I reminded myself to breath and turned my head to the right. In the corner, murky water from a crevice in the cave wall dripped into a full bucket, the excess droplets sizzling in the coals of a small fire. Beyond it, a long tunnel crept off and disappeared in the distance.

"Finally, he wakes," a low voice echoed ahead.

Malachi.

"Where—where am I?"

"Do you like it?" He motioned around the room, keeping his face just beyond the light's reach. "It was quite important to me that your final resting place be...private, so you might erode and decay in your loneliness. That is what you fear most, is it not? Dying alone? It must be. Why else would you have followed that insufferable woman to this realm like a lovesick puppy, straight into the arms of your own defeat?"

I lurched forward. "Let me go, coward."

"Oh, that ship has sailed, *Lyvias*. Or should I say, Copernicus?"

He took a step closer. The flames reflected in his shiny leather shoes. So he finally figured it out. Took the bastard long enough.

"I know who you are and of your naive mission to restore balance to the kingdom as your forefathers before you. But need I remind you," he sneered, "they failed just the same as you. I suppose in that regard, you upheld the Talonborn legacy perfectly: utter failure."

"You bastard—"

"Accept it. You have lost. This little façade of yours, this childish game: it is over. There is nowhere left for you or your disgraced queen to hide."

I sucked in a breath, wincing at my bruised ribs. "Where is she?"

"At this very moment? Likely mourning the loss of her new love, I would assume. Poor thing took the news quite hard. Understandable, really, considering you snuck off in the night, your sole explanation penned in a letter about how you no longer wanted her. Seems abandonment is a sentiment she is familiar with."

My stomach dropped as my fingers constricted around the chains. "You monster!"

"Ah, ah, is that any way to speak to your king?"

"The day Anathema crowns you king is the day all sanity is lost. It'll never happen!"

"That is where you are wrong. See, as the next eligible Lord in the cycle, it is my right—no, my *duty*—to wed the future queen."

Lies. He was lying; he had to be! There's no way Death would allow such a thing, unless...unless his pact kept him from intervening. "If you touch her, I swear—"

"Touch her?"

Malachi stepped forward, his shadows dispersing as he glared down at me. I receded. The sight of him was so heinous that I considered for a second if it was a trick of the light. It simply couldn't be real. My lip curled as I beheld my enemy's true form for the first time: marred beyond repair. Risen burns encased every visible inch of skin; pink, oozing blisters riddled his face. The club's flames had melted his ears clean off and corroded through his left cheek to reveal two rows of charred molars. My eyes widened, and I bit my tongue. While he hadn't died, he must have wanted to. The corded muscles in his temples—his jaw clenched and grinding—told me it took everything in him to remain standing in that moment. But his hatred proved more powerful than the pain. He reared his mutilated fist back, ready to smash me square in the mouth, when a second figure emerged from the shadows.

Nasheesh caught his hand. "Save your strength for the heathen queen. Allow me?"

Malachi considered his offer, a war of violent desire and the reality of his condition raging in his expression. Finally, he relinquished. Nasheesh's serpent-like stare fixed on me as he removed a bludgeon from his robe, bashing it across my cheek. Again. And again. My shoulder—clearly dislocated—swayed from the crushing force, sending shock waves across my body with each new blow.

"Not only will I touch her," Malachi snarled at Nasheesh's side, "but I promise you this: I will *shatter* her. Destroy her body, mind, and soul. I will take and take every minuscule semblance of pride she has and force her to bow at my feet as I slit her throat!"

Blood and spit dribbled down my chin as I peered up at him through swollen eyes. A laugh built in me. "Fucking...idiot...you're no match for her power."

"For now, maybe. But when I devour her soul?" He pushed the advisor aside and leaned into my face. "Take her power as my own and cast her corpse at Chaos's feet? There is not a being in this realm or the next that will be able to stop me."

"You're bluffing."

"You think so, do you? Answer me this then. Say if one discovered a way to, I don't know, circumvent Fate, would that sway your disbelief?"

He dropped his face an inch from mine, and an unforeseen glamour fell from his eyes. In them, I saw the courts of Anathema reflected back at me: demon, vampire, and shapeshifter—all in one somehow. My veins turned to ice. The world shifted on its axis as the last pieces of his sinister plan clicked together. Odin's hybrid abilities truly had been a test: an experiment to see if a lesser being was able to hold such power without splitting in two. But a Lord? They'd be able to endure *far* more. Malachi had already absorbed the power of three courts, leaving only one. The reapers. And the feral smirk on his face ensured me he'd set his sights high for that particular sacrifice.

He circled me, his hands clasped behind his back. "You know, it's true the Ancient Lores were locked away for their ravenous taste for mortals. But fill their bellies, and you would be surprised how quickly they can become an ally, willing to disclose the darkest spells lost to time. Even ones capable of overthrowing Fate's divinity to insert a new, more powerful Reigning Reaper line. *My* line."

"It's not possible. The Old Gods would never allow it—"

"The Old Gods are dead! If they still held sway over this realm, they would never have allowed atrocities to ascend the throne! They would have eradicated King Shadra decades ago. They would have seen my strength and rewarded it!" His shoulders shook, singed hair falling into his face. "I am the new god, and you will submit to my will!"

He crossed the cave in two strides and retrieved a red-hot iron prod from the fire. A psychotic grin tore the already cavernous hole in his cheek, but he didn't flinch.

"Will you bow to your king?"

I sucked the blood leaching inside my cheeks into the back of my throat and spit it straight in his eye. "You are no king!"

He wiped it off, simultaneously burying the poker in my shoulder. A scream ripped up my throat, but I swallowed it down. I wouldn't let this asshole have the satisfaction of seeing me break. With my hands white-knuckled on my bindings, I gritted my teeth through scalding pain as the smell of burnt flesh filled the air, like roasted meat over a fire pit. Smoke and iron and char. Malachi pulled the poker free, burying it in my other shoulder before I could blink.

"Fuck," I muttered under my breath. Sweat beaded on my forehead.

Fate, Mother Goddess, if you're out there...help me, please!

This time, he didn't remove it. The tip bubbled in my skin as he walked to the fire, looked to me, and suspended the full bucket over the flames.

"It would have been far less painful to bow," Nasheesh said with a cocky smirk.

"Indeed." Malachi smoothed his tie. "Now if you'll excuse me, I have a wedding to attend."

Malachi doused the flames, and their footsteps receded into the distance. Alone and defeated, I released my pent-up scream into the surrounding black. As the poker cooled—my body trembling—a hollowness settled in my gut. It was over.

I'd lost.

Cadagon's belief in me had been severely misplaced. I was no hero. I was weak. Useless. Fate hadn't smiled on me like my mother had claimed. The Goddess had *abandoned* me the same way she'd abandoned Anathema, despite Juniper's attempts to restore faith in the Old God's power. Now, not only was my kingdom primed to fall, but the woman who possessed every part of my existence, who'd loved me in spite of all my broken pieces...she—she could die believing I'd abandoned her as she thought her father had.

I shouted into the void until my sore throat couldn't take it any longer and hung my head.

I'd lost *everything*.

Chapter Eighteen

VENGEANCE

A scuffle against stone tore me from my fever dream.

"Hello?"

I waited, listening intently. One second, then another, and my shoulders sagged. Rats, most likely, ready to descend upon me and pick my bones clean, which would be a blessing honestly, sparing me months of my body eating itself from the inside out. Already my gums throbbed from thirst, so let them come and free me from the torture of my own failure. Adding insult to injury, a violent cough rose up, tar catching in my throat. My pact with Death: also a failure. Kim was in danger, and I could do nothing about it but die slowly.

Another shuffle in the distance stirred me, this one heavier. I squinted, searching. "Hello? Anybody there?"

Silence gave way to rapid footsteps, and a glimmer of light flashed down the tunnel, here then gone. My pulse clapped in my ears. Was I hallucinating? Had hysteria set in so soon? The steady, relentless *drips* about the cave resumed. Right, I'd lost my damn mind; I'd cracked, shattered, and— Heavy thumps drew nearer; the light suddenly returned.

"Your Highness! There you are," a man called.

My stomach jumped. Not just any man... "Adari? How did you find me?"

Magic hissed from his fingertips like a roaring torch as he stepped around me, busying himself with my shackles.

"Your magic is hard to miss." He snickered. "Stunning, really: the thick burgundy of it. Unique, but a tad forceful if I may say. It nearly choked me out in my sleep before leading me here to you. I apologize for my delay, but these tunnels are quite vast."

"I—" My words caught in my throat. "Thank you for coming for me."

"Thank the Goddess. Her gifted sight is the sole reason I was able to find this place. She has a fondness for you, you know."

"Well, she has a funny way of showing it."

"What can you do? The Old Gods are, at the very least, cynical in their approach. But I would never have found you without her help."

I offered up a silent apology for my lack of faith.

Lend me your favor one last time, Fate. Don't let me be too late.

The chains *clinked* a second later, and my wrists fell free like an answered prayer. I folded my dislocated arm into my lap, massaging the deep cuts in my wrists left behind by my bindings. My knees shook as I pushed to stand, the adrenaline coursing through my veins lending me strength.

"Kim?" I asked through clenched teeth.

"We must hurry. The ceremony is about to begin."

There was still a chance then, however small. My teeth gnashed as Adari wrapped my good arm over his shoulder, and we started down the twisty tunnels.

I'm coming, baby. Hold on a little longer.

We wound this way and that, around and down and up, following the guiding mist of Kimber's and my blood pact magic. Its fleeting trail solidified its intent: the time had come to deliver on my promise to kill Death.

Rickety scaffolding caught my eye as we stepped out into the cloudy night. The moon peeked through in disrupted bursts, illuminating the mouth of the mine behind us. What a vile but clever place to hide your enemy, considering nobody would simply wander into a dilapidated cave. Far too dangerous.

Thank the Gods Adari had.

With each step, his light burrowed into me, gently stitching bits of broken flesh and bone together inside me like a spider weaving silk. "You're healing me?"

"The best I can, yes. But when this is over, I bid you to return to me. There are some things that cannot be mended so quickly."

My curiosity piqued; I marveled at the luminescent tendrils dancing beneath my skin. How? Just...how? Healing magic stemmed from Elysium. The only way Adari could possess such abilities was divine favor. To be born of the realm of eternal night, and yet possess both Death's and Fate's strengths was nothing short of miraculous. Gratitude rushed through me, and my spine straightened as the worst aches receded. This man—this stranger who owed me nothing—he'd saved my life.

And now, I'd use it to save another.

We rounded over the hill leading into the castle courtyard, and I gripped Adari's shirt collar, peering through the garden gates at the lamenting scene. Kim stood on the alter, Death at her side arguing with Nasheesh. I removed my arm from Adari's shoulder.

"Find Suri. Tell her I am here and to keep a watchful eye."

"Yes, Your Highness." He bowed and disappeared around the courtyard wall.

And so it began: the start of the end.

I cracked my neck, heading through the arched, rose-covered gates. My power flowed freely, ready to release the wrath I'd swallowed down like bitter chocolate sticking in my throat. I *would* reclaim what was mine. I swore on my mother's grave: Malachi would be fucking buried six feet under this night, even if it meant I went with him.

Kimber was an absolute vision of power and vengeance, scythes clutched in her hands. I steadied my breath. I'd made it in time. I dragged myself around the backmost chairs, and my steps faltered. Malachi's shadows coiled around Kim's ankles, slithering up her legs.

"Do you agree to this union?" Death asked. "To binding your soul to the court of power and sharing your rule with Malachi Avarti?"

My spine stiffened, mouth turning to sandpaper. Avarti? As in...*Nasheesh Avarti?*

You've got to be fucking kidding me! While I'd known they were in this together, I couldn't for the life of me figure out what they aimed to gain by their alliance, but now it made perfect sense. The advisor had been pulling the strings the entire time. Vying for his son to take the crown. My crown. *My* bride! I picked up the pace, my knees giving out every other step. But I persisted.

"Speak up," Malachi hissed.

"Don't you dare order me," Kim seethed in response.

I cleared the backmost chairs, heads turning towards me with hushed gasps. The whispers spread like wildfire, each one granting me more confidence.

That's right. I'm back, bitches.

"Princess, you *must* answer," Death prodded.

"I—I..." Kimber stumbled. "Well, I—"

"I object!" I boomed from the center aisle. "It is my right, and mine alone, to stand by the queen's side."

To my astonishment, I believed my own words.

Every eye fell on me, but the only ones I saw were hers. My vision tunneled straight to her smile which pinned me in place. She ran to me, blatant relief washing over her as she prodded my face in fear I might evaporate into thin air at any second. Her gentle touch settled in my bones like a healing tonic.

"You came back," she whispered.

I cupped her cheek in my palm. "I'll always come for you."

She hiked my arm over her shoulder to steady my swaying steps.

Nasheesh shot up from his seat and laced his shaky hands together. "Sire, this is blasphemous; the ceremony has already begun!"

"What is blasphemous," I snarled, "are the lengths you went to keep me from being here today, Nasheesh Avarti. Tell them: how you sought me out in the dead of night, stole me away, and saw to my torture by your own hand."

Voices from the crowd tangled together in a mess of objections and questions. I honed in on Cadagon who offered me a half grin. It was gone in a flash, but that small gesture confirmed my suspicions. I'd fleshed out the one who'd bound him to secrecy, and now we could end him for good. To think, the one who'd forced him into a blood pact was the very same man who stood at his side pretending to have the king's best interest in mind while secretly puppeteering his every move. A wolf in sheep's clothing.

Death addressed his people. "Calm yourselves. Malachi Avarti, step down."

"I—I had no knowledge of this," Malachi lied through his teeth.

With a snap, Death sealed his lips, and armed guards stood at attention for their orders.

"Guards, see that these traitors remain firmly planted in their seats without any further disruptions. I want them to see their own failing firsthand before they lose their sights completely." Cadagon turned to Kim and me. "Lyvias, Kimberly, please take your rightful places."

Death continued the ceremony as I drank Kim in, and my rapid pulse calmed. Her irises flamed anew, stealing the air from my lungs as sparks flashed in her shadows like embers twisted in a violent wind. My *gods*, she was radiant. This image of her—glistening black gown hugging her curves in all the right places—would stay with me forever. Gravity no longer cemented me to this plane: she did. A wave of pride swept through my chest.

Queen of Anathema, at last.

"Royal heirs," Cadagon boomed, "take one another's hands and repeat after me. 'Bound in blood and rite, I will lead my people through eternal night.'"

Kim's shadows nipped at my fingertips, and we repeated what was asked.

"Together," I mouthed.

She nodded, returning my silent encouragement.

Death raised his hands to the masses. "Once again, we come to a pact in blood."

Kimber sliced her palm open—the scent of her blood making my head spin—before setting the blade's edge on my own. Pinpricks crawled up my spine in time with the fresh incision, and the invisible cord tethered between us drew our hands together. Our blood sank and swam in the other's veins, the most unusual euphoria spreading through me. Finally, our magic returned united, bursting over us like a supernova, and the residual, starry mist swept about her hair. To anyone else, it was simply the wind playing with the strands of her ashen hair, but I knew better. Our pact was about to be fulfilled, and the bond we'd made knew it. Grew ravenous.

"By night and balance bestowed to me by Fate herself, I deem this marriage bound," Cadagon called. "Both of you take a knee."

His gaze never strayed from mine—locked on with obvious intent—and he removed a charred-bone crown from an ornate box. Everything he wanted to say but couldn't lay in one final, silent exchange. His finger tapped the bone halo. The singe marks...they were by design. He knew. Knew what I'd done to take down Malachi. How I'd almost succeeded. A challenge flickered in his weathered stare: *Finish this.* I offered him a pained smile, and he settled the crown atop my head.

Gods, don't let me fail him.

He nodded before turning to his beloved daughter. Pure pride and adoration showed on his face as he removed his crown, placed it on Kim's head, and whispered something for her ears alone. I wondered then if she saw it: the deep love he had for her. The deals he'd made in her name. Wondered if, maybe, her last seconds with her father could be ones worth cherishing and not ones that'd mar her soul with regret.

I battled my mind, the urge to tell Kim everything dropping like a brick in my stomach. If I told her before the deed was done, before unchangeable actions were put in play, I could spare her the guilt. The shame. But Death's attention flickered to me in warning.

You made a promise, boy. His words slithered across my skull.

Though it killed me inside, I had to deliver if I wanted to ensure the sacrifices he'd made were worth it in the end. I heaved a breath. His legacy would live on.

"Now rise, Queen and King of Anathema," Cadagon said, "and seal your nightly union with a kiss, like your forefathers and mothers before you."

My heart swelled. I peeled back Kim's veil with shaky hands, took her in my arms, and sealed our union with a deep kiss.

My best friend. My queen. My home.

Let her see you. Death's words waded through my mind again. *The real you, Copernicus Talonborn.*

He was right: the time had come, no matter the consequences. I stepped back—my arms loosely circled around her hips—and bit back a scream as my body rearranged into my true form. Into me. Though quicker than other transitions, the shift locked my jaw nonetheless. Muscles shredded and reformed, ligaments clicked together, and bone shifted. The final rib locked in place in time with my shoulder—the reconnecting joint making me hiss—and I held my breath. This was it. No more hiding. No more secrets. Right then and there, the most important person in my life would either accept me or strike me down.

In tandem with the crowd's gasps, Kimber's eyes opened, and her face tangled in an imperceptible expression.

She swallowed hard. "Cooper?"

"My Queen." I bowed.

She snatched my sleeve, pulling me close, a million questions written on her face. Time slowed as I awaited her decision. The ensuing chaos of the courts dissipated around us as Death's booming orders bought us time.

"What is happening?" she asked, tears pooling in her wide eyes. "How are you here? How...just, how? Was...was it you all along?"

Before I could get a word in, she dove into my arms, pressing her face to my chest. I sighed, and relief washed over me. She saw me the same as she always had. I wanted to spend forever there: in her arms, telling her the things I'd been damned to keep quiet. To explain how and why and when. But the guest's objections grew louder and Death's voice sterner. Our reunion—sweet and painful in the same breath—would have to wait. I squeezed Kim tight.

"Almost," I finally whispered in her hair. Her honey scent drifted over me as I kissed her forehead. "I'll tell you everything, Kim. I promise. But you have to trust me right now. End this madness, Lady Death. You're the only one who can. I'll be waiting when the ashes settle."

She followed my sight line to Cadagon and shifted on her feet. She knew what came next. What we'd sworn ourselves to.

"I don't know if I can do this," she muttered.

Hell, I didn't know if I could either, but the wheels were already in motion: the characters cast, the plot laid out, the ending at our fingertips. Though my conviction wavered, for her I would do what I'd always done. I'd put on a brave face, swallow my fears, and get shit done.

"Together?" I asked, and rubbed my thumb along her jaw.

A wicked grin splayed across her face as she squeezed the scythe in her grasp. "Together."

I wrapped my hand around hers, closed my eyes, and drove the blade to the hilt in Cadagon's chest. I dropped my hold immediately, bile crawling up my throat. The air of peace emanating from him only turned my gut more. Because me? I felt no peace. I ached, burning up inside. I'd delivered on my promise like I said I would.

And it wasn't fucking fair.

My nails cut half-moon shapes in my palms; the fresh slice from the ceremony reopened. I studied the droplets rolling down my forearm to distance myself from the brutal scene. Death choked on his own blood as his shadows took firm hold of my leg. Even actively dying, he made sure I knew he harbored no ill will—showing me he didn't want me to hurt—but I still did. Promising to deliver his death was one thing, but I never agreed to watch him suffer.

I counted the seconds until his magic fizzled in his veins, abandoning him for its new host. Kim welcomed it wearily. Her stance faltered slightly; but when her birthright sank into her bloodstream, flowed under her skin, and took root, she softened. She looked upon her father with pity as his body went still.

Goodbye, old man. May you rest among the stars.

My head hung in the wake of his loss, a knot forming in my throat. Life had never played fair in Anathema, but this...this was something altogether unjust: to care and serve and love as he had only to die at the hands of the one who had inspired such affections in him. My mind raced—threatening to undo me—until Kimber's fingers feathered around my jaw. Right. We had to be strong. Our kingdom needed us.

We turned to face the insanity unfolding among the crowd. In mere seconds, the guests bristled with the onset of a riot. Talk of treason and assassination abounded.

"I warned you about her!" Duke Jarlin pointed his skeletal finger. "I warned you all that she was not fit to lead, but no! You wouldn't consider my words as truth, and now look."

Baneful swells leached from him, slinking towards Kim with deathly intent, but her power rose to meet his challenge. Her shadows permeated the scene and slunk about in intoxicating geometric patterns, sharpening to daggers. I tilted my head. Strange: how they appeared to possess life and intention of their own. One motion from Lady Death, and they descended on Jarlin, turning him to ash in a blink. Goosebumps prickled my forearms.

My hand found its home in Kim's. "You are absolutely terrifying, my Queen."

Hellbent on revenge, she ordered the guests to return to their homes. I chuckled. Oh, Malachi and Nasheesh had no idea what fresh hell was coming their way.

"Guards," she snapped, "take the new king and find the advisor's son by any means necessary, but return him alive. I'd like to have the joy of ending his life myself."

I kissed her cheek. "Give him hell."

With a wink, she evaporated into pure shadow.

The guards flanked me as I entered the castle courtyard. Their armor *clinked* in time with their synchronized steps, unnerving me. I cleared my throat and scoured for any trace of magic Malachi might have left behind, but with the recent departure of so many people, it was impossible. The sheer number of magical trails—their potency intensified by fear—made me dizzy. I pinched the bridge of my nose. Where would Malachi go? Where would he hide? Somewhere few would see him, where he could fly under the radar and disappear—

A silhouette flitted past in my peripheral towards the cemetery, a second figure following a step behind. *Gotcha, sucker.* I walked to the pointed, iron gate, and my fingers latched onto the rough metal as I searched. A scream rang out from the foggy smattering of tombstones. But not Malachi's.

"Suri..."

I made my decision in an instant. New crown heavy atop my head, I summoned the guard captain. "Split up and search the courts. Malachi will be looking for a way to escape. We *cannot* let him slip from this realm."

I whirled around at the sound of a second blood-curdling cry. Another familiar voice. Duchess Nova.

"Would you like me to accompany you, Highness?"

I shook my head. "No. I need all available eyes on the hunt."

"Yes, Sire."

The guards divided and disappeared down the walkway towards the arching paths. With them gone, there would be no witnesses to the destruction I was about to inflict on the disease of a woman. Nobody to question my ruthlessness or judge it.

I climbed the mounting hill with wide, steady steps. Halfway up, I spotted Suri near the top, pinned face down under Nova's boot. The duchess held Suri's hair in a tight grip, her neck arching under the strain. *Oh, hell no.* I started towards them, the reality of my recent beating slowing my pace.

"You weak, vile thing!" Nova sneered. "Not even I could make a diamond out of a lump of useless coal like you!"

"Shut your mouth!" Suri slammed her head back into Nova's chin.

Nice one! Got her!

Nova stumbled back, and Suri took her to the ground in a fury of fists and wrath. They tumbled over one another, but with a sinister smile, Nova dug her fingertips into Suri's eyes. Cheap fucking move. My friend cried out, clutching her face.

"Oh, Suri, you should know your place by now." Nova towered over her. "Right there, in the dirt at my feet."

"Conniving bitch!" Suri yelled.

"The elite do not play fair with peasant trash. It is simply beneath us. *You* are beneath *me*."

Careful not to alert the duchess, I rounded the nearest tombstone, positioned myself, and kicked out Nova's knee. Twisting her arms behind her back, I forced her to kneel. "It is *you* who is beneath *her*."

"Please! Please spare me, my King! I—"

"Spare you?" I chuckled. "You mean like you spared all those innocent women and children from a life of servitude at the hands of your pig colleagues? Not a chance."

"They forced me." Nova panicked. "I would never—"

Suri slapped her across the face. "Liar! I witnessed the evil you wielded time and time again."

"My friend," I said with a smirk, "would you like to do the honors?"

"With gods-damned pleasure."

Her tinctured and demonic magics tangled in her fingertips, and she took Nova's face in her hands.

"Look at me," Suri demanded.

Duchess Nova thrashed to free herself from our holds, but to no avail.

"I said, 'Look at me'!" Suri ripped Nova's chin up and unsheathed a dagger from her waistband, tracing its sharp tip across Nova's collarbone, splitting the flesh wide open. "This is for Lana." The blade trailed down Nova's arm; a river of red and screams released under its edge. "For every person whose soul you crushed under your heel." Suri slashed across the duchess's breasts, fatty tissue spilling out. "For every innocent you tried to destroy."

Without remorse, she buried the knife in Nova's throat.

"Fate," Nova choked out as the blood at the edges of her lips trailed down her neck. "Help...me."

Suri leaned into her face. "Fate has abandoned you. You are completely and utterly alone."

Nova's lip quivered as Suri drove the dagger in farther, and the once proud duchess lurched forward, the life draining from her eyes. Dead. Where she belonged. I let her body crash to the ground like discarded trash and collected Suri in my arms.

"You do not know how long I've wanted to do that," she sobbed against my chest.

"She's gone. You're safe."

Suri's blade clanged at our feet. I held her tight, rubbing small circles between her shoulders as she wept. Her mission was complete. Those she'd fought so hard for—herself included—were finally free.

A sudden jerk tugged at my center. My vision blurred, layering into two somehow: here and somewhere else at the same time. The flash of a longsword ghosted past. A clang of metal clashed in my ears. I shook my head and tried to clear it away when Kimber's blood-covered hands came into view like they were my own. The knot in my center yanked again.

Fuck.

I didn't question it. Kimber needed me. Now. I could sense it in my bones, my teeth, my skin, my blood. No, not mine anymore: ours.

"I have to go." I picked up Suri's blade and started towards the gate with hurried steps.

"Where?" Suri called after me.

"To find my wife."

CHAPTER NINETEEN

A BRUTAL END

My heart sank into my toes as I absorbed the brutal scene. Kim—her hair knotted in Malachi's fist—sat on her knees fully at his mercy. *Fuck...* Odin reverted from beast to human form and towered over her at Malachi's side. I smirked as he turned his back to me. *Perfect shot.* I unsheathed my dagger. Keeping low to the ground, I carefully picked up the pace.

Kimber lurched in the Lord's grip. "You can't kill me."

"You're wrong," he replied, his blade at her throat. "You see, your coronation was never fully completed. The ceremony was interrupted which means..."

My steps faltered. *Oh gods, please don't let it be true.* If the ceremony wasn't completed, that meant Kim was still part mortal. The pressure mounted in my chest as I flanked to the right and positioned myself, ready to lay down my life if it came to that. This wouldn't end with their victory. They couldn't win.

Kim met Odin's gaze. "Do it then. Go on. Do it!"

"Easy now." Odin stepped in front of her, preparing to strike.

But in doing so, he'd given me the perfect damn opening. Goddess be blessed. I slipped from the shadows like a wraith.

Odin brushed a thumb across Kim's lips, taunting her. "We wouldn't want to—"

I sank my blade through the base of his skull, and a second later, he crashed at my feet.

"No!" Malachi shrieked from the depths of his soul.

I chuckled and stepped over Odin's body, ripping the blade free in a gush of blood. Ha. Stupid bastard really thought he'd stood a chance. Guess he'd never got it through that thick skull of his that I don't take kindly to people touching what's mine.

I started for Malachi, wiping the blood off my blade with a slide of my fingers. "Sorry about your mate. But I couldn't very well let him live after he attacked my queen, could I?"

"You *monster*," Malachi wept.

He pressed his blade to Kim's neck, a crimson line rolling down her throat.

"Let her go, and I'll let you keep your life," I lied.

"Filthy Talonborns. Righteous pricks," he seethed. "Mate for a mate."

"Sorry, I don't make deals with dead men." I raised my blade, lined it up, and hurled it straight into the demon Lord's face before he could flinch.

He pawed at his free-hanging jaw.

"You can't...kill me..." he muttered.

"Shut your lying mouth before I cut out your tongue!" I turned to Kim, my expression softening. "Lady Death, I believe this kill belongs to you."

"Such a gentleman." She winked.

The buzz in the air quieted all at once, and an eerie, hollow silence replaced it. But as we dragged Malachi—kicking and flailing—back to the path, the silence gave way to a sharp voice ringing out from the void below. My knees locked in place as it whispered in a sing-song tone: *Kill one master, and another shall fill his place. The Lores shall reign supreme.*

Chaos.

A scare tactic, Cooper. Nothing more. Get your head in the game.

"Any last words?" Kim asked, a depraved grin spreading across her face. "Maybe an apology?"

"Never," Malachi seethed.

"May the void show you the same kindness you showed me."

In a fierce display of justice, Kim sliced him clean open, dropping him into the void below. She dove into my arms, relief sweeping through my chest as her arms tightened around me. She was safe. It was all over.

"You did it," I whispered, and squeezed her.

"What if we didn't get them all?" she asked in a hush. "What if this was only the beginning, and there are more out there biding their time to strike—"

"Impossible. Between you and me, our enemies never stood a chance. We're free, Kim. *You* are free."

We cherished those stolen moments wrapped in each other's arms, the fight slowly purging from our systems. But as we made our way down the path back to the castle, I swear I heard laughter rising from the depths below our feet.

I dangled my feet over the castle roof, and my chest tightened. Kim and I knew each other like the back of our hands. We'd grown up together, and yet the silence tangled between us like awkward acquaintances. It unsettled me, but I understood. I'd lied. She probably had a million questions whirling in that pretty head of hers about who I truly was and what my intentions were. But tonight, my sins would step into the light. And though I faced the very real possibility that she might not want me—that sneaking around might have caused irrevocable damage—the weight on my shoulders began to lift. Hiding things from her was, by far, the hardest thing I'd ever done.

Tonight, I would tell my best friend everything.

She cleared her throat. "Is this your first time in Anathema? Or..."

"No, I've visited." Once, right after Amelia had rescued me—short-lived as I'd barely touched down before she'd hauled me away again—and in every memory and dream throughout my time in the mortal realm. In that sense, I guess I'd never truly left. I pursed my lips. "But I always knew I'd return one day to fulfill my duties."

"Duties. Right."

Her head fell, the embarrassment from the night we'd shared together plain on her face. It hit me like a sack of bricks: she really didn't know how I felt about her.

"I know what you're thinking," I said, "and no. You were never a duty to me. You've always been the reward."

"That night...that's why you stopped me, right?"

Heat flooded me, and the truth slipped out before I could stop it. "Yes. I wasn't about to be inside you and not have you scream *my* name. Don't tell me you question my feelings for you, Kim. You're smarter than that."

I relished the tick in her jaw as a blush dusted her cheeks.

"How is this possible?"

The events leading up to this night poured out of me from there. How Juniper had lent herself to our cause countless times. How she loved Kim in a way I had nothing but respect for. On occasion, Kim would ask me to go deeper, like in regards to Death, but that story wasn't mine to tell. It was his.

She bristled. "After what he did to you, your people, you're going to defend him?"

"I can prove his innocence," I said, reaching for her hand. "But first, can you hear me out? Let me tell you what I have to share? I can explain everything if you let me."

"Fine. But for old time's sake. The verdict is still out on your guilt, got it?"

"More than fair."

Time slipped by as I explained how her mother had saved me and how I'd lost my parents to the flames in the massacre. To my relief, the more I talked, the more she relaxed. Maybe I hadn't lost her after all. With each new fact, the bond between us mended a step further until we reached the final piece. The hardest bit to swallow: her father.

"None of it was his fault," I said.

She squinted at me. "But I saw it the day I read the realm. He conspired with a demon to ensure all the shifters had been wiped out like he'd ordered."

"It's not what it looked like. But that part is not mine to share."

"If it wasn't how it seemed, then why didn't Cadagon tell me the truth? Explain it?"

"He did."

I dug in my jacket pocket, swallowed hard, and extended the letter to her. She searched my face before taking it. Her sights traced down the page and tears welled in her eyes until it became too much.

"I was so cruel to him," she sobbed.

"You freed him. He knew you were ready, knew you'd be the leader Anathema needed. He wanted this."

She didn't fight me. Didn't argue. Instead, she leaned into me, and I wrapped my arms around her. I'd have given anything to take her pain away. Hell, I'd make another deal with Fate if I thought it'd mend her broken heart, but Cadagon wouldn't have wanted it that way. He'd have wanted her to feel her way through it, mourn his loss, and move on to the future he had wished for her. She shook herself out of the moment, not ready to process Death's truth just yet. And honestly, I couldn't blame her. I didn't know what to do with it either.

"When did you do it?" she asked. "Kill Lyvias?"

I stiffened. "The night I saw him disrespect you on the castle stairs. Nobody calls my woman a cancer and fucking lives."

"Wait, you saw that? How?"

"If I tell you, will you promise not to murder me?"

"I will promise you no such thing."

"Okay, okay," I sighed. "I'm...I'm Poe."

She hauled off and slapped my shoulder. *Just like old times.* We shared a laugh as the last of the tension melted away, and I decided to let that energy linger. The rest of what she needed to know—the whirlwind details around the meat market, the Ancient Lores, and the Shroud—could wait a little longer, until she'd had time to process. The air calmed, and she searched my face, her smile fading as she traced a finger across my jawline.

"Want to know something?" She asked.

"I don't know." I grinned. "Do I?"

"How about I give you a hint?"

She drew near. Her lips lingered an inch from mine, and my heart began to race all over again. I closed the gap nice and slow, letting the spark between us catch fire. For so long, I'd dreamed of this moment. To be wanted by her. And as she glided down my body—her touch electric—it became crystal clear how much she wanted me. But I also knew how hard it was for her to do what she was about to, and the last thing I wanted was for her to sacrifice even an ember of her light to please a man's needs. Especially mine.

"You don't have to do that," I breathed. "I just want you."

Her hand continued to pry at my zipper. "Let me show you how much I love you."

"If you insist, my Queen."

CHAPTER TWENTY

A GODS-DAMNED PROMISE

Adari found me in the royal study overlooking the cemetery the morning after our triumph. With a reverent gleam in his eyes, he presented me a wax-sealed envelope.

"I was asked to hold onto this until your victory was secure," he said, a quirk at his lips. "I believe now is the right time."

"What is it?"

"A gift from someone who never once doubted you. I hope it brings you the peace you deserve, Highness."

He bowed and went on his way without another word. Brow pinched, I turned the envelope over in my hand, and my breath hitched. I knew that signet: Cadagon. Another letter? How very *him* to get one last word in from beyond the grave. I popped the wax seal and traced my finger across the dented words in the parchment.

You will find my wedding gift not ten minutes through the Evermoor Woods. When the weight of your new crowns grows heavy, I hope you will find solace there as I often did. Please tend to the garden. It might very well be the only thing I have done right in my life. Live simply. Live well, my children. I am so proud of you both.

- Your Father

My heart ached. What I wouldn't give to see that cocky smirk on his face as he beheld the strides already made to unite Anathema and restore her balance. I could picture it clear as night: the chuckle rolling through him when he discovered our enemies had fallen. The sheer possibilities of what could have been washed over me, and I swallowed my grief. Perhaps in another world. Another life. I tucked the letter into my coat pocket.

We could have been a family.

Sleep evaded me. I turned on my side, and my sights danced over my wife, her skin drenched in the hearth's warm amber glow. The sight took my breath away. Lost in a dream, her lashes fluttered—peaceful and serene. I caressed her cheek with a feather-light touch, slipped from our bed, and pulled the tousled silk sheets over her. My treasure. My prize.

I made my way through the castle, heading for the shapeshifter path to clear my mind. Breathe. We'd accomplished our goals, and yet I couldn't wrap my head around it. Couldn't believe we'd actually done it. Suri insisted acceptance would come with time, though I admit I wasn't entirely convinced. So for the time being, I'd focus on simpler, more welcomed matters, like Cadagon's elusive wedding gift.

I drifted through the Evermoor Woods, captivated by its tranquil beauty. For the first time since arriving in Anathema, I felt safe. Secure and present in the moment instead of constantly looking over my shoulder for the next threat. I heaved in a deep breath of piney air. Yes, change was on the horizon. Already the trees were starting to recover as their toxic leaves drank in new, balanced air. Wildlife ran about in giddy exploration. Even the moon shone brighter.

Anathema was healing.

I emerged from the trees into a clearing littered in black rose bushes, a path winding through its center. The crash of waves reverberated in the distance, and I followed the sound like a siren's call over the hill opposite the dreaded revel den, thank the Gods. "Alright, old man. Let's see what you got."

I flipped the lock on a white picket fence. Planter boxes and clay pots dotted the yard, the lush blooms within swaying in the briny ocean breeze. Warmth built in my cheeks. Death had nurtured life here. A beautiful oxymoron: just as he had been. He'd tended to the soil and pruned the plants to perfection. Though he'd left us, this part of him—the true, gentle pieces he'd been forced to hide away—lived on.

I waded in farther, losing myself in the sheer variety of flora. Reds and purples, thorns and shrubs. But most impressive of all was the lone, potted bush perched on a crescent-shaped platform in the garden's center. Foreign to Anathema's innate darkness, the white roses intrigued me. A plaque jutted up from its soil: *To Eternal Love and New Beginnings.* My lips quirked up as the petals' sweet scent carried around me.

Cadagon, you old softy.

I cast my sights to the old Victorian house reaching for the clouds at the cliff's edge. Amazing: how it had somehow survived the massacre. Or maybe Death had rebuilt it? Whatever the reason, it—

A flash of white caught my eye on the far end of the porch, and I started up the stairs. "Hello?" Silence returned my call, but a steady crunch of footsteps lured me closer. In a vegetable garden overlooking the cliff, a woman in a white robe tended to her crop. A knot tangled in my throat. "Mother..."

Barefoot with her hands sunk into the moist dirt, she sang a song I hadn't heard in over fifteen years. Bewitched by her voice, I settled on my knees at her side.

Fate be blessed, and bless us too, that we might serve the will of you. And if it be within thy plan, may your nurturing light spread across the land.

The difference between my last glimpse of her and this one made my heart swell. She was so calm and carefree. So happy.

Again, I looked over at the house locked away since my youth, and memories seized me. Tears blurred my vision as Cadagon's intention took root in my soul. That man...he'd given me more than a simple gift. He'd filled a part of the gaping hole my mother's loss had created in me, despite it never being his responsibility. Death, in all his kindness, had given me the desire of my heart. *My dear boy, you have always had a home.*

His words solidified in me as I sat there—fingertips in the moist earth—listening to my mother's joyful songs. Remembering. *Feeling* the way Cadagon had encouraged me to. Years he must have spent rebuilding my childhood home from scratch after it burnt down. He'd breathed new life into its charred bones.

The same way he'd done with me.

I let hope creep beyond the walls I'd built inside myself, acceptance steadily setting in. My life, my future, had turned out far grander than my wildest dreams. I'd built unbreakable friendships with loyal, passionate people I hadn't seen coming. Made a home in a world full of wonder and adventure. Most of all, I had a partner with which to share my heart, who was not only worth dying for, but worth *living* for. I finally knew where I belonged.

I'd found my destiny.

After returning to the castle, I tossed together Kim's and my belongings in two bags, fetched my bride from her slumber, and stole us into the night.

"Where are we going?" she asked.

"You'll see."

Excitement buzzed between us as we walked the moonlit path through the woods hand in hand. Together: the same way we'd always done.

Embodying my deepest fantasies in her lacy robe, she meandered through the garden.

Her black-tinged fingers plucked a red rose, and she pressed her nose to the petals.

"Beautiful," she sighed, and met my gaze. "But what is this place?"

"A gift. From your father."

At the mention of him, her expression tightened, conflicting emotions evident in her distant stare.

"He loved you so much," I murmured. "But I'll let you in on a little secret."

She raised a brow. "Oh yeah, and what is that?"

"Nobody could possibly love you as much as I do."

I swept her into my arms, her laughter tickling my neck as I carried her up the front steps. Pausing at the door, I leaned down and kissed her deeply, and she returned my affection with heavy breaths. Enamored, I stepped over the threshold.

"Welcome to your honeymoon, my Queen."

"And yours." She skimmed a finger along my jawline. "My King."

I started up the stairs to the second story with her legs wrapped around my waist, our mouths devouring one another. In the backmost bedroom, I laid her down and made my way to the French doors, opening them to the incoming storm. Raindrops and wind chimes and waves swept in like a symphony. Ivy twisted across the balcony banister covered in dew, and I picked a leafless stem.

"I wonder who used to live here," she said.

"This was...this was my home." I flicked a match to light a candle on the nightstand; the spark reflected in a full-length mirror.

"Here?" She pushed up on her elbows. "But...how? I thought everything burned in the massacre."

"Turns out even broken things can be made new with enough patience. And that's what I plan to do here," I whispered, and ran my thumb along her bottom lip. "Patiently remake this bond between us into something new. No more masks or half-truths. No more holding back. Just you and me as we are in this moment. That is, if you'll have me?"

I took her hand and got down on one knee.

"What...what are you doing?" She clutched her chest.

"Kimberly Ann Bradshaw, would you do me the honor of making me the luckiest damn man in existence?"

"I...but we—we're already married."

"On paper. But I want this to be real. I want to know that every morning when I wake up and reach for you—those big, beautiful eyes falling on me—that you chose this. That you chose me."

"Coop, it's always been you."

"Then, marry me?"

She extended her hand with a giddy nod. "Are you kidding? Of course I'll marry you."

I tied the bit of ivy around her finger in a bow, and her lips crashed into mine. My wife. I crawled over her, pinning her beneath me. Our tongues tangled together—her desire burning hot and fast—but I'd waited too long to hear those words not to savor the taste. To sip her passion in small, calculated mouthfuls.

I broke from our kiss, my hips settling between her thighs. "Do you trust me?"

"Of course I do," she breathed.

"Then can you do something for me?"

"Anything."

"Relinquish control. Let go."

She nodded with hooded eyes, and I seized control, trailing kisses down to her collarbone. More. I craved *more*. My mouth watered at her scent, and I realized then the future I faced. This part of Lyvias—the thirst, the fangs, the unquenchable desire—would stay with me forever: the consequences of the ritual and my cross to bear. But I had a hunch someone might be willing to tame the beast inside me, or better yet, feed it.

I nipped Kim's neck with sharpened teeth. "I want to taste you, drink you in."

"Drink your fill. I am yours, completely."

I sank my teeth into her—heart pounding—and her sweet blood trickled down my throat like warm honey. Her gasp in my ear made my cock pulse. I pulled my lips free to glance down at her, licking her blood off my teeth.

"It's like you were made for me."

Her mouth fell open as I slipped my hand into her already wet panties. My thumb swirled around her swollen clit while my free hand made quick work of removing her silk top. Her peaked breasts bounced free, and a moan tore through me. Mine. All mine. I sucked her nipple into my mouth—my thumb and tongue swirling in tandem—and her hips bucked at the friction. Her breaths grew ragged. Without warning, I buried three fingers in her, sweeping them in come-here motions.

"That's right, baby. Come for me."

"Oh, fuck!" she cried out.

She bit her lip, bearing down on my fingers as she crashed over the edge. I needed her. Needed to bury myself inside her. I yanked my shirt over my head, and she pushed closer to trace the fresh burn holes on my shoulders. A pained expression eclipsed her face, but she didn't ask who or why. She already knew. Instead, she placed a soft kiss atop one before making her way to the next, all the while fighting with my pants. She popped the last button, staring me straight in the eyes as she licked her palm and slid it down to wrap around the base of my cock. My eyes rolled back at how *perfectly* I fit in her hand, as if we had been predestined to fit like missing puzzle pieces.

She began to pump as her thumb swept over my head. "You're so thick."

"You'll know just how thick when I fill that tight little pussy of yours."

To this, she forced me to lay back on the bed, discarded her thong, and straddled me. Her bare center on my shaft nearly had me coming on contact, but I fought it. *Far too soon.* She guided my head to her entrance, but I caught her wrist and shuffled out from under her. "Patience, my Queen."

"I'm no good at that," she grumbled, her naked frame crumbling on the mattress.

Oh, but she would have to be, because I had an idea. A damn good one at that. I made my way to the room's edge and dragged the mirror next to the bed.

"Show me how much you want this." I grasped my rock-hard length. "Show me how wet you are for me."

With a wicked grin on her face, she spread her legs wide. I bit my lip, stroking myself as I watched her play. Her brow creased, her fingers gliding in and out, and her knees began to quiver.

"Fuck, that's hot," I muttered.

"Yeah? You like that? You like watching me pleasure myself for you?"

"Oh, hell yeah, but I'm going to need you to come here. Now."

I grabbed her ankles and dragged her to the edge of the bed. Looking down at her, I positioned her head at my waist. "The next time you come, it'll be on my cock, understand?"

"Yes."

"Yes, *sir*," I demanded.

She grabbed my ass. "Yes, sir."

She sucked me into her mouth with force, taking me all at once.

"Shit—Kim, your mouth is fucking heaven."

My fingers tangled in her hair as her tongue skimmed across my head before driving me back in her throat again and again. Her moan reverberated around me, making my stomach drop. I was going to burst. *No. Not yet.*

Taking firm hold of her hips, I switched our positions. After sitting down on the bed's edge, I guided her to stand facing away from me and met her gaze in the mirror. Slow and soft, I teased her entrance with my length, eliciting a sigh from her parted lips.

"Do you want this?" I asked, watching her stance lower towards my lap.

"Gods, yes," she heaved.

"Then be a good girl and sit."

I slammed her down on my cock, filling her completely, and she screamed out. *Holy...* So tight. So wet. So *perfect.* I became feral, thrusting myself harder and harder into her. My hand wrapped around her neck, gently guiding her attention back to the mirror.

"Look at you," I growled. "Look how well you take me, baby."

Her muscles clenched, her back arching in time. "Cooper, I'm going to come again."

My name on her tongue only encouraged me more. I collected her hips in a firm grip, driving her down. My head swam. This woman was going to destroy me. And I was going to fucking let her.

"Say my name again," I ordered.

"Cooper."

I rolled my hips deeper, watching my cock slip in and out. "Oh shit, yeah."

"Harder!" she screamed.

"That's it. Take it."

"I'm coming!"

Together we cried out as the passion grabbed hold. The euphoria ripped across every nerve in my body, and I collapsed, my forehead coming to rest on her quivering back. I fought for air. Of all the times I had imagined her relinquishing control and handing her closely clutched dominance to me, I'd never once imagined it would be that powerful. That ground shaking. Absolute madness in the best way. I hugged her close, kissing up her spine.

"I love you," I whispered.

"I love you more."

There was no chance in hell that was true, but I let her have it. She slid me out of her with a gasp and started towards the bathroom. Again, I caught her wrist.

"And just where do you think you're going?" I asked.

"To shower?"

"Funny, because I don't remember saying I was finished with you yet."

She grinned. "Is that a threat?"

"No, baby. That's a gods-damned promise."

Fully spent, Kim snuggled close and tucked her head against my chest. We laid there, blissfully content, our laughter giving way to comfortable silence aside from the crash of the waves seeping in through the cracked doors.

I laced my fingers through hers. "You kept your promise."

"What promise?" she asked.

"You said you'd always be my home."

"Always."

Our magic emerged—first from her, then me—and met between us to melt together. Without thinking, I swiped a finger through the warm mist.

"You know, you've never told me why you do that," she murmured.

"Do what?"

"Go somewhere else. Drift."

I chuckled. "I'm right here."

"No. I mean, it's like you're looking at someone. You're here but...not."

The burgundy fog swept through her hair, tousling it a bit, which had quickly become one of my favorite views. Her: wild and free.

She smoothed her hair back down. "I love it here, but it's drafty..."

With a shiver, she snuggled closer, tucking the sheets up over us.

"It's not a draft. Our magic can be a little...distracting at times. And handsy when it comes to you." I smirked down at her. "Seems to be especially active tonight. I can't imagine why that might be."

"Ha, my shadows can certainly be distracting, but with focus—" She startled. "Wait, *our* magic?"

"From our pact, yeah. You really don't see it?"

"No, I don't see it. How do *you* see it?"

The image of June's bright light as she encouraged me towards my destiny sharpened in my mind's eye. It was time Kim knew. "Juniper."

"June? But how...why? I—I don't understand. You met her?"

"Right before you said goodbye, yes. The sandman dropped me in the Shroud, and she found me. Saved my ass, actually. I told her you'd opened *The Book of Shade* and she needed to get to you."

"What did she say?" Kim propped herself up.

"She said she knew that day would come but wanted to keep you for herself just a little longer. She wanted me to tell you how much she'd miss you. How much she loved you."

Kim nodded and kissed my chest.

"After that," I continued, "she granted me oracle sight to flesh out those who meant you harm. She's pretty amazing. I get why you fell for her."

It's funny: the admission didn't hurt like it used to. There was no twinge of jealously. No hard feelings. It was simply fact. They'd loved, and they'd loved hard; but there were no insecurities brewing in my mind about Kim regretting ending up with me. She loved me hard too. I felt it in her touch. Saw it hanging there in her eyes like a promise. We were simply meant to be.

"When did you first notice it? Our magic?" she asked.

"After our first pact, but it changed when we completed the marriage ritual. When we combined our blood, it melded to become something both you *and* me. Honestly, I don't know how, but it's grown on me. It's special. It feels like...us."

"But we fulfilled the original agreement. Why would that blood pact magic still bind us?"

My stomach jumped. I hadn't considered that, but she was spot on. We'd ended Death as we'd sworn to do, though neither of us had expected to suffer such guilt from it. Such grief. The pact had been fulfilled.

I pursed my lips. "Huh, good question."

"What does it look like?"

"A burgundy mist, but it has this opalescent sheen. The longer it lingers, the more conscious it becomes somehow. Alive in its own right. It flows between us when it chooses, but it definitely favors you. Seems to enjoy teasing you." I tugged her hair playfully. "Can't say I blame it. It's pretty damn fun."

"Har-har."

"Honestly, I haven't seen anything like it aside from when Odin and Malachi were near each other."

"What do you mean?"

"Odin's magic was a kind of shimmery turquoise. Every other form of magic in the realm is more...translucent, I guess you could say."

"Odin's magic?" She sat up straight. "Coop, hellhound abilities are a genetic thing not a magical affinity. Hounds don't wield magic. That's why he always shifted during any altercation. More protection."

"Well, it wasn't Malachi's. His affinity was as dark and twisted as they come. If it wasn't his, then—"

I stopped short, the wheels in my head turning. The second part of my mother's proclamation of how Fate had smiled on me rushed back: *She gave you a special gift. You see, she took part of that big heart of yours, and she gave a piece of it to another.*

The magic around us sparked with new intensity as reality wove together in my mind. If Malachi and Odin had it...if Kim and I shared that same bond...

"We're mates," I whispered.

Kim's brow pinched. "What?"

"Our magic: it had nothing to do with the pact. It was always ours. It's why I followed you here. It's why I've always been drawn to you like a moth to an open flame, willing to burn if it means I can be even a touch closer to you." I pinched her to look up at me. "You are my soulmate."

Tears welled in her eyes as the dots connected. All this time—the days, weeks, years—where we simply couldn't stay away from each other; the intensity she'd felt in finding a cure for me; and the ensuing heartbreak of letting me go: it all finally made sense. From day one, our souls had called to each other.

"Fate made you for me," she purred.

"And you for me."

Our lips met in a consuming kiss. Our hearts: finally one.

EPILOGUE

Anathema's crescent moon grinned down, its pale light spilling over a sea of desserts and easy conversation in the castle gardens. Kim, Suri, and Adari sipped from their teacups between bouts of laughter, rattling on about some game we "simply had to play." Lana and Tovas sat locked in a heated chess match, her posture straight and proud. I sighed, soaking in the scene.

My home. My family.

The Goddess had worked her magic, piecing together the foundations for a new Anathema seamlessly. Tovas and Adari had graciously stepped into their new roles as Lords of the demon court and—after searching high and low for her parents—had taken Lana in and decreed her the formal heir to Wentworth Manor. Their daughter. Suri, in all her stubborn glory, had taken her sweet time in accepting Kim's and my invitation but had finally agreed: royal advisor to the crown.

Our kingdom was at peace.

Kim met my gaze, her lips mouthing, "I love you."

"I love you more," I whispered back.

"What do you think, Coop?" Suri asked.

I blinked back into the moment. "About what?"

"About a trip to the mortal world? I have always wanted to see what all this talk of mortal heathenness is about."

I smirked. "I think that could be arranged."

"Tovas, Lana, and I would love to join you," Adari added.

Kim chimed in. "I don't know. There's still so much to do and—"

"And we will handle it," I said, and rubbed my thumb across her forearm. "But I think even you can agree we've earned a little respite."

Kim smiled. "You're right."

Magic drifted across the table—Adari taking notice in time—and we turned to find a silhouette darting in the shadows. *The hell...* I stood with my dagger drawn. A guard stepped forward and bowed, his face wrinkled in concern.

"Your Highnesses, I present Lord Drystan."

He ushered the vampire Lord forward before disappearing in the direction he'd come. Kimber took her place at my side in a heartbeat, her hand slipping into mine as Drystan lowered his rigid shoulders in greeting.

"I apologize for my impromptu appearance, Your Highnesses," he said, "but I have a matter I fear needs your immediate attention."

Kim and I shared a panicked glance. Something was off.

Her grip tightened around mine. "What is it?"

"I—I am not entirely sure." Drystan said. "If you would be so kind as to come with me, I will show you."

I considered for a second if it might be another trap. Another enemy we'd missed somehow, but Drystan hadn't once been in the wrong place at the wrong time. Technically, I had no reason not to trust him. Yet. We followed him to the vampire gate—my grasp on my dagger's hilt unwavering—and wandered through the leafless trees. A thick layer of fog stuck to the forest floor, the stench of decay permeating the air. It didn't make sense. Just weeks before, the woods in the shifter realm had shown signs of healing. Why now did the trees in the vampire court rot instead?

We drifted farther and farther in. My stomach turned the more time slipped by—Kimber's visible concern rocking me further—and my fists clenched at my side. What in the Gods' names could require our attention this far outside the town line? But then I saw it: the iron gate to the mortal realm caked in rust...and open.

"I never gave my consent to reopen access to the mortal world," Drystan confirmed, "and yet, here it is: gates wide open. I simply have no explanation."

"Who else would have the ability to do this?" Kimber asked.

"From within? Only you, my Queen. But from outside…"

I started a slow pace towards the gate, lightning crashing through the sky on the other side. *Those clouds…* I swallowed hard.

"Kim," I called, and motioned for her to join me.

"What it is?"

I pointed to the sky swirling into a vicious storm overhead. "Do you see what I see?"

"Violet clouds…"

It hit us both with the same biting force. While the gates had been opened wide to another plane, what greeted us was neither mortal sky nor mortal soil. A knot cemented in my throat.

We were standing on the precipice of the Shroud.

"How is this possible?" I whispered.

"I—I have no idea," Kim said. "But this ends now. I refuse to have my peace stolen from me again."

She raised her hands. Her shadows slipped from her fingertips and slithered up the iron bars, stringing themselves across the gap to cinch it together. Slowly, the gates began to close.

Drystan let out a relieved sigh. "Thank you, my Queen. I promise I will keep a watchful eye on this; and should anything change, you will be the first to know."

"Please do, Lord Drystan. You were right to summon us," Kim said.

Their conversation turned to static as the hairs on the back of my neck stood on end. Through the gate across the flowery field at the tree line's edge, a figure emerged, the horrific sight gluing me in place. Ten feet tall and cloaked in a swirl of screaming sandmen, the being crept closer. Chains jutted from the darkness, attached to an army of corpses dragging their broken ankles beneath them. Sheer horror trapped me in my own skin. My mouth refused to open; words stuck in my throat like paste.

In a blink, the being and its army stopped five feet short of the gate. While the Reigning Reaper's eyes crackled in living flame, this being made their fire—both Cadagon's and Kimber's—look like mere sparks.

Hellfire and screaming faces danced within the figure's hardened stare from four feet above, the rest of its features cloaked in darkness. A bony hand jutted from the chaos and cemented a hold on the gates, preventing them from closing and sending Kimber's shadows cowering back to her.

She stood motionless at my side. What the ever-loving fuck *was* this thing? Its skeletal face emerged from the flurry of sandmen overhead, and it hit me instantly: a primal sense of knowing. Maggots clawed their way to freedom from the deepest layer of soil beneath my feet to slink into the ancient being's shadows as it hunched down over me.

In a voice layered with ten thousand others, the figure screeched, "Deliver me the sleeping key, or I shall unleash a plague upon thee."

Death's words snapped off the treetops as they boomed through the kingdom, blotting out the moon in their wake.

The Old Gods had awoken.

ACKNOWLEDGMENTS

First and foremost, thank you to the love of my life. Without your comfort, support, and constant compassion, I wouldn't be where I am today. Quite simply, this book wouldn't exist without you. Thank you for encouraging me to shoot for the stars. I love you, baby!

To my editor and best friend: thank you, thank you, THANK YOU for ALL you do! You are an absolute blessing, and I cannot wait to work on more books together! It's an honor to be your sister and client! (Authors reading this: trust me when I say you want to hire this woman!)

Gramma, thank you for putting up with my shenanigans and allowing me to blabber to you about all my bookish ideas at all hours of the day. Your support means the absolute world to me! Thank you for believing in me.

To my Aunt: thank you for always talking me off the stress roller coaster and reminding me of my strengths when I feel like the sky is falling. You, dear one, are irreplaceable!

Tia—my own Jiminy Cricket—you are amazing! Having you as my friend, my confidant, and my PA is a dream come true. Thank you for all the late-night calls, laughs, and always encouraging me to step out of my comfort zone to "do the scary thing."

To my Raven Babes: thank you for being on this wild journey with me. You all inspire me so much! You guys are the best, and I cannot thank you enough for all you do!

And last, but not least, to you! Yes, YOU, reading this right now. Without you, none of this would be possible. I appreciate you taking the time to read my words and explore my worlds. I sincerely hope you found a home in these pages. I cannot wait to introduce you to the chaotic world brewing in the Shroud next. Yup, that's right...we're taking a little trip to the in-between. But shh...that's our little secret. For now. ;)